JUST ONE MORE THING

DOM HASLAM

DE LANDRE PUBLISHING

ALSO BY DOM HASLAM

So Long, Marianne

CONTENTS

Doubt is not a comfortable condition, but certainty is an absurd one.

— VOLTAIRE

TREE HOUSE

Kit inserted the long, silver deadlock key into the keyhole, turned it and pushed open the magnificent, wide, heavy gloss black door to their new home. The kids yelped and rushed past him and his wife Alison, dashing up the stairs while shouting at each other about who was going to have which bedroom.

Once in the front hall, Alison stepped in front of Kit, turned to face him and took both his hands in hers. 'I know I've had my doubts about this move, but I'm really proud of you for making it happen. I hope we'll be happy here.'

Kit smiled but was already gazing past Alison's golden hair, savouring the vaulting expanse of space in the hall, despite its dusty, musty odour and tired décor; it was positively stately compared to the narrow, cramped entrance of their previous home. 'We're definitely going to be happy here,' he said, marvelling again at how his recent promotion had transformed their lives.

'You took ages getting the keys,' said Alison, looking up; the kids' footsteps thumped above as they charged from room to room, interspersed with cries of delight as new discoveries were made in the house's many rooms.

'Yeah, sorry about that, there was a final call to those idiotic solicitors. Thank god it's over.'

'Oh, I met the previous owner Mrs Gunn while I was waiting for you. She's moved in next door.'

'You *what*?' said Kit, his brow shifting forward.

'She's living next door in the bungalow. She was telling me this house was built in 1889 and that she lived here for sixty-eight years. Can you believe that?'

'Mmmm,' said Kit, now staring out the hall window at the house next door. She was *living there*? Why hadn't anyone told him? Their solicitor had explained how their house once had a very large garden which the owner recently split in two to build a small bungalow next door. The annexation of what should have been his impressively spacious garden had grated on him, only now to discover that the author of the vandalism was living right there on the very land denied him. He didn't like it. Not one bit of it.

They strolled through to the darkened lounge, Kit shaking his head at the sight of the threadbare mauve carpet and the fading, flaking, peacock-blue textured wallpaper which together conspired to suck all the light and energy from the room. 'Looks like Mrs Gunn not only lived here for sixty years, but kept the original furnishings too.'

'Stop it,' said Alison, smiling.

Kit walked over to the big bay window and ripped back the heavy, bottle-green curtains; a cascade of dust enveloped him and he staggered backwards, swearing, blinking and coughing. Once recovered, he admired the sheer size of the panes of glass in the window and the views they afforded, and allowed himself a moment to digest what he'd achieved. Their last place had been a modern build, three bedroom semi-detached. It had served them perfectly well, but had been entirely devoid of character and just so ordinary in every way. When he'd looked around this place for the first time, it'd been like peering into another world, its grandeur, space and solidity giving a rarefied atmosphere of potential which was the precise opposite of the parsimony and flimsiness he was used to living in. The huge, knee to ceiling, lounge windows in front of him, with their leaded, geometric, pastel green stained-glass panels at the top, were just one of many of the house's original and bold Victorian features he'd fallen in love with, but looking out of them now it annoyed him how the imposing beech tree in the front garden blocked out most of the light; some of its branches were so long they almost touched the window. His plans for a bright, modern interior wouldn't look like he'd imagined them with that tree there. As he shook his head, a movement in his peripheral vision caught his eye: a flash of silver hair just along from the beech tree on the opposite side of the recently built garden fence. 'I assume that's Mrs Gunn,' said Kit. 'Guess I best go and introduce myself.'

As he descended the steps of the house, he had to avert his eyes from the white early-morning sun, still low in the crystalline light blue sky and shining directly at him under the canopy of the beech tree. He stepped to one side so that the tree's huge trunk, which was deeply lined and rutted like an elephant's hide and must have been twelve feet in diameter, blocked out the glare. The silhouetted trunk sprouted two huge branch limbs halfway up, each reaching outwards and upwards, like a crooked cross against the morning sun.

He approached the garden fence and peered over: Mrs Gunn was kneeling away from him in a flowerbed, wearing a powder-blue smock. A tabby cat prowled next to her. 'Hello?' he said.

No reaction.

'Hello?!' he called out louder.

Mrs Gunn rose unsteadily and shuffled towards him with a pronounced bowed back that caused her to stare at her feet. 'Hello,' she said, turning her head sideways to look up at him from under a fringe of white-blue hair. She wore a vivid, pink lipstick which contrasted with her pale skin and bled into the fine wrinkles at the corners of her lips.

'I'm Kit. I've just moved in next door.'

'You're *what*?' asked Mrs Gunn.

'My name is Kit,' he said, slowing down his speech to make sure he was understood.

'Oh, I see. Well, my name is Violet. Pleased to meet you.' She shuffled her feet a little to try to get a better look up at him. 'I do hope you're going to be happy in the Rectory.'

'Well, it's a very fine——'

'Just remember you're only the custodian.' She jabbed a crooked finger at him to emphasise her words. 'The house stood here before you and I arrived and will be here long after we've left. Same as the beech tree, which was planted when the house was built. Magnificent, isn't it?'

Kit glanced at the tree, but it just reaffirmed his view that it was far too large and encroaching on his house. Turning back, he saw to his horror that the plaque by Mrs Gunn's front door said *Rectory Lodge*. 'You called your bungalow Rectory Lodge?' he asked.

'Yes, well, after sixty-eight years in the Rectory I felt entitled to retain some connection to the place.' Kit wanted to shake his head, but nodded half-heartedly instead. 'Now, there's something I wanted to talk to you about,' continued

Mrs Gunn. 'Someone's left your bins at the front of the house, but they belong at the rear. The bin men come on Tuesdays and you should take the bins out through the gate in the *back* garden. The bin men drive their lorry up the back, so there's no need for you to use the front.'

Kit glanced at the bins. He wasn't sure whether Mrs Gunn's comment was a request or an order. 'Right, okay,' he said neutrally.

'And you see the camellias over there?' she asked, pointing again.

Again he turned to see what she was talking about.

'They need deadheading, or else they won't flower again properly.'

'Right,' said Kit. 'It was nice to meet you,' he added hurriedly. 'I'd best pop back and see how the unpacking's going.' He turned to leave.

'If there's anything you want to know about the house, just ask. Nobody knows the Rectory like I do.'

Kit didn't reply, he just walked away. He'd been looking forward to today for months, this house purchase being one of the great achievements of his life, one of the reasons he'd pushed himself so hard at work all these years, but Mrs Gunn had taken the gloss off it. *And* he'd just given her £1 million; for that he expected a clean break with the previous owner, not all her do this and do that nonsense.

Reaching the front door, he realised he'd left the key inside and so knocked to be let in. After a few seconds of no response, he banged hard on the door with his fist. 'Can you let me in!' he shouted.

As he heard his wife struggling with the lock and handle inside, he tutted and said, 'Come on!' just as the door swung open.

'How did you get on?' asked Alison.

'I don't like her,' said Kit, walking past.

'Why? What did she say?'

'Nothing important, but she clearly thinks she still owns this place from the way she spoke to me.'

'Well, she seemed pretty harmless to me. Anyway let's not worry about it. Come on, you've hardly looked around yet.'

As his wife walked upstairs he stared again at the ancient and outdated decorations and furnishings, and experienced again the damp earth stench of decay and decrepitude seeping into him. He'd always planned to upgrade the house, but now a new sense of urgency surged through him: he'd wipe clean every trace of that old bat.

THAT EVENING, KIT SAT DOWN AT THE HEAD OF THEIR sturdy, solid oak dining table with a blank piece of A4 paper and his favourite, black Montblanc fountain pen. They'd made good progress with the unpacking, but he was too tired to do any more. As he stared down the length of the table, a satisfied smile formed on his lips; they'd never been able to utilise the extension leaf of the dining table in their former house, except on special occasions like Christmas lunch when they didn't mind being squashed, but here it could easily be left in place permanently, such was the size of the room.

Now to plan the renovation. This very room, as sombre as a long forgotten cobwebbed tomb, with its horrible creepy chandelier casting spidery shadows everywhere and looking like it might fall on his head, seemed a fitting place to design the changes. And by god he loved change. It'd made him what he was today. It always made him cringe when he thought back to his younger self. At school, he'd been the quiet, nerdy one too shy to join in. Worse still, his surname was Bunyan and a group of kids, who even more humiliatingly had been younger than him, had taken to calling him 'Onion'. Christopher Onion. For as long as he could he'd tried to ignore them, but they'd been so persistent. 'My eyes are watering from the onion,' they'd say, giggling, while walking behind him, or else, 'Peel the onion!' One day they'd congregated near him in the playground and simply chanted, 'Onion! Onion! Onion!' Unlike before when he'd mainly been alone when they'd abused him, this time his friends and classmates were nearby and also started laughing at his discomfort. The accumulated tension rifled up his spine into the base stem of his brain and even before he knew he was about to erupt he'd screamed 'I AM *NOT* AN ONION!', clear white visible all around the irises of his manic eyes. After a brief startled silence, the kids had spurted out with laughter, pointing at him and slapping each other's backs that he'd been reduced to pleading that he wasn't a root vegetable.

And what were those kids doing now? Probably tradesmen, or taxi drivers. One thing was for certain: they weren't fucking board directors of international advertising companies earning over a quarter of a million pounds a year. Fucking retards.

When he'd left university and joined his first advertising agency he'd *still* been so wet behind the ears. Those boring white shirts he'd worn and that bright red tie. He grimaced as he recalled that awful occasion when one of the cocky young guys in the office had said, 'Hey, look at Chris, dressing like an accountant again!' and everyone had started laughing, just like in the playground at school. His clueless fashion sense had been matched by his naivety, blindly thinking there was something special about his colleagues, that they were somehow more 'creative' than him, more worldly.

But it all changed one fateful day. It was during a client meeting with a building society about their brand. They'd spent all morning trying to convince the client of the need to dump their boring, dated, stuffy corporate image and embrace something completely fresh and new, but the client had been resistant, saying their customers weren't ready for it. 'It's not about you pandering to what your customers think,' his boss had said, 'it's about you *telling them* what to think. They'll be led by you as long as what you say feels authentic.'

It had been Kit's eureka moment. He'd walked out of that meeting with a sense of wonder and power, because for the first time in his life he realised that his destiny lay in his own hands. No one would ever laugh at him again. Within a few days he'd given in his notice, feeling it would be easier to reinvent himself at a new agency, with completely new people who knew nothing about him.

What a few weeks it had been. Gone was his bad hair, replaced by something the stylist had called a 'high fade', shaved at the sides and rear and tapering up into a thick, sculptured rug, like a teddy boy. Next came the glasses, a pair of thick black-rimmed Buddy Holly style ones, the style he still wore today, giving him an air of sophistication and authority. And the clothes, all tailored, fitted and dark: midnight blue, charcoal, British racing green, mahogany brown. He'd spent a fortune, but every penny had been worth it.

And of course the name change. On his first day at the new agency the man in security had asked him how he wanted to be referred to on the company's systems and email. 'Is it Christopher, or Chris?'

'It's Kit actually.' No one had ever referred to him as Kit before in his life. It didn't matter; they'd referred to him as it from that day onwards.

He stared down again at the blank piece of paper. He'd already booked the builders to start next month on smashing down the wall between this room and the kitchen, thus creating a thirty-six-foot-long kitchen diner. Thereafter, the plan was to install new folding French windows to saturate the merged room in natural light. Now he began to capture in words the overall mood and atmosphere he hoped to create throughout the house: clean, modern, contemporary, space, light, symmetry, balance. He followed this with some of his design ideas: reflective surfaces; exposed metal, glass and brick; chrome; long, low furniture; neutral colours accented with sparse, punchy, striking features; one room with a bold coloured wall such as plum, or charcoal with a burnt orange for contrast?

Looking around the morbid, depressing interior of the dining room with its spooky faded crimson walls made Kit even more determined. The mustard coloured carpet was so scuffed it was a wonder there weren't weeds visible cracking the floorboards. Old bat. Under a heading called 'To go', he wrote: all traces of Mrs Gunn; horrible old kitchen and bathrooms; darkness – e.g. carpets and curtains; beech tree.

Cutting down that tree would send the message to old bat Gunn to keep her nose out of it and why the hell anyway should he pay £1 million for a property and then have a fucking tree block out all the light? Then it hit him: shit, hadn't the solicitor said something about the trees being protected? He rummaged through the solicitor's papers in his tan leather satchel until he found the 'Local Authority Search' letter. It said:

There is a Tree Preservation Order which affects some or all of the trees at the property. This means that it is a criminal offence to cut down, lop, uproot, damage or destroy the trees, except with the consent of the Planning Authority.

'Fuck it,' he muttered.

Alison entered the dining room holding two glasses of red wine. 'Hi, I was just sorting our stuff in the bedroom. It's amazing to have so much space. What are you up to?' She handed Kit a glass.

'Just starting the planning for the renovations. Are the kids alright?'

'Yeah, they're settled,' said Alison, sitting down. 'Listen...' She placed a hand on Kit's shoulder and waited a moment until she had his full attention. 'I know I wasn't always convinced about this move but seeing how happy the kids are and seeing again what a great house this is makes me think perhaps it *is* a good move.'

'I'm pleased,' said Kit. 'I truly believe we'll be happy here. It's got so much potential and this time *we* get to design how it'll look.'

'I suppose so. Here, let me see your thoughts.' She turned his piece of paper through ninety degrees, but shortly her eyes scrunched into a squint before she looked up at him. 'You've written *beech tree* under *To go*?'

Kit sat back in his chair. 'It's just a thought; it blocks out so much light.'

'But it's so beautiful,' Alison said, half chuckling at him through incomprehension.

'Why are you laughing?' asked Kit, his face hardening.

'I'm just saying, I like the tree. Besides, it's protected, isn't it?'

Kit shrugged his shoulders. 'Is it?'

'I'm sure it is. And it's been here since the house was built, according to Mrs Gunn.'

'Who cares what *she* thinks?'

Alison pulled in her chin. 'It isn't about her, it's about respecting what's here.'

'Jesus, you sound like her.' He crossed his arms over his chest. 'Plus there's the safety aspect…'

Alison leant forward. 'How do you mean?'

'You've seen how close the branches come to the house. What happens if one snaps off in a storm and smashes through one of the kids' bedroom windows?'

'But it's been here for over a hundred years, why's it suddenly going to lose branches?'

Kit shrugged.

'Anyway, it's academic,' said Alison. 'We're in a conservation area and I'm sure it's protected. We can always get it cut back a little. Let's just concentrate on the inside of the house, shall we? I hope you're going to listen to my ideas too?'

'Of course,' said Kit, a little defensively.

'Well, I'm afraid charcoal offset with burnt orange sounds revolting. Sorry. I'm happy to indulge your minimalist fantasies a little, but the place also has to have some warmth. It's a family home.'

The door to the dining room opened silently, allowing a shaft of light to fall in. Kit and Alison turned. Their daughter Megan stepped forward hesitantly in her pale blue nightie, clutching her fluffy toy tabby cat. Alison stood up and put her arm around her. 'I thought you were asleep, Darling.'

'You're not going to change the house, are you? I love it as it is.'

'Oh, Megan. We're not going to do much, we're just going to create a wonderful new kitchen. You can help us choose how it looks. Come on, let's get you back to bed.' Alison led her by the hand upstairs.

Alone again, Kit clicked on the diary on his phone and typed in the following for the next morning:

8am – Call tree surgeons about beech tree.

THE TWO-TONE RING OF THE DOORBELL SOUNDED. ALISON was out all morning at the gym followed by lunch with friends, while Kit was working from home, which he only did rarely as he thought there were too many distractions, and because he didn't like his staff doing it. He rose and walked to the front door.

'Hi, I'm Kevin; come about the tree.'

Kit assessed him: scruffy, two days' worth of grey stubble, pot belly. They shook hands, Kit making a mental note to wash his later. 'Shall we take a look at it?' he asked, ushering Kevin outside. Their footsteps crunched on the crisp carpet of the beech tree's recently fallen dry, brown orange leaves as they took up position under it. It was a clear, late autumn day, just a few wisps of light cotton cloud in the pale blue sky, the glare of the bright white sun filtering through the branches of the tree, causing Kit to shield his eyes.

'It's a magnificent tree,' said Kevin.

Kit didn't respond. He'd met one tree surgeon already that morning, but he hadn't been right. Kevin moved about under the tree's canopy, leaning back to look up and assess its trunk and branches. As he did so, Kit observed his van:

old number plate, dented bodywork, the wording on its side flaking away in places.

'Of course, you know this is a conservation area?' said Kevin.

Kit nodded.

'So this tree must be protected. The council won't let you do much just because it's blocking out some light.'

'But we can cut it back?'

Kevin shrugged. 'A little. We could ask for a few feet, but in my experience they'll only agree to about two or three.'

Kit knew this already from his prior research and from the previous tree surgeon, but it still angered him. 'It's bloody ridiculous. You would have thought I would have more say over a tree on *my* land. Isn't there some sort of safety issue here, with it being so close to the house? I mean, look at that branch there, it's just a few feet from my son's bedroom.'

Kevin squinted while looking up to where Kit had pointed. 'It's very rare for these trees to lose large branches. I can't see the council agreeing to remove it.'

'So there's nothing I can do about this damn tree? Nothing at all?'

Kevin turned, walked along the drive to where it met the street and stopped, looking down at his feet. Kit followed, to find him staring at a drain. 'The only time I've seen permission given to cut down a tree like this is when its roots were damaging drainage pipes or causing subsidence,' said Kevin. 'Looks like your drains might run near the tree's root system. Had any problems of that sort?'

'I'm not sure,' said Kit. 'I've only just moved in. But if I could prove my pipes were being damaged, I might be able to take the tree down?'

Kevin shrugged. 'Maybe.'

Kit allowed himself to imagine it. All that new light released into his house. His vision of modern living realised. Clarity and cleanliness. And think of old bat Gunn's reaction! He turned towards her bungalow and his heart jolted: she was standing at her bedroom window looking straight at him fierce faced, her sharp eyes like the points of two ice picks. Kit gave her a slow, knowing, quarter smile before turning his back on her and moving a step closer to Kevin, close enough to smell the stale tobacco odour clinging to him. He lowered his voice. 'So, can you help me? I'm willing to explore *every* option.' A silence followed; as it lengthened so the tension rose, like a thickening of the air.

Kevin's eyes narrowed and his voice dropped to a confidential whisper. 'I might be able to help. I'd need to contact a pipework contractor. He'd need to dig up a bit of your drive to prove there was an issue. Take some photos. Then I would put the application in to the council. Only *if* there was pipe damage, of course.'

'Of course,' said Kit, nodding slowly, 'only *if*.'

Kevin brought a hand to his jaw and stroked the stubble on his chin against the grain. 'I know a pipework guy who can help,' he said eventually, causing the tension to ease a little. 'I could have a word with him. But all this doesn't come cheap…'

'No, I'm sure it doesn't. But I would consider it money well spent if it achieved the right result.'

'And you wouldn't be able to claim on your insurance for any pipe damage, you know that? I don't think any of us wants insurance men sniffing about, do we?'

'Of course not. It would remain solely a matter between us. And your pipework expert. You trust him, right?'

'With my life,' said Kevin. Kit held out his hand and Kevin shook it. 'I'll be in touch with the quote.'

Kevin climbed up into his van and turned the ignition; the engine rattled and when it caught, a puff of sooty black smoke belched out from the exhaust, before he scraped the gear into first and drove off.

As Kit walked back to the house, he glanced again next door: Mrs Gunn was still standing in her window, her face pale and drawn. Kit smiled broadly; Mrs Gunn turned away without acknowledging him.

'Holy shit,' said Kit, staring at a letter while sitting on a new retro American diner high chair at the newly installed breakfast bar in their now extended kitchen. The kids were at school, while Kit had delayed going to work to wait for the long anticipated letter from the council, which he'd just opened.

'What is it?' said Alison, standing up from loading the dishwasher.

'The council have rejected permission for the new French windows. They say it changes the character of the house and they've received an objection from a neighbour.'

As Alison read the letter over Kit's shoulder, it started to shake in his hands. 'That fucking *old bat*,' he muttered, standing up.

'What?'

Kit turned to face his wife. 'It's Mrs Gunn. That fucking bitch put in the objection.'

'You don't know that. It could be any of the neighbours.'

'Oh, come on, Alison! Get real. Of *course* it's her.' He strode towards the window while pointing at Mrs Gunn's bungalow. 'The way she's always sneaking around her garden peering over the fence and checking up on us. She was permanently stationed there when they were knocking through the dining room.'

'She was upset. She didn't like seeing her old house changed so much.' What she hadn't told Kit was that when she'd spoken to Mrs Gunn on the day the builders came to knock down the dining room wall and informed her of their plans, she'd become very pensive and had eventually begun to cry. She hadn't told him because he hated Mrs Gunn and she feared it would give him some sort of sick satisfaction.

Kit paced up and down, still clutching the letter from the council. 'I'm going round there to give her a piece of my mind,' he said, starting for the door.

'Stop!' shouted Alison. Kit stopped dead in his tracks. She strode up to him and grabbed him by the arm to force him to turn around. 'Just leave it! Look around you, will you? We've got everything we ever dreamed of. *Everything.* Surely we're not so desperate that we need to charge round to confront a lonely old woman in her eighties? You'll give her a heart attack. Can't we just let her live her last few years in peace and change the house afterwards?'

'She'll be dead quicker than she thinks if I have anything to do with it.'

'Kit! That's a terrible thing to say. And besides, *if* it was Mrs Gunn who complained – and you've got no evidence it was – have you considered why she might have done so?'

'What do you mean?'

'Has it crossed your mind that as well as the drastic renovations she might also be upset that you *still* insist on taking the bins out the front, which you know she hates.'

'How can you compare where the dustbins go with our dream home? You sound as senile as her.'

'She is *not* senile. I've had some very nice conversations

with her and she hasn't had an easy life. Her husband left her when her children were young and she had to bring them up on her own.'

'Oh, so you're friends now are you?' said Kit, his green eyes glistening with anger behind his glasses. 'Nice to know you've got time to natter all day while I'm hard at work earning all the money.'

Alison took an involuntary step backwards. She looked her husband up and down as if he were a stranger who'd just wandered off the street into her kitchen. 'In case you've forgotten, I gave up my career to bring up our children. *And* I more or less bring them up on my own.'

'Making packed lunches and doing the school run is *not* the same as being a company director.' He tutted, before pulling back his sleeve to examine his watch. 'Shit! I'm late for my train. We'll discuss this later.'

Shortly afterwards the front door slammed shut and a melancholy quiet settled throughout the house. Alison sat down, but the silence emphasised her laboured breathing, like someone at the onset of asthma. How *dare* he belittle her efforts with the children and at home. How *dare* he! And did he *really* believe he'd ever have achieved even half his successes at work if she hadn't been doing absolutely everything at home?

She stared out of the window at the beech tree standing resolute and strong against the blustery autumn wind, before placing her elbows on the table and dropping her head down into her hands. It was all so ridiculous! Kit had become so, so... controlling over the last few months. You would have thought becoming a company director would have somehow relaxed him, made him feel he'd made it. It surely gave them financial security for life. It had allowed them to buy this house. On the contrary though, he barely listened to her anymore, and kept ignoring all her ideas about the house. When she'd very reasonably pointed out to him recently that she hadn't agreed to the colours the painter was applying in the living room, he'd shouted at her that he was sick of how ungrateful she was and was he not allowed some say in his own house for once?

On top of all this she rarely saw him anymore because of the long hours he kept at the office and the persistent business travel, often overseas. On the rare occasions they spoke, he talked down to her these days, as if he was addressing a slow child, and any comments she made were met with winces and grimaces as though she was unnecessarily inconveniencing him. She prayed to god he didn't treat his staff at work like that, but suspected he did. Then there was his temper, which had always been bad, but was now constantly on a hair trigger ready to be detonated by the slightest thing which didn't go his way: screaming at everyone if the TV controller was lost, shouting that no one gave a damn when mud from shoes made it into the hall, swearing loudly if a shirt wasn't ironed properly.

She stood up to try to take her mind off it and walked to the window but, feeling a little woozy, had to steady herself by placing a hand on the wall. The beech tree was losing its battle to hang on to the last of its leaves, the final few swirling and falling, before being propelled upwards on surging squalls of wind, and falling again. A dab of white caught her attention: Mrs Gunn was just the other side of the fence, staring up at the beech tree.

'WHAT TIME ARE YOU OUT THIS MORNING?' ASKED KIT, standing at the new chrome island in the middle of the extended kitchen.

'The usual, about half eight. Why?' asked Alison.

Kit quickly shook his head. 'I was just wondering, that's all.' He left the room and went upstairs.

Alison began clearing away the cereal packets. She shouted to the kids, 'Noah, Megan, are you ready to go?' before putting the packed lunches into their school bags, but was distracted by Kit's question about what time she was leaving. Why did he care what time she was leaving to go to the gym? And now she thought about it, his working from home all day to meet the new gardener was a little odd considering how he hated working from home.

Underpinning her suspicions was the fact that her relationship with Kit continued to deteriorate. Just last night they'd argued after Kit had arrived home late from work and Alison had ventured that perhaps Noah should give up his guitar lessons as he had too much on and was clearly tired and unhappy. Kit had simply said, 'No,' and seemed to think that settled the matter. When she'd challenged him he'd immediately flown off the handle, accusing her of undermining him as a father and that he should have the final say 'for once', which was ridiculous given that he increasingly refused to countenance any of her opinions.

Noah and Megan appeared in the kitchen, ready for school. After dropping them off, she drove to the gym and began her spinning class with her friends Katie and Suzanne. Focussing on the instructor's commands and the strain of physical exercise had the effect of clearing her mind a little but towards the end of the class the doubts crept back in: Kit *knew* she was staying out for lunch today with Katie and Suzanne after the gym, he *knew* he had the house to himself until early afternoon. What was he up to?

In the changing room after the class she told Katie and Suzanne she felt unwell and would have to skip lunch. Once back inside the silent little capsule of her car, shielded from the hostility and unpredictability outside, a contemplative state drew down on her. She gazed at some water droplets sat suspended on the windscreen, her eyes drawn to how each refracted the grey white light in similar but unique ways. Her stare fell to her hand on top of the steering wheel and the waxy pale lunula crescent at the back of her thumb nail where it met the skin. She became conscious of the faint, sugary odour of the lilac cardboard air freshener hanging from the rear-view mirror, before the dread fully gripped the muscles in her gut again as she considered what Kit might be up to… but there was also the fear of how he'd react if she challenged anything he'd done. He would inevitably erupt in anger again and what if the cumulative effect of her querying him resulted in him losing it completely? What was he capable of? She stared through the car windscreen into the far distance without seeing anything at all as a terrible realisation hit home: she was afraid of her husband.

She gathered herself, knowing she had to face this, and drove home, but turning into her street, she immediately sensed a change: more light, like something vast had been pulled back, then saw a battered old white van in their driveway, a man up a crane and the top of the beech tree gone!

She pulled over and ran into the front garden shouting, 'Stop! Stop! You've made a mistake!' but couldn't be heard because the man up the crane was using a growling chainsaw to slice through the tree's main branch. Another man in a disgusting set of dirty overalls stepped in front of her to keep her back.

'Careful, love, it's dangerous!' he shouted.

'Stop! You must stop!' she shouted back.

'We can't! The owner wants it cut down!'

'*What?!*'

She saw Mrs Gunn on the other side of the garden fence and ran over; her bloodshot blue eyes were lacquered with tears which hadn't yet fallen.

'I'm so sorry, it must be a mistake!' Alison shouted.

'No, your husband ordered them to do it.'

Alison ran into the house, to find Kit standing by the lounge window looking outside and smiling to himself.

'What's happening?! You have to stop them!' The sound of the chainsaw still rumbled noisily in the background.

'I can't stop them, they've almost finished,' said Kit without looking at her; he was staring unblinking at the tree being cut down and smiling, but something strange had happened to his face, its features almost clown-like: the fixed upwards grin; the wide, high cheekbones; the shining, staring, vacant eyes.

'But the tree is protected, we'll be prosecuted.' She pulled on Kit's arm to get him to come outside.

He shook himself free, but continued to stare, transfixed, outside. 'No, our sewage pipes were being damaged by the tree's roots. We got permission from the council to cut it down.'

'What? What damage to the pipes?' she asked, stepping in front of Kit to try to make him look at her. It took a moment for her to process everything. She'd challenged Kit a month earlier when some builders had arrived and dug up part of their drive, but Kit had said the water company was simply doing a routine check.

How many other lies was he hiding? 'What's got into you, Kit?'

Kit was still staring at the tree and smiling in that strange, rigid way. He was oblivious to her, like he'd retreated into an inner compartment of his mind and preferred it there.

'Kit!' she shouted. 'Kit! You've completely lost your mind.'

Finally Kit turned to her, the backs of his eyes flinting. 'I haven't lost anything. I've won.'

'You what?'

'You heard me. I've won. No one stops *me* anymore. Those kids at school tried when they called me an onion. People at work tried but it just made me stronger. Now you and that old bat next door are trying to stop me, but it won't work, do you hear me? It won't work because this is *my* house! *I* paid for it. I *knew* you'd be against me cutting down the tree, just like that harridan next door, but I'm sick of taking orders, do you hear me? I paid £1 million for this house, so *I* decide if the tree stands or falls. *I* tell people what to do. Do you hear me? *I* tell them and they fucking well obey!' Kit hadn't blinked while speaking and still didn't now; Alison took an involuntary step backwards. At that moment the chainsaw ceased and they stared at each other in silence.

Alison broke the stare by glancing outside and gasped; Mrs Gunn had her arms wrapped around the trunk of the tree, hugging it to protect it from further assault, the trunk being all that remained.

Alison ran outside and Kit followed. The workman with the chainsaw had descended from the crane and he and his colleague were talking to Mrs Gunn, asking her to please step aside so they could complete their work.

'Get back,' said Alison to the workmen as she approached, uncomfortable with the way they were crowding the tiny old lady, who still had her arms wrapped around the tree. She barged past the men and put her hand on Mrs Gunn's shoulder. 'It's alright, Violet, they've stopped, I won't let them cut any more.'

Mrs Gunn's head swivelled; she was trembling and tear streaks wetted the fine wrinkles under her eyes, a sight which redoubled Alison's anger at her husband's treachery. She slowly ushered Mrs Gunn away from the tree. 'It's been there since the Rectory was built,' Mrs Gunn said as she was moved, sobbing.

'It's over now, it's all over,' said Alison. 'Let me speak to the men.' She turned to the workmen, who had backed away towards their van. 'You have to stop. I don't care what my husband has told you to do, it must stop now.'

The workmen wouldn't return Alison's hostile gaze; they glanced down at their feet, like guilty schoolchildren. Alison turned back to Mrs Gunn to make sure she was alright, when suddenly the growl of the chainsaw erupted.

All eyes turned: Kit had lifted the chainsaw in two hands and rushed towards the tree trunk.

'No!' shouted Alison.

Kit drove the chainsaw towards the trunk, but it bounced back off the wood and as it did so he lost control of the heavy tool; his hand fell off the top handle, it dropped downwards and the shrill whining of the blade intensified to a frenzied high pitch as it caught on Kit's flesh and sliced into his lower leg. 'ARRGHHHH!' he screamed as he fell backwards to the floor, his arms flung out to either side, like a crooked cross.

Mrs Gunn rushed forward and collapsed on Kit, but her weight on the chainsaw, such that the high pitch of its blade suddenly stuttered into a horrific clunking sound as it made contact with the bone in Kit's leg.

The workmen ran to Mrs Gunn and lifted her and the chainsaw away, as Alison fell to Kit's side. 'Oh my god, oh my god,' she said.

He rolled from side to side clutching his leg with vivid bright blood soaking his hands, all the while making animalistic grunting and snorting noises.

One of the workmen called for an ambulance while the other kept an eye on Mrs Gunn, who kept saying, 'I was trying to help him, I was just trying to help.'

Alison cradled Kit's head in her lap; he was still clutching his leg but his groaning calmed and he began mumbling a phrase to himself over and over again. She ran a hand over his forehead to comfort him and said, 'It's over, it's over, help is coming,' as Kit continued to repeat the same phrase. She leant forward to hear what he was saying.

'I am not an onion, I am not an onion, I am not an onion,' and seeing his face Alison realised to her horror that it wasn't over, for once again he'd retreated into the inner compartment of his mind; the clown's face returned with its fixed grin, and wide cheekbones, and shining, vacant eyes staring unblinking to where the trunk of the beech tree still stood.

SEEING IS DECEIVING

The baby monitor crackled: Jane reared upright from the sofa, her head jerking upward. A soft mewing could be heard and she waited paralyzed... before it cut to silence. Thank god. She was too exhausted to go up there again.

She clicked back on Facebook, anxious to upload the photo. She'd taken over twenty of Molly that morning and thankfully one had come out well. She wasn't sure it necessarily captured her daughter faithfully, but it was by far the cutest. As she searched for it, the now familiar dread washed through her abdomen again and she lifted her eyes to look at Gary, but surreptitiously. Sitting there as usual not saying anything. Staring into his mobile as usual. Sipping his wine without a care in the world *as usual*. What was he thinking about? *Who* was he thinking about?

Something was going on. Or some*one*. In recent weeks – or was it months? – he'd retreated into himself and she didn't know why. Tonight was a case in point. There was a time when their evenings meant spending quality time with each other: cooking and eating together at the kitchen table; conversing about their respective days and Gary making her laugh; plotting their plans for the future… it seemed like another life, like another couple, for here they were again sitting on opposite sides of their small, dark, shoebox-shaped living room in silence, the only sign of life being their tightly concentrated faces illuminated by the ghost light of their phones.

What was he looking at? *Who* was he looking at? She tried to take her mind off it by clicking on Facebook, but was immediately distracted by a post from Verity, Gary's ex from university. Even on their wedding day, there she'd been, speaking confidentially with Gary whenever she looked around, but – thank god! – she'd met someone a year ago. Better still, from the previous Facebook photos she'd seen, he not only looked like quite a catch – handsome in a slightly foppish way and a successful architect apparently – but they also appeared genuinely happy together. Verity's new post showed photos of their new house, an Edwardian semi with lots of original features such as red lattice brickwork, intricate cornicing, and large sash windows which bathed their tasteful furnishings in an abundance of natural light. Such happiness and affluence would usually depress Jane and make her question her own life's decisions and achievements, but seeing it embodied by Gary's ex with her partner comforted her, as it finally put to bed the threat Verity had once posed.

Gary rose and started for the door, and almost as an afterthought turned back to her and said, 'Fancy a wine?' She shook her head in disgust. 'Oh, sorry, I forgot,' he said. 'I'll get you a tea.' He walked off to the kitchen.

She reached down and stroked her tummy. How can a man forget his wife is three months pregnant? It was yet another damning piece of evidence. Added to which were his words from last night when they'd argued about one of Molly's pick-ups from nursery. 'I can't believe that with all I do for Molly, you can't show some flexibility,' she'd said.

'I *do* show flexibility. We *share* the childcare. *And* you've forgotten who the main breadwinner is.'

She'd been too startled to respond and kept hearing repeats in her head of his line. 'We *share* the childcare.' What cheek. He was out the door each morning before Molly got up, only saw her one evening in the week and maybe changed two nappies on average at weekends. That constituted *shared*, apparently. Her own list of responsibilities was endless: getting Molly up and dressed and ready seven days a week, cooking all her meals and washing up afterwards seven days a week, putting her to bed six days a week including bath time, teeth and bedtime stories. Checking her temperature and administering Calpol when she was unwell, taking her to the GP and to jabs, reading endless books about food for babies and toddlers, making sure nappies and wipes were in the weekly shop and with them wherever they went, researching and buying the travel cot – and putting the bloody thing up and taking it down when they went away! Applying for her passport, liaising with nursery, pick-up three days a week, cutting her nails, washing her hair, brushing her hair, ridding her hair of nits, taking her for haircuts – it struck her that her responsibilities to Molly's hair *alone* constituted more work than the entirety of her husband's contribution. Buying new shoes, buying new clothes, selling or passing on old clothes, washing clothes, drying clothes, folding clothes and taking them back upstairs, as well as washing *his* clothes and ironing *his* shirts. Changing the sheets on Molly's bed and washing them, taking her to birthday parties, organising her recent second birthday party, researching age-appropriate presents, comforting her whenever she was hurt or afraid (Molly never went to *him* for comforting), constantly feeling guilty when going to work and leaving Molly (she'd be amazed if *he* ever experienced any guilt) and last but not least worrying over and over again about every single last component of Molly's tender young life in the knowledge that the buck stopped with *her* as the primary carer, the worry compounded by the crushing certainty that if she missed any one of the million things on the never-ending to-do list then her husband sure as hell wouldn't remember. 'We *share* the childcare.'

Running through the inequities of their contributions reminded her of one of the things she now most resented about Gary: Molly's birth had barely changed *his* life at all. She conceded he loved Molly dearly, and pictured her giggling hysterically while riding on his back as he whinnied and neighed pretending to be a horse, and him lifting her high in the air repeatedly with a whooshing sound pretending she was a rocket travelling to the moon. But why did he get to play fun dad, while she was relegated to chores and responsibilities?

He ambled back into the room with a full glass of red wine and handed her a mug of tea.

'Thanks,' she said.

'You're welcome,' he replied. 'What's this?' he asked.

'What?'

'That,' said Gary, pointing at her mobile phone, which was face up and showing photos of Verity.

'Oh,' said Jane, heat reddening her face. 'It's just Facebook.'

'But why are you looking at Verity's photos?'

'We're friends on Facebook, okay? She posted some photos and I was looking at them.'

Gary reached for her phone. 'Let's see,' he said.

She snatched up her phone and clicked off Facebook. She didn't like the thought of him knowing she'd been looking at Verity's photos, let alone *him* staring at them. 'It's nothing. Just photos of her new house.'

Gary stood momentarily still, before returning to his chair and dropping into it with a thud. He immediately reached for his mobile and brought it to his face, its glow again throwing an eerie half-light onto his face, such that the exaggerated shadows of his features – his nose, his frowning brow, his heavy-set chin – made him look like a man lurking with intent down a poorly-lit back alley at night.

She stared at him until eventually he looked up. 'Don't worry,' he said, 'I'm not on Facebook, I'm reading the news.'

The trouble was, Gary so rarely seemed really *present* these days. For a while she'd persuaded herself that his increasing distraction was probably some sort of reaction to fatherhood. She'd tried talking to him about it, but he kept just shaking his head and tutting and saying, 'I'm fine.' It had crossed her mind whether stress at work was causing his behaviour, but he'd reassured her that everything was in hand.

She'd then thought perhaps his moods were *her* fault? Can a man ever see his wife in the same light after having to buy her breast pads at the supermarket, or being informed of perineal tears, or confronting an afterbirth? Or perhaps all the attention she'd given Molly had made him feel unwanted or unloved? Perhaps her lengthy physical recovery after giving birth and resulting lack of a physical relationship had emasculated him? Or worse still she feared the explanation lay in the daily reveal in the bathroom mirror. She'd never been a slim girl, but since childbirth her stolid, pear-shaped body had swollen and slackened and now appeared grotesquely misshapen in places, particularly around her midriff. She kept meaning to do something about it, kept meaning to reduce her calories or take some exercise, or upload one of those fitness apps, or book a Pilates class, but all her good intentions kept being swamped by her daily chores.

If it *was* her looks, that surely meant he could be tempted elsewhere? Oh god. Unable to bear thinking about it, she picked up her cup of tea in two hands, holding it to her chest for warmth.

'I'm out tomorrow night,' said Gary.

She traced back in her mind for any evidence that he'd previously mentioned it. 'You never said.'

'Didn't I?'

'No, you didn't. I would have remembered.'

He scrunched his shoulders. 'It's no big deal, it's just a work do.'

His casualness annoyed her as much as his abandonment of her. 'Why go then?'

'I'm sorry?'

'If it's *no big deal*, why go?'

He reached for his wine and took another large slurp; his glass was already almost empty. He must have done another whole bottle tonight; another complaint to add to the list. 'It's someone's leaving do, it's important I go,' he said.

'Whose leaving do?'

'Dan.'

She'd never heard of him. 'Where are you going?'

Critically, he paused before replying. 'Er… The Bank of England. It's a pub on Fleet Street.'

'But you never said.' She couldn't believe that all his staring into his phone and his now going out after work were unrelated. 'So you're going to leave me to deal with Molly on my own *again*.'

He tipped back his head while upturning his glass, draining the last of his wine. 'Jesus, Jane. You seem to think money grows on trees. My job demands I socialize occasionally, okay?' He stood up and walked out; moments later she heard the plop of a cork releasing from another bottle, only he didn't return to the lounge.

She sat stock-still in the near darkness, her heart thumping under her sweatshirt as her fears crystallised into a certainty: Gary was seeing another woman.

THE FOLLOWING EVENING SHE SAT RIGID AND ALONE IN THE darkened living room in her winter coat and scarf, waiting for the doorbell to ring. Occasionally she heard a car approach and turn the corner outside, as it did so its headlight beam momentarily sweeping through the shadows on the wall, like a searchlight scanning the perimeter fence of a prison at night.

On her non-work day she normally got some chores done, but not that day. Weeks of growing fears about Gary, and the overwhelming prospect of a new baby in a few months' time, had finally defeated her. She'd barely slept the previous night, even spending an hour at twilight searching the property apps for modestly priced flats for her, Molly

and the new baby should the worst come to the worst. She'd
spent the day in a sorrowful daze, surrounded by half done
things, like cold cups of tea undrunk and the washing
powder packet taken from the cupboard but standing
unopened on the side.

All she could think about was what Gary might be up to.
And *with whom.* She'd again had one of her paranoia fits
about the women in Gary's office, which came to her
occasionally whenever she remembered the time she'd been
in there to show his colleagues Molly just after her birth.
She pictured them all, just like they'd been that day, lined up
like harlots in the harem. His secretary Julia with her big tits
and bright lipstick; surely he wouldn't stoop so low? That
young girl Jessica he often mentioned in passing, so petite
and demure; what if she developed a crush on Gary as her
boss? And of course the most dangerous one of the lot:
Bina, big-eyed, slim, exotic and clearly absolutely certain of
her effect on men; Jane wanted to scratch her eyes out!

He could be out with any one of them tonight. All while
she was chained to the house and caring for *his* daughter!
Carrying *his* unborn child! It was intolerable! But then she
had an idea: she could check up on Gary *tonight.* Moments
later, she'd called a babysitter.

As she waited for her now she clicked on Facebook
again, meaning to upload yesterday's photo of Molly, but
her old school friend Gemma had just posted photos from a
weekend in France: just look at her long, luxuriant blonde
hair, so rich and lustrous, blowing in the Parisian breeze.
She reached up and tucked a strand of her own thin, lank
hair behind her ear, hair which she'd once just about got
away with calling strawberry blonde, but was now more
accurately a lifeless colour, like watered-down gravy poured
over her skull. God, Facebook was so annoying; the more

you resented someone's post, the more you had to 'like' it for fear if you didn't it might betray your real feelings. She pushed her thumb to the screen and reluctantly turned the 'like' sign from grey to blue. Gemma already had seven 'likes' and had only posted a few minutes ago.

The doorbell's harsh buzz blared and Jane stood to let the babysitter in. She seemed nice enough, but Jane still hated the forced niceness and having to show her where the Calpol was kept and how the baby monitor worked, and worse still when the lady looked her up and down quizzically and asked, 'Going anywhere nice tonight?'

'Er… just to see a friend,' she replied, suddenly conscious of how she must appear with her bloodshot eyes, greasy lank unwashed hair and dressed in food-stained tracksuit bottoms.

She strode to the tube station, figuring the quicker she got this done the quicker she'd get back home to Molly, adjusting her hat and scarf as she went to shield herself from the bitter, biting cold and freezing drizzle. The glare of the lights in the tube station foyer affronted her eyes as she entered and rushed down the steep-stepped escalator to the District Line platform below, standing at the very end of the platform and pulling her scarf above her nose to reduce the chances of anyone recognising her. Soon a train arrived and as it rattled along the tunnels into London, Jane kept seeing images of Molly waking and crying, her innocent face puckered in confusion and distress after discovering a complete stranger leaning into her cot from above. God, she hated being separated from her daughter, but she *had* to know the truth! She wouldn't be kept in the dark any longer!

At Temple Station, she hurried up the stairs, but carefully, as their smooth concrete surfaces were slippery with rainwater trampled in by commuters, and once in the street, checked her phone for directions and walked up the road to Fleet Street. She wondered when the fear of discovering the truth would start, but her anger and sense of purpose were ascendant. She deserved the truth! The sign of the Bank of England, lit from a spotlight above, came into view through the misty rain but still no fear, rather she drew deep breaths of saturated frosted air into her lungs as she climbed the steps and thought how alive she felt. *She* was in control for once.

Opening the heavy door with two hands and stepping inside, the heat and musty smell hit her; she immediately lowered her head, fearing being recognized, and walked to the bar. There, she furtively glanced around; the pub was quiet, with no sign of someone's leaving party. The barman approached her.

'Has anyone booked a function room tonight?' she asked. 'I'm looking for a leaving party.'

'There's a party in the room next door.' He pointed to where it was. 'It's booked under the name Glazer.'

'Thanks.' She walked to the door, but hesitated once her hand touched the handle and she heard the hum of conversation from beyond. Now the fear gripped her: what if he was just the other side of the door? How would he react? Would he ever forgive her? She squeezed the handle tighter; this wasn't about *his* feelings.

She pulled her scarf back up over her nose, pulled the door open and stepped inside; she again lowered her head and made for the bar, acutely conscious that everyone was dressed smartly and she couldn't have looked more out of place in her tracksuit bottoms and trainers. She pulled her mobile from her pocket and pretended to look at it, ignoring the barman, keeping her back to the throng. After a few seconds, she turned; everyone was talking in their groups and ignoring her, thankfully. She scanned the room, but could see neither Gary nor anyone she recognised from his work, before a tall, dark-haired woman in a white blouse appeared in front of her, her thin painted lips curled upward at one side in disdain. 'Can I help you?' she asked.

'Is this Dan's leaving party?'

'I'm afraid you've got the wrong place; this is my birthday party drinks.'

'Right, sorry,' said Jane and headed for the door. Seconds later she was outside, bent over with her hands on her knees and panting like she'd been holding her breath the whole time inside. Drips of icy cold rain trickled down the back of her neck. She *knew* Gary had lied.

ONCE HOME, SHE RELIEVED THE BABYSITTER AND RUSHED upstairs to Molly, who was sound asleep, but something about her tranquility lying in her cot – her flawless skin like fine powder, the stillness of her closed almond shaped eyes – and the contrast with the madness and deceit of her own life was too much to bear. She staggered through to her bedroom and collapsed on the bed, weeping with great guttural yelps which she tried to suppress lest she wake Molly. What sort of life could her daughter possibly hope for in a world populated by sociopaths like her father, so willing to betray those closest to them? She closed her eyes tight and tried to forget everything, forget Molly, forget Gary, forget her custodial sentence of a life, focusing solely on the warmth and closeness of the winter coat, hat and scarf she still had on, enclosing and protecting her, keeping her safe, until eventually her breathing slowed…

Sometime later the thump of the front door closing

woke her: Gary was back. As her groggy, half-asleep mind
cleared a little she began to wonder what she would say to
him, but then heard footsteps on the stairs. Shit, she was still
dressed! She stood and ripped off her clothes, stuffing them
under the bed and slipping under the duvet just as he came
in… she heard him moving about in the darkness and
knocking into his bedside table, which surely would have
woken her had she been asleep. He tutted and turned on his
bedside lamp. She sat up.

'Oh, you're awake,' he said.

She stared at him, the man she'd once loved, as he
removed his clothes. She could smell the bitter sweet alcohol
on him, but was it just booze, or were there also the more
fragrant notes of a perfume? 'Where have you been?'

He sat down on the bed, twisting his torso to look at her,
his eyes half closed. 'You what?'

'I want to know where you've been.'

'I told you, it was a work do.'

'Yes, but *where* was it?'

He sighed. 'What does it matter?'

'I don't believe you.'

'What?'

'I don't believe you were at a leaving do at the Bank of
England.'

'I don't know what you're talking about. We went to…
to Daly's Wine Bar, and had a few drinks, alright?'

'That's not where you said you were going. You said you
were going to the Bank of England.'

'Did I? Well we didn't, we were in Daly's.'

She was *sure* he'd said the Bank of England. Hadn't he?
Now she doubted herself. Surely the recce all the way into
town hadn't been for nothing? Oh god. She fell back on
the bed and turned away from him, tears welling in her

eyes but not daring to cry properly for fear he'd think her crazy.

Gary lay down on the bed, shuffled over and put his arm around her. She tensed at the touch of his warm, clammy skin and thought about pushing him away and accusing him outright, but what evidence did she have? Had it all been her imagination, her paranoia? She didn't know. She didn't know anything anymore. Her body swelled with the need to sob, but she strained and held it in.

Gary's hand shifted around her midriff until it lay flat against her swollen belly; she held her breath, not daring to move. Slowly, Gary started to stroke her tummy, stroking their unborn baby. Surely such a gesture wasn't possible from an adulterer? *Surely*?! She slowly let out her breath again.

She desperately longed to trust him, but when she searched deep within herself to ask whether she believed he was telling the truth, she just didn't know. She tried to clear her mind to think only of Molly and the baby, her innocent children, and remaining strong for them, remaining steadfast and secure for them, and ever so slowly she began to relax, despite her husband's gently caressing hand.

SHE ORDERED A DOUBLE ESPRESSO, STANDING AT THE TILL IN a baseball cap, scarf and coat, never taking her eyes off the entrance to her husband's offices across the road throughout the process of paying for and collecting her drink and walking to one of the tall seats by the counter running the length of the front window. She glanced at her watch – 5.43pm – and quickly back up again. She couldn't miss him. She'd called him on his office number at about a quarter to

5pm, just before setting off, to check he was still there. She
needed this sorted tonight or she feared for her sanity. The
days since last week's trip to the Bank of England had been
a living hell; half the time she still doubted him but had no
evidence against him, and the rest of the time she doubted
her own mind. She hated herself for the way she kept
checking his phone for evidence of wrongdoing whenever
he left it unattended; but surely *he* was to blame for her
doing so?

So when last night he'd again unexpectedly announced
an evening out – this time with an old university friend
called Richard who she'd never met and couldn't recall
Gary ever mentioning before – she'd immediately gone
upstairs and booked the same babysitter. She'd twice asked
him where he was going, but both times he'd said, 'We
haven't decided yet.'

Suddenly he appeared from his office – he looked
different somehow at a distance and in a new setting, like a
stranger – and in reflex she stood up, her lungs opening to
allow air to flood in as she walked to the door, all her
faculties and senses firing with adrenalin. He started walking
westwards along Fleet Street; keeping a close eye on him she
crossed the road so that she was about twenty feet behind.
Did his leaving the office alone rule out an office romance?
Or would two people in an office romance never be so
stupid as to leave the office together?

Walking down Fleet Street to Strand, she expected him
to walk on towards Trafalgar Square, perhaps for Covent
Garden, but he turned left by Saint Clement Danes church,
heading towards Temple tube station. Keeping him in sight,
but not daring to get too close, she followed, then sped up to
narrow the gap as he entered the station and descended the
steps onto the westbound platform, which was heavily

populated with commuters giving her plenty of cover. She stood behind a heavy man in a grey suit and as the first train pulled up – a District Line to Wimbledon – she glanced over to see him boarding, so did likewise into the same carriage but through the doors one along. Why was he taking his home commute train? Surely just a coincidence? He'd sat down; she remained standing with her scarf over her face fifteen feet away, making sure she stood on the same side of the train as him to reduce the odds of being inadvertently spotted.

The train passed through the obvious stops to change line or to meet someone: Embankment, Westminster, Victoria, eventually approaching Earl's Court; if he stayed on here, he was surely going home? How would she explain the babysitter?! The train slowed and stopped and the doors opened. Shit shit shit, he wasn't moving!

The train pulled away: West Brompton, Fulham Broadway, Parsons Green; still he remained seated. Fuck! Perspiration matted her hair under her hat as her heart clenched and unclenched inside her chest like a fist; what stress was she putting on the baby?!

Their home station was next. Or perhaps he was staying on to Wimbledon to meet his friend there?

The train slowed into Southfields and Jane readied herself while looking at Gary out of the corner of her eye. The doors opened, but he sat still; suddenly he stood and walked off the train. Shit shit shit. She gave it a few seconds to let him move on and just as the beeps started to signal the imminent closing of the doors, she stepped off onto the platform. She followed him as he made his way along the platform and up the stairs.

In a few minutes' time he'd arrive home to find the babysitter and not know what on earth was going on. What would she tell him? Perhaps she could say she'd been feeling stressed about the pregnancy and needed a friend to talk to? But who? Oh god, she needed to get her story straight…

He turned *left* out the station. Why left? She hurried to the exit and saw him thirty feet or so down the road. She let the gap increase a little and again followed.

Surely he would have mentioned it if his friend was so local? Wouldn't he? After two hundred yards he turned left again down a residential road and Jane lost sight of him. She sped up and as she came to the junction, slowed and glanced left: he was standing a hundred feet away facing a house, he looked left and right – Jane's heart stopped in case he saw her – and stepped towards the house, disappearing from view. She walked slowly down the street, trying to isolate which house it had been, expecting to find him standing at a door, but he was nowhere to be seen. Did he have a key? Had the door been unlocked and he'd gone straight in?

She walked a little further, approaching what she thought was the house, a semi-detached period property; it looked vaguely familiar, although in the darkness it was difficult to tell. The lights were on and the curtains open in the front room, but she couldn't see anyone inside. The interior was tastefully decorated with a neatly stacked floor-to-ceiling fitted bookcase on one wall and a large antique gilded mirror over an original cast iron fireplace with William Morris design tiles on the other. The gate to the side of the house swung open on the wind and hit the wooden garden fence with a thud; had he entered that way? Sensing some movement down the road she looked right; an elderly man walking a small dog approached and, feeling acutely self-conscious just standing and loitering in the dark, she returned up the road from whence she'd come. At the junction, she stopped and pretended to consult her phone, allowing the dog walker to pass. She looked back down the road. Should she return to the house? And knock on the door? She couldn't, she just couldn't, they'd think her mad. She stood paralysed for a few moments, before reluctantly turning, and setting off for home.

AFTER RELIEVING THE BABYSITTER AND CHECKING ON Molly, who was asleep, Jane flopped onto her bed. As her breathing subsided and her pulse slowed, a sense of resignation began to settle inside her like a clinging, damp fog. Maybe her fears had been all her own making, but if not she'd know soon enough; when he returned she'd ask Gary where he'd been tonight and the matter would be settled: either he'd confirm his friend Richard lived locally, or else he'd make up a story about some other venue and she'd know he'd been lying.

She took out her phone and clicked on Facebook, only to see another post from Verity, Gary's ex, showing her and her fiancé standing in bright sunlight in their neatly manicured small garden with a comment about how nice it was to have outdoor space after years of living in a flat. Her nose scrunched in disgust at the way people so carefully selected photos which pretended to casually update everyone on their news, but in fact had been painstakingly chosen to generate as much envy as humanly possible.

Her concentration cut back to Gary and all the commitments they'd made to each other: their marriage day and their solemn vows in front of the gathered congregation, indeed in front of God; the birth of their daughter, their beautiful, innocent mutual creation, and all they'd done since to cherish and protect her precious, tender young life; the fact she was pregnant again and needed him now more than ever as the miracle of life slowly grew inside her. Surely he wouldn't risk *all that* for a brief, grubby affair? *All that* traded for a frantic few seconds of disgusting sweaty clinch and sordid little squirt? My god, it wasn't possible, surely? But what if it wasn't just an affair, what if he was planning a *future* with someone else? She pictured again the harlots in the harem of his office, all lined up with their false smiles and sinister intentions.

She stroked her lower tummy as it clenched repeatedly in worry. As had happened throughout the last few days, a powerful guilt gripped her at the thought of her unborn child suffering from the stress and anguish of its mother. What effect would it have on the baby's development? You read such terrible stories: of genetic deformity, and stunted growth, and abnormality, and misshapenness. What if it had all been for nothing and Gary had been innocent all along?

She clicked on Facebook to take her mind off it and remembered she *still* hadn't posted the recent photograph of Molly. She did it now, experiencing a little shot of excitement as the photo went live and she anticipated just how many people would soon be experiencing this insight into her life. Unlike most people's, *her* post was justified; if you couldn't be proud of your own child, what was the point in anything?

Perhaps everything would be alright. Perhaps Gary *would* confirm he'd been with his friend Richard at his nearby house and her life would return to normal. Perhaps it had all just been in her head all along, her imagination running wild. The first 'like' of Molly's photograph appeared, then another, and another, each one a tiny confirmation of… of acceptance. Momentarily she felt capable, felt *normal* and that simple feeling caused a deep squeeze of emotion in her core and as she stared down at the Facebook photograph of Molly on her phone a single tear fell from her eye onto the screen.

She undressed, got into bed and soon dozed off, only to be shocked awake sometime later by a brassy blast of the doorbell. Had Gary forgotten his key? Her bedside clock said half past midnight. She rose, picked her dressing gown off the hook on the back of the bedroom door and pulled it on. The doorbell rang loud again. 'I'm coming!' she shouted.

She descended the stairs and opened the front door, only to see a policewoman: adrenalin shot through her system. 'What? What is it?'

'Can I confirm you're Jane Isleworth?' the policewoman asked, expressionless.

'Yes, yes, that's me,' said Jane, nodding vigorously. 'What is it? What's going on?'

'Can I come in please?'

Jane backed away to allow her entry. 'What's this about?'

'It's about your husband.'

'He's okay, isn't he?' Her mind fizzed off terrible images of him being knocked down by a car, or mugged, or knifed.

'He's safe, if that's what you mean. I think it's best we sit down.'

'Okay,' said Jane, suddenly nauseous and weightless and unsteady on her feet. She showed the policewoman through to the kitchen and they each took a seat at the small pine table, the single overhead light giving the room an eerie, hazy, sodium glow, intensified by the pitch darkness outside abutting the curtainless, single-glazed window.

The policewoman removed her hat and looked Jane

clean in the eye. 'I'm afraid your husband was arrested earlier this evening and is currently at the police station answering questions.'

'Oh my god,' said Jane, bringing her hand to her mouth. 'What for?'

'I'm so sorry, this isn't going to be easy for you, but Gary's been arrested for trespassing and on suspicion of stalking.'

The word *stalking* hung in the air, like the slowly subsiding resonance of a large bell after being tolled. Jane sat very still, just the blinking of her eyes and the rise and fall of her chest visible. Eventually she said to the policewoman, 'Who was he stalking?'

The policewoman looked down at her notepad and flipped the first few pages. 'A Miss Verity Jones.'

Jane shrieked like a wild animal whose claw has just been crushed in a trap, her head collapsing onto the table as she wept uncontrollably, gasping for breath between wretched, wrenching sobs. The policewoman pulled her chair closer and put an arm around Jane's shoulder to comfort and calm her. They stayed that way for some time, Jane repeatedly saying, 'No,' with varying degrees of volume and intonation, but all drenched in misery.

'What was he doing when he was arrested?' asked Jane eventually, sitting up a little.

'I'm so sorry, but earlier this evening Verity's partner thought he saw someone in their back garden and when he checked he found your husband. He restrained him, but then Gary broke down and confessed everything.'

'Oh my god,' said Jane, shaking her head. 'Where? Where's Verity's house?'

The policewoman consulted her pad again. 'Seymour Road.'

'Is that close by?'

'Yes, it's just the other side of Southfields tube station.'

Jane keeled over like someone winded from being unexpectedly punched hard in the stomach, clutching her midriff. 'What else has he done?' she spluttered. 'Please, I need to know, what else?'

'We're hoping you might be able to tell us. Have you noticed him doing anything unusual recently? Anything at all?'

Despite it all, her instinct was to protect him. 'He's been very distant recently… and he's been out some evenings… but I'm not aware of him doing anything like, like… stalking.' Mention of the word *stalking* crushed her spirit all over again and she wept with great juddering yelps.

After a while the policewoman eased Jane upright and said, 'Listen, I'm sorry to have to push you on this but is there anything else you can tell us about Gary's behaviour? It's really important we know everything.'

'I'm not aware of anything,' she said, shaking her head. 'I'm not aware of him doing anything other than what you've told me.' The inner lining of Jane's stomach ached like it had been scraped raw with some sort of blunt metal instrument. 'What do *you* know about what he's done? I mean, apart from his arrest tonight, what else has he done?'

'We really don't know yet. Your husband has assured us that tonight is the first time this has happened. He said he became fixated with Verity after seeing all her recent posts on social media.'

Jane couldn't get enough air into her lungs and clutched her chest as she started gasping.

'*Breathe*,' said the policewoman. 'Try to breathe slowly.'

Jane couldn't comprehend it all, but a sense of deep shame started to tug at her for her own constant use of

Facebook, at her own preoccupation and anxiousness to forever log-in to discover all the details of other people's lives, and to gawp and judge and envy, although... although surely just *looking* at the site wasn't the same as... as whatever Gary had been doing?

It was all too much and the devastation again crushed her, causing her to weep uncontrollably with a series of distressing high-pitched wails. The policewoman again put an arm around Jane and repeatedly said, 'It'll be alright, it'll be alright.'

THE POLICEWOMAN EVENTUALLY RECEIVED A PHONE CALL from the police station, following which she explained to Jane that she would stay with her until Gary returned home. She confirmed that the police were satisfied that Gary posed no immediate danger to Verity and that he wasn't yet going to be charged, pending further inquiries to validate his statement.

During the hour that followed, sitting in the cold of the kitchen with a red tartan blanket wrapped around her shoulders and holding a cup of tea for warmth and distraction, the policewoman talked Jane through where she could find support and advised her that social services would be in touch, as was standard procedure whenever a parent of a young child was arrested. Most of it passed Jane by, such was her preoccupation about the future and the filthy public shame now staining her family. Eventually she heard a key scraping in the lock of the front door; she reared upright, her eyes trained towards the hallway.

The policewoman gave Jane a hug and went to meet Gary, speaking to him briefly in the hall in a low voice before leaving. Gary shambled into the kitchen, head down, and slumped into the seat at the kitchen table that the policewoman had been sitting in.

He looked dreadful: drawn and haggard, his face completely colourless, his eyes lifeless and cold, the very image of a man in a police mugshot whose expression betrays his knowledge that his life will never be the same again. She wondered to what extent she knew him at all and a surge of anger swept through her. She was about to shout at him, but the baby moved in her belly; instead she rested her hand atop her bump and composed herself. She stayed still and silent, refusing to lose her temper or to cry in front of him, indeed refusing to show any emotion at all.

Gary broke down and cried out, 'I'm so sorry, I didn't know what I was doing!' Jane remained silent, staring at him. 'I promise you, I only went round there once. I'm not the monster you think I am!'

'Do you still love Verity? Tell me the truth.'

'No! No, I don't love her, I swear, Jane, I don't. I just became obsessed. It was all her posts on Facebook, constantly showing off about her new boyfriend, and all their holidays and their engagement and their new home. It was like she was taunting me. Please, Jane, I swear it will never happen again.' Jane sat motionless. 'I love you, Jane, and Molly, and our baby. Please, Jane, you must know, I love my family.'

She couldn't process it, let alone trying to work out what was going on inside Gary's head. It was all too much. She'd need time to think it through and the implications for her and the children. There could be no future for her and Gary, surely, but she couldn't bear the thought of being alone and her children fatherless. She refused to think further about it, trying instead to think of something, anything, to hold onto to make things better. One small action came to mind, a tiny step whereby she might begin to recover from having her world collapse and slowly start to rebuild. 'Where's your phone?' she asked.

'What?'

'I said where's your phone? Get it out now.'

Gary reached into his pocket and pulled his phone out. Jane did likewise with hers.

'We're both going to close our Facebook accounts right now. And I mean *forever*.'

Gary nodded and they both clicked on the app and searched through its settings to close their respective accounts.

Once done, Gary again broke down, sobbing with his head bowed and unable to look Jane in the eye. 'You and Molly mean more to me than anything,' he said in a pained high-pitched voice. 'I don't know what I was thinking, it was as though I'd lost my mind.'

Jane sat wordless and motionless, her hand still atop her tummy. After some time, she rose. 'I can't deal with this now. I'm going to bed. You'll have to sleep on the sofa.'

'Please, Jane, don't leave me here like this.'

'You're lucky I'm letting you stay here at all, after what you've done. We'll speak tomorrow.'

As Jane took a step towards the door, Gary whimpered and slid off his chair onto the floor with a thud, reaching out and clutching her ankles. '*Please* Jane, I know you'll never forgive me. I love you, but you'll never forgive me.'

Jane stepped out of Gary's hold and he collapsed fully onto the floor, a streak of translucent green snot dribbling from his nose and his face knotted in anguish. Amongst the fierce and surging thoughts and emotions of her exhausted mind, she just wanted to find a place of sanctuary. She knew any journey to recovery with Gary would take months, even years, if ever, but seeing him grovelling for mercy brought to mind not just the failure of this one man, but all the weaknesses of mankind. 'No one is beyond forgiveness,' she said and went upstairs to bed.

UNIVERSAL SUFFERAGE

'Oh, for god's sake,' said George, spotting the long queue snaking left and right up to the check-in desks.

He'd just arrived at Heathrow Airport with his wife Emily for their first holiday in over two decades without their children. They joined the end of the queue. Every so often it shuffled forward and George would pick up their suitcase and place it two feet further along the line. He blew out his breath in frustration.

'Please,' whispered his wife. 'Be patient.'

He shook his head, still unable to process the referendum result. It made him look like a fool, heading for a holiday just when he was needed most in the office, but he'd very reasonably booked it safe in the knowledge that surely the Prime Minister, who clearly had a first-class mind, would never have allowed such an idiotic ballot to take place unless he knew what the outcome would be: a clear Remain win. Not only that but all the experts had been clear: Remain *would* win. Not a single credible voice had predicted otherwise. But when his alarm had woken him abruptly at 5am and he'd turned on the radio, he couldn't believe what he'd heard: the UK had voted Leave, his stomach knotting instantly followed by a nauseating disorientation as various certainties he held dear fell away. 'Just how many idiots are there in this country?' he kept asking himself as he showered, dressed and double checked the plane tickets and passports. The radio had soon provided the answer: over 17 million people had voted Leave.

The queue inched forward. George had that early flight wired feeling of exhaustion and dehydration, his heavy eyes assaulted by the departure hall's bright lights and TV monitors, and too many people in close proximity. It wasn't helped by the noisy family in front, a couple with two young children, all wearing sportswear heavily embossed with the manufacturers' logos. There was a certain irony to this, thought George, as judging from the pot belly of the father, he clearly didn't use his sports apparel for any form of exercise. Nor the scrawny, undernourished mother, with her hollowed-out cheeks and sharp bones; probably a heavy drinker and smoker. George's eyes were then drawn in grim fascination to the tattoos littering the length of the father's arms, proudly shown off by the white sports vest he wore. They spoke in an accent which George couldn't quite place but was definitely northern. He leant towards his wife and whispered, 'I bet they voted Brexit.'

'Shhhh,' said his wife, glaring at him. 'We're meant to be on holiday.'

The queue crept forward. Just how difficult can it be in the twenty-first century to scan a passport and issue a boarding card? It amazed him that they hadn't invented a machine to do the job in seconds so the airlines could dispense with the clearly ineffective operatives manning the check-ins. As George pondered this the Brexit couple's kids became restless: the young son – perhaps aged three and with lime green snot bubbling from his nose – kept wandering off, causing the mother to repeatedly stride after him to grab him by the arm and drag him back; the daughter – perhaps aged seven – kept whining, 'Can I have the iPad?' over and over again. Sportswear. Tattoos. Computer games. Snot. Welcome to Brexit Britain.

ONCE CHECKED-IN, GEORGE DIALLED INTO A CONFERENCE call with his colleagues in Human Resources; he'd put the call in the diary a week before the referendum, 'just in case'. On the call, he asked his number two, Fiona, to action and lead the (admittedly rather lightweight) contingency plans they'd drawn up in case of Brexit: reviewing the nationalities of their workforce; scenario planning for potential new immigration laws; considering employee communications, particularly as many of their employees were young people from the Continent. And to think all this was avoidable! It staggered him that his county had actually *chosen* this madness! Fortunately, George had spent the last five years carefully building a team around him that he knew he could trust and whom he'd fully empowered to take responsibility. He considered his ability to delegate to be his greatest strength as a leader.

After the call, he and his wife made their way to departures, only to be met by another long queue leading up to the scanners and security; George's shoulders slumped and he breathed out heavily through his nose. 'Jesus, this is hell on earth.' He couldn't help but reflect on the agony of this travelling experience compared to the business-class travel he undertook regularly as part of this job: the chauffeur-driven Mercedes saloon courtesy car picking him up from home ('Let me help you with your bags, Sir'); the immediate transfer through to the first-class lounge with complimentary Wi-Fi, freshly brewed coffee, freshly squeezed orange juice, fruit, croissant, pastries and newspapers. And definitely not a Brexit voter in sight!

George consulted his phone: total carnage! The UK stock market had just opened and millions were being wiped off its value by the minute. Speculation was rife that the Prime Minister might resign! Story after story confirmed the idiocy of it all, and he blamed the likes of the ghastly Brexit family he'd seen in the queue. *You've caused all this,* he thought, *you actually chose this! Despite all the clear warnings from all the experts so much more qualified than you, you still thought no, my life's shit, so I'll fuck up everyone else's...*

'Shoes off, please,' came a voice close by, George glancing up to see a joyless, overweight security guard thrusting a black plastic tray at him. He hated the indignity of all this, having to remove his shoes and belt and having a stranger frisk him, and for what? A knife? A bomb? Surely one look at him should satisfy them: white, fifties, beige slacks, polo shirt, blue sports jacket, side parting, clean shaven. Hardly the profile of a mass-murdering terrorist.

Having walked through the scanner (mercifully it didn't bleep) he retrieved his tray and was threading his belt back through the hoops of his trousers when he heard another man's voice, 'Is this your bag, Sir?'

George glanced around to double check that the guard meant *him,* but then saw him holding *his* bag. 'Yes, that's mine, why?'

'Can you step this way please, Sir?' said the guard in the formal monotone of an order rather than a question. He looked like a military type, square jawed and empty headed. George tutted and checked where his wife was: sitting on a bench a few feet away putting on her shoes. 'Can you *please* come here,' said the security guard.

'Okay, okay, I'm coming.'

The guard stared at George, deadpan. 'Did you pack this bag yourself?'

'Of *course* I did,' said George. Another glare from the guard. 'I mean yes, sorry.' Fuck, he hated this! The jobsworth proceeded to check his bag with completely unnecessary exactitude, taking out every item in turn, examining each methodically from all angles and carefully placing them in a pile to one side. After three or four long minutes during which George felt the eyes of fellow passengers crawling all over him, the guard was done. 'Thank you, Sir, you may proceed,' he said, stepping back from the counter.

'*I'll* repack everything then, shall I?' asked George.

'Excuse me?' said the guard, stepping forward again.

Heat rushed up the back of George's neck; he wouldn't be bullied by an officious halfwit prick in uniform. 'Let me ask you something,' said George. Turning, he caught sight of the Brexit family and pointed at Mr Brexit. 'You let *him* go through without checking *his* bags. Am I really a more likely drug trafficker than *him?*'

The guard's eyes flicked to Brexit then back to George. There was a brief silence. 'I think I may have to take you through for further quest—'

'What's happening, George?' said his wife Emily, appearing and glancing alternatively at her husband and the security guard.

George quickly decided he wanted the confrontation over. 'Okay, I'll pack my bag now.'

The guard gave George a sardonic little smile. 'Very good, Sir.'

THE AIRPORT HAD BEEN DESIGNED SO THAT ONCE PASSENGERS cleared security, they were forced to walk along a winding route through a large, brightly lit duty-free shop to get to the departure gates. Clever, thought George, the way they herded the unthinking into their shop and made them pass every type of merchandise, forcing temptation upon them. Of course, the company he worked as Human Resources Director for – an international fashion chain – had to spend millions on marketing, advertising and public relations to entice customers in, but he'd do exactly the same if he ran airports. Besides, a certain type of traveller craved making purchases in duty free as part of their holiday experience… and then it dawned on him: the duty-free shop was stuffed full of Brexit voters! See how they swarm excitedly around the cut-price booze and fags, agonising over which brand to choose to shorten their own lives. See how their unsupervised children rush to the sweets and chocolates and implore their parents to buy, buy, buy, thus guaranteeing their own malnutrition. Oh the irony of such a Brexit paradise existing at the very point of departure to their packaged *European* holidays! You couldn't make this stuff up!

The duty free had the usual stifling heat, glaring lights and heady perfumed air of all such shops in every airport the world over and George wanted to get out as quickly as possible. As he made his way towards the exit a young, pretty girl with clear skin and an Eastern European accent smiled at him and invited him to try some aftershave, which he accepted. Poor girl. She was exactly the type of hardworking youngster trying to better themselves by doing a poorly paid job involving long hours which most Brexiteers considered beneath them.

Once through duty free, George and his wife came face to face with a cut-price pub chain outlet that he wouldn't be seen dead in. The place was packed. He could have forgiven the customers had they been drinking tea or having breakfast, but most of them were drinking lager from tall glasses. At 8.30am! He pondered this momentarily: these people thought boozing before 8.30am was *normal*, just part of the routine of going on holiday, same as buying cheap junk from duty free. There were 17 million such people in the country and they were now leading the policy agenda! George stopped dead in his tracks, the same wooziness and disorientation he'd experienced at 5am returning as a sudden realisation struck him: *he no longer believed in democracy!* Indeed it was more than that: the muscles in his shoulders and jaw tensed as a visceral desire rushed through him to lash out at democracy, to hit it and kick it and beat it until it owned up to its failure. Ugly, disgusting democracy, giving free rein to Brexit racism and bigotry, and the febrile mob rule now sweeping the country. What next? Concentration camps for illegal immigrants? Public executions for Saturday night entertainment? If you weren't careful, democracy was simply a rush to the bottom, to the most despicable inclinations of mankind.

~

GEORGE AND HIS WIFE FOUND SEATS OUTSIDE THEIR departure gate. She started reading her novel while he checked his phone again for the news: 'Bloody hell, Cameron's resigned!'

'Really?' said Emily, sitting up. People around them picked up on the news and started conversing animatedly and looking into their phones.

'Unbelievable! The country's falling apart!' George found footage of the Prime Minister's resignation speech and Emily leaned over to watch too. Once it ended, George said, 'I hope the idiots who voted Leave are happy now.'

'Probably for the best we're getting away from it all,' said Emily, returning to her novel.

'Someone needs to get a grip and reverse the decision.'

Emily looked up from her book, keeping her finger on the page. 'You can't *reverse* it; that would create at least as many problems as it would solve.'

'Are you joking? It's clearly a massive mistake. Someone's got to stop it before the whole county implodes.'

'It'll pass.'

'*What?!*'

'I just think any disruption will probably be short term and then we'll get back to normal.'

'I can't believe how blasé you are about it. It's our futures at stake.'

'Oh, come on, George. No one's died. This country has faced far graver situations in the past and come through.'

'But it's our children's futures.'

Emily gave him a sideways glance and took up her novel again. '*You* were the one who wanted a holiday without the kids; I wanted them to come. Besides, I really don't want to talk about it. How about you make yourself useful and get us some breakfast?'

George set off and returned a while later with croissants and two Italian coffees from the single culinary outlet of any quality he could find. As he sipped his coffee he once again checked his phone for the news. There was talk of the country's credit rating being downgraded! A petition had started to have the referendum re-run and thousands were signing it every minute, which George now did also. Another petition had started supporting London forming a separate city state; George couldn't work out whether it was serious, but he hoped it was. London *is* a separate state: a state of enlightenment. Cosmopolitan, vibrant, young, liberal, multicultural. A place of goodness, decency and reason. These were things worth fighting for! If not the country risked becoming like the north, all bleak and dark and backward... in fact the Brexit vote confirmed it was worse than that, such places were clearly also full of bigotry and hatred and racism and... *evil*. Yes, that was it. Beyond London lay places of pure evil.

A profoundly unpleasant odour caused George to look up: the Brexit family was taking the seats opposite and eating McDonald's! Fucking hell, couldn't they be more considerate, stinking the whole place out with that stench of grease. Imagine feeding your kids chips and burgers at 9am! No wonder they were all short and fat. Everything about the Brexit family was... *nasty*.

He sipped his coffee, which made him contemplative. Whenever he wanted to feel better, George would picture a status graph in his mind, with home location on one axis and employment on the other. The location axis had London and the South East with the highest rating, because it was clear: all the most talented, educated and cultured people lived there, and his house in Fulham put him right at the centre of it. The South-West came next because Devon and Cornwall were beautiful and there were nice places like Bath down that way. The Cotswolds were picturesque, as were the nice parts of Wales such as Pembrokeshire, although clearly most of Wales should be avoided at all costs. One could comfortably then bypass Birmingham and head somewhere pleasant such as the Peak District or the Lake District. After that, things got bad… real bad. Hull. Oldham. Scunthorpe. Rochdale. You didn't need to visit these places to know how awful they were. One look at the Brexit family confirmed it.

Along the employment axis of the status graph the professions scored highest: doctors, engineers, lawyers, accountants, teachers and of course specialist experts like himself. In a meritocracy such people had rightfully risen to occupy the most responsible positions. Bankers had a strong rating, but he wouldn't rate them higher than himself despite their stratospheric earnings, because there'd been too many banking scandals, so he considered them tainted by their obvious greed. Similarly landowners and the aristocracy had a reasonable score but only a reasonable one because their wealth and influence were purely an accident of birth. Then came the grubbier end of capitalism such as sales and manufacturing and construction, and those in limited but useful employment like cleaners, couriers, caterers and security, some of whom worked hard to improve themselves but who generally needed constant monitoring, as he knew from hard experience. Finally came the indolent and lazy such as the unemployed and the workshy sponging off benefits. He assumed the Brexit family was in final category. In fact the Americans had quite a neat term for the likes of the Brexit family, a term which George would never use in public, but he thought quite accurate: they were *white trash*. And voting Leave confirmed it.

George's phone pinged, notifying him of a new email. The message was from Quentin, his boss and CEO, and the man he hoped to succeed. The email was to all the directors and talked about the actions Quentin was taking in response to the Leave vote and about the employee communication going out later that day to try to reassure everyone. He stressed the need for leadership and clear thinking during such a volatile period, but then towards the foot of the email he'd written, 'We could have done with you here today, George.' A fierce heat rushed into George's head. The fucking little shit! He'd cleared his holiday *with Quentin* weeks ago. Typical Quentin, fucked off because he'd actually have to do some real work for once.

George's phone rang: it was the office. George answered it.

'Hi, George, it's Quentin. Sorry to disturb you on your holiday. I'll try to be quick. It's been mayhem here today.'

'I can imagine. It's all a complete shambles. I can't believe there are so many idiots in this country.'

The Brexit family father looked up from stuffing his face with burger and stared at George. George didn't care. It was a private conversation and he would damn well say what he pleased. If trash like Brexit didn't like it, then serve him right for landing us all in this shit. He looked directly back at Brexit and spoke up. 'Most of the cretins who voted Leave had no idea of what they were voting for.'

Brexit stared back. George looked away, preferring any sight to that of Brexit digesting the horsemeat or whatever it was in that rancid burger.

'Indeed,' said Quentin. 'Listen, have you put your department's contingency plans into action?'

'Yes, we had a call this morning.'

'Good. Now listen. At the emergency board meeting earlier we discussed this Brexit mess, but there was also another thing we discussed...' Quentin paused.

'Yes?'

'It's your new productivity app.'

'What about it?'

'It's on hold.'

'*What?!*'

'I'm sorry, George, the decision was unanimous.'

'Yeah, a decision conveniently taken without me there.'

'And whose fault is that?' A brief silence. 'Look, I don't want to get into an argument, I just wanted to update you, out of courtesy. We're not scratching the idea, we're just saying that with over half the staff being foreign and now worried about their futures here, now isn't the right time to be asking them to log into an app five times a day to improve their productivity.'

'But they can't be trusted to work efficiently.'

'It's *too much*, George,' said Quentin. 'We can't bring such a thing in when half the staff are in danger of being deported. Please.'

Silence. In the same way as hearing about the Leave vote's victory at 5am had forced a horrible reality upon him, so this news was equally unpleasant, as it would inevitably hamper his positioning as Quentin's successor.

'I'm sorry, I've really got to rush. Give my best wishes to Emily.'

Little shit, thought George. Quentin had always been resistant to his productivity app. He didn't grasp its potential to be transformational. Everyone knew the staff in their shops were underutilised and inefficient, but no one had the guts to do anything about it.

George went online again, the rolling news confirming more and more turmoil: Scottish politicians pressing for a fresh independence referendum, the pound in freefall, Nigel Farage admitting that the claim that a Leave win would mean reclaiming £350 million a week for the NHS hadn't been accurate! 'It's fucking outrageous,' he muttered to himself. Looking up, he saw Mr Brexit reading *The Sun* and talking to his wife.

'For the first time in a long time I'm proud to be British,' said Mr Brexit.

He was proud! Proud to have brought the country to its knees! George's adrenalin was sparked and he turned to his wife and said in a clear voice, 'I can't believe so many stupid people voted Leave.' He turned back to Brexit to see if he'd heard.

Brexit looked up from his newspaper. 'Have you got a problem?' he asked.

'What, other than the whole country going down the pan because some idiots voted Leave?'

'It was a free vote, wasn't it?'

'Yes, but some people didn't know what they were voting for.'

'Like who?'

'Stop it, George,' said Emily. 'We're on holiday. The last thing I want is you arguing with strangers about politics. And you're being rude, telling people they didn't know what they were voting for.'

'It's okay, we're just having a discussion.' He turned back to Brexit. 'You're kidding yourself if you think this is going to make things better. Have you seen the news this morning? The GPD is sinking by the minute.'

'That's your GDP, not mine, mate,' said Brexit.

George shook his head. There was no point reasoning with these people; rationality and logic clearly dissolved on contact with them. 'The irony of course,' said George, 'is that the very people who voted Leave are the ones who'll suffer most because of Brexit. When the economy dives it'll be you lot losing your jobs first.'

'What do you know about the lack of jobs where I'm

from? Or the housing shortages, or overcrowded schools and hospitals, or immigration changing the places we grew up in—'

'Ah, it's all about immigration, I knew it!'

Brexit stared at George with focused contempt. 'It's called democracy. Even you must be able to understand that.'

George's lips thinned; he didn't like the tone of Brexit's voice. 'When democracy becomes the ignorant voicing their bigotry and envy, then you're right, I do doubt it.'

Emily had sat forward and turned to stare pointedly at George; eventually he looked at her.

'What?' he asked.

'It sounds like you're saying only certain people should be allowed to vote because you think only certain people are intelligent enough,' said Emily. 'Or else perhaps you're saying some people should be disqualified from voting because they dare to disagree with you?'

'Well, given what's happening to the country, it's clear that certain people shouldn't be allowed to vote.'

Emily's eyes narrowed. 'I think it's highly insulting to claim only people like you are fit to vote.'

'Don't tell me you're agreeing with *him*?' George nodded in the direction of Mr Brexit.

'I'm just saying there was a free and fair vote. Everyone understood what they were voting for and Leave won fairly and squarely. And I'm asking you not to throw all your ignorant prejudices at people simply because they disagree with you.'

George saw that Brexit was nodding and smiling. 'Don't smile at me like that, you halfwit scumbag.'

Brexit stood up. 'You *what?!*'

George stood up.

'George!' said Emily. 'Sit down. How dare you insult the man like that.'

'He's a fucking knuckle-dragging gorilla,' said George, taking a step forward.

'I'll not be spoken to like that,' said Brexit.

'I'll speak any way I like to an *imbecile*.'

'George!' said Emily. '*I* voted Leave.' There was a pin sharp silence. 'Does that make me an *imbecile* as well?'

George pushed his head forward in disbelief as he looked back and forth between his wife and Brexit. 'You've all lost your minds, you've completely lost all reason!'

'It's you who's lost his mind, mate,' said Brexit.

A white flash of rage shot through George's head and before he'd consciously decided upon violence his fist had connected flush on Brexit's temple, who slumped with a thud into the laps of his children, who shrieked in panic.

Brexit quickly righted himself, his face contorted in hatred and cocked an arm back, ready to unleash.

'No!' cried out Emily, staring at Brexit. 'Please?'

He made eye contact with Emily. He was breathing deeply. They held the stare, and after a few seconds, he slowly lowered his arm and took a step backwards. He looked at George. 'There was a time when I would have killed you for what you've just done, but for the sake of my wife and children, and your wife, I won't. But by god I *will* be pressing charges against you.'

'I'm going to find security,' said Mrs Brexit, rushing off.

The only motion as George and Brexit stood facing each other was Emily bending to place her novel in her handbag and collect up her belongings.

'What are you doing?' asked George.

'I'm leaving,' replied Emily.

'Leaving where?'

'Leaving *you*.' She stood upright. George still had the same perplexed look on his face as when he'd heard his wife confirm she'd voted Leave. 'That's right. Our marriage is over. Today is the final straw. You have nothing but hatred and contempt for everyone. I can't live with you anymore. This man here,' she said, pointing at Brexit, 'he actually listened to me and refused to fight. A complete stranger respecting me more than my own husband.' She turned to go.

'You can't leave. We're about to go on holiday.'

'You're not listening, George, as usual. I am *leaving you*. For *good*. And trust me, when I make a decision, I never go back on it.' She strode off.

George stood still, head bowed. Like any couple, he and Emily had argued occasionally over the years, but she'd never before threatened to leave him. Soon the room started to sway, the horizontal line where the floor met the wall seesawing first this way then that, like a boat pitching in rough seas, and he sat down as a disgusting dry retching sensation started in his throat and in the pit of his stomach as the realisation hit home: Emily *always* did what she said she would do; their marriage *was* over.

He felt a hand on his back and looked up. It wasn't a hand of comfort. It was a security guard. 'Please don't move, Sir. A serious allegation has been made against you and the police are due to arrive any minute.'

George's head dropped down, his eyes coming to rest on a yellow, polystyrene McDonald's container with a half-eaten burger in it. He muttered words which only he heard. 'Oh god, what have I done?'

VIRULENCE

'The boys aren't *still* playing Minecraft are they?' asked Mary, entering their narrow lounge to find her husband alone watching TV, children's toys and books littering the floor around him.

Duncan shrugged his shoulders while staring straight ahead; he didn't even turn his head to acknowledge her presence.

Her stress level clicked up a notch; it was clearly solely down to her to monitor the children's screen time. 'But they've been on it for over two hours. I thought we said we'd limit it to an hour?'

'Okay, I'll speak to them about it,' said Duncan, but didn't move. 'I just want to see this press conference.'

'And where's the twins?'

'They're watching TV in our bedroom,' said Duncan.

Mary blew out her breath in frustration; *more* screen time. Her neck twinged as it stiffened, her head lilting to one side. 'Don't you think we need to… to *interact* with our children a bit more?'

Duncan raised an arm in the air to silence her and pointed to the TV, still without looking at her. 'Listen,' he said.

The Prime Minister looked into the camera. 'And I must level with you, level with the British public; more families, many more families, are going to lose loved ones before their time.'

'Bloody hell,' said Mary. 'Did you hear that?'

Duncan shook his head. 'I can't believe this is happening.'

'It was only a couple of weeks ago they were telling us it wasn't serious,' said Mary, 'that we should just carry on as normal but wash our hands properly. Now this.' She couldn't recall a Prime Minister ever speaking in such solemn terms, almost as if they were now helpless in the face of this biblical plague. Her thoughts turned to her four children; thank goodness the virus didn't seem to affect kids.

'My dad is screwed if he catches this virus,' said Duncan, suddenly staring apprehensively at her. 'I need to call him.' He stood up and walked past her to the telephone in the hall.

An expression of disgust passed like a shadow over Mary's face at mention of Duncan's dad. That revolting man. She only tolerated him because he was the only family Duncan had other than her and the kids. She had a theory about people, one which applies to everyone you know, your friends, your colleagues, but most particularly to your family: they're either net contributors to your life, or blood suckers draining you of energy. Everyone falls into one of the two categories, and she frequently got shot of the blood suckers. Take *her* parents: they were kind, positive, they remembered all the kids' birthdays and sent cards and presents, they offered to host at Christmas, they constantly wanted to help and take stress away, but without being too pushy or prying. Net contributors. Duncan's dad Peter fell squarely into the latter category: a blood sucker, a putrid drain burbling and belching as he drew your energy away, as well as being a sexist misogynist semi-alcoholic.

Mary watched a bit more of the press conference. The government appeared to have no control whatsoever over the spread of the virus.

'I called him,' said Duncan, returning to the lounge.

'Is he okay?' she asked, half hoping Duncan would confirm that, no actually, he's got this terrible virus and has been admitted to hospital.

'He's still going to the bloody pub every day. I said to him, please can you stop going there or you'll catch it, but he just told me to stop fretting.'

The familiar tightness travelled even further up Mary's neck and into the back of her head. Another notch. Here was classic Peter: faced with the worst health crisis in over a century he could have done what *her* parents had done, make a clear decision to social distance within reason and reassure their daughter they would be careful, thus *reducing* her stress and taking one worry away. But not Peter. Oh no. He just carried on mingling down the pub, irrespective of the additional concern this caused Duncan. It was almost as if he revelled in being so bloody-minded, as if it gave some sort of perverse purpose to his miserable life, his only impact being the extent to which he riled other people.

'Can you *please* go upstairs and play with the kids?' she implored Duncan, who grimaced but started for the stairs. 'And get them off those bloody screens.'

She walked back to the kitchen to finish dinner. The pasta was gurgling and steaming in the pan and now overdone, so she drained it over the sink, sighing at the complexity of dinner: her nine-year-old Ben liked his pasta with red pesto, 'but not too much'; her seven-year-old Scott liked his with Marmite stirred through, even though she couldn't recall where that strange habit had started; her five-year-old twin girls, Chloe and Annie, liked theirs plain with cheddar cheese grated on top, so she always gave them a side of carrot sticks and cherry tomatoes to try to force some goodness inside them. And all of them preferred garlic bread to pasta, so she had to strategically delay the delivery of that to the table until halfway through the meal otherwise they would only eat the bread.

After serving it all up in bowls she walked to the kitchen door and shouted up the stairs, 'Dinner's ready!' After ten seconds of no response and no movement, she shouted as loud as she could, like a person suddenly attacked from behind by a mugger and screaming for someone to save their life, 'DINNER'S READY!'

MARY SAT CROSS-LEGGED ON THE FLOOR OF HER BEDROOM with the iPad on her lap. She logged into her email account and winced as she saw all the emails the school had sent through for home schooling. One more notch. She clicked on the first email – the one relating to Ben – and saw twelve Word documents attached! Twelve! She clicked on a few; there had to be at least forty or fifty pages in total! Just for Ben! Just for one week! She'd have to print out the same for Scott and for the twins, and *then* read them and digest them. And how long would this home schooling last for in any case? Months? Years?! A spasm of pain shot up her neck and she rubbed it with her hand. The pain brought to mind the endless discussions with Duncan after they'd had the two boys. She'd wanted to stop at two children, but Duncan had wanted a third, and kept repeating how unhappy he'd been as an only child and how he'd always wanted a large family. She'd eventually relented, only to have twins. She loved the girls with all her heart, but always felt spread so thinly these days and thus always falling short of each child's respective needs. She worried they weren't getting the love and attention they needed. What effect was it having on their development? Each time she turned her back the boys were bickering or fighting and it was getting worse the older and bigger they got. And whenever she spent much needed one-on-one time with one of the girls – reading them a Mr Men book or giving them a quick cuddle – the other twin would immediately become anxious and jealous. Her children seemed so needy and less self-assured than other kids their age and often just so, so… unhappy. But what could she do about it, given how little time she had? Tears gathered in her eyes as she clicked 'print' for the first home-schooling document.

An hour later she returned downstairs to find Duncan hunched over his laptop in the kitchen. On the way downstairs she'd seen the boys again playing Minecraft in Ben's bedroom, while the twins were watching a Disney film in the lounge. *More* screen time. She banged down the thick wad of papers she'd printed onto the table. 'You haven't started the roast then?'

'I'm reading work emails,' said Duncan, without looking up.

Up two notches. 'Well, your dad can go hungry then,' she replied.

'For fuck's sake!' said Duncan, standing up and striding over to the counter, grabbing the peeler and starting to peel the potatoes aggressively, bits of potato skin falling to the floor. 'You've got no idea, have you? Since when were you *furloughed* and your wages cut and told you weren't needed? It's been so long since you worked you've forgotten the pressure that goes with working for a wage.'

She studied his words for a moment, thinking them through. Firstly, as he'd been furloughed, he wouldn't actually now be working for his wages. Secondly, they'd jointly agreed three years ago that she would give up her job because of all the work needing doing at home, despite her being the higher earner, because there was no way *he* could have coped being responsible for all the kids. But she said nothing.

Instead, she started to lay the table, while casting her mind back to her career. She'd struggled through six months of work after the twins before it all became too much. Before kids, she'd loved her job as a buyer for a supermarket chain, but her memories of it were now tainted by how it ended: her inability to concentrate on the most basic tasks in the office because of the weight of responsibilities at home, the crick neck she began to suffer while sat at her desk pondering what to try to complete before rushing back for pick-up, the arguments with Duncan over him giving her more help at home. And of course the terrible occasion of sheepishly entering her boss's office to confirm her resignation, struggling to get her words out while desperately trying to hold it together, before choking up and breaking down in tears, her humiliation and defeat complete.

'I'm sorry,' said Duncan. 'I shouldn't have shouted. I'm just feeling really stressed, especially about our finances.'

Mary was also worried about money now that Duncan would only be getting 80% of his salary while furloughed, which would take them from just about coping to not coping at all, but if she mentioned her concerns that would just augment Duncan's anxiety. 'We're just going to have to be careful with our money for a while,' she said instead. 'We're saving some on the kids' clubs which are cancelled, such as swimming and football.' She didn't mention the massively increased food bills which would rack up during lockdown, or the fact the kids all needed new clothes and shoes. She'd read something in the press about mortgage holidays during lockdown, and made a note-to-self to look into it. Another notch.

Duncan carried on peeling the potatoes and carrots with a forlorn expression, his mouth slightly parted and sloping down to one side, and his chin jutting, as if he might start crying, or dribbling, or both. She wondered how he would cope during lockdown; not well by the look of him. She sighed silently; it would be down to her to take responsibility for the crucial necessary actions these coming weeks and months.

Her thoughts returned to their overdrawn bank account. Every month they went overdrawn, which often caused Duncan to lose his temper, like when another bill landed on the doormat, or when he saw Amazon parcels arrive, even though they were all necessities for the kids rather than the frivolous buys he initially thought they were. She didn't mind cutting back on expenditure on herself, but it broke her heart to have to skimp on the kids. Clothes, bikes, books, scooters, iPads, Lego, toys. All were substandard, or hand-me-downs, or second-hand, or broken. Money worries permeated every aspect of their lives, like the mottled brown damp clinging to the walls of the poorly insulated rooms at the back of the house.

Some time ago she'd mentioned in passing their money problems to her parents, who now regularly sent her a cheque for a few hundred pounds. She hated having to cash them, and worried that she was denying her parents a well-earned holiday or nice meals out, but the fact was they needed the money. By contrast, Duncan's dad *increased* their costs, by coming over for dinner every Sunday and never offering to pay or bring a bottle. *And* there was his yearly insistence on accompanying them on their UK holiday, which *they* paid for! Sometimes he would compensate them, but never for the amounts they'd incurred, and other times he simply 'forgot' to pay. How convenient. Blood-sucking energy drain.

Later that afternoon, as Mary carved the roast pork, the doorbell rang out. 'You get it,' ordered Mary to Duncan, tightening her grip on the handle of the carving knife as she awaited Peter's imminent entrance.

'Hi, Darling,' said Peter as he came into the kitchen, sporting his usual faded denim jacket and swept back greying blond Brylcreemed hair; she had to brace herself to resist recoiling as he kissed her on the cheek while reeking of booze and fags. As usual, he hadn't brought a bottle of wine. He had an uncanny knack of arriving just minutes, sometime just seconds, before the food was served and as normal sat straight down at the dining table, leaning back with his legs spread, like some kind of abusive husband returning from a long shift and demanding to be fed immediately.

The kids entered the kitchen and each gave Peter a hug. 'Chloe and Annie are growing up to be right lookers,' Peter said. Mary's neck jarred, knowing where this was headed. 'I bet you *love* having all the boys chasing you,' he said to them, with a gravelly chuckle. Two notches up. She *hated* the way he always commented on the twins' looks, as though that was all that mattered in a woman, and the way he sexualised them by talking about boyfriends. They were five years old for fuck's sake!

Peter spent the meal gorging himself in the manner of a man who had enjoyed five pints of lager down the pub. Which of course he had. 'You couldn't get me a tinny could you?' he asked Duncan at one point. Another notch. Had he asked *her*, she'd have told him to get it himself; she'd found it harder and harder to be civil to him over the years as her loathing of him had increased.

Although she maintained basic manners with Peter for Duncan's sake, she'd considered her relationship with him essentially dead since last Christmas when both sides of the family had been congregated in the living room opening presents on Christmas morning and Peter had hugged Chloe, before opening his arms wide to Annie, 'Come on, Darling, give your old Grandpa a hug.' Annie's face slumped – she was shyer than Chloe and had possibly picked up on the tension in the room whenever Peter was around – so she grabbed hold of Jane's leg instead, looking up to her for support. Despite Peter's beckoning, Annie refused to hug him, and his mood suddenly turned like a flicked switch. 'Don't you love me anymore?' he asked repeatedly, each request more pointed and accusatory than the last. Thereafter he kept referring to Chloe as, 'my *favourite* granddaughter,' even staring directly at Annie as he said it. Poor Annie's expression at being bullied this way – plaintive and open faced in bewilderment and fear – was still etched in Jane's memory. Eventually, her dad had spoken up after another comment from Peter while they were having lunch, 'Peter, I don't think it's appropriate to favour one of your grandchildren over another.'

Peter's scowling stare of hate had been such that Jane thought he was about to rise from his seat to assail her father. 'And who the *fuck* told you to interfere in my relationship with my grandchildren?' he said instead. Duncan had stepped in to diffuse the situation, but the Rubicon had been well and truly crossed.

Every Sunday lunch was now conducted in fear of Peter blowing up again, although that day they had coronavirus and the forthcoming lockdown - which started tomorrow - to discuss. You would have thought such a deadly serious subject matter might have led to some unanimity and consensus, but Peter still managed to wind her up when they discussed Duncan being furloughed. Peter just trivialised it, saying, 'Just take a good holiday, Son, you deserve some time off.' No suggestion that Duncan should help look after the kids now that they were being home schooled. No, that wouldn't occur to a sexist pig.

Later in the meal, Peter had taken another swig of lager and said, 'Well, the lockdown better be lifted by August, as I want my holiday with my grandchildren.' She suddenly sat rigid in her chair as the realisation struck home: she couldn't do it. She couldn't do *another* ten-day holiday with him. She turned over her memories of past holidays like pages in a horror album: his comments about overweight women in bikinis on the beach, 'those that shouldn't wear them do; those that should don't,' followed by that horrible husky cackle of his; him lighting *another* cigarette indoors, her *again* politely asking if he could smoke outside and him rolling his eyes and tutting; putting his arm around a waitress's waist in the restaurant and ignoring her clear expression of discomfort. No! She wouldn't do it. And last year there'd been that joke about disabled people he'd told, and his constantly banging on about Brexit, and foreigners, and 'loony left' politics, any comeback from her or Duncan met with immediate belligerence, and her children wide-eyed and confused and afraid. No. No. No. She wouldn't do it. Not on top of looking after four children, and applying their sunscreen, and remembering their hats and rash vests, and packing wetsuits, and the girls crying when their ice creams melted, all the while *him* never lifting a finger but instead slouched against the kitchen counter in their holiday home, or slumped in a deckchair on the beach cracking open another tinny, and his letching and leering, and belching and grunting. No. She would *not* do it.

'So, you're going to obey lockdown, aren't you, Dad?' asked Duncan during dessert.

Peter shrugged. 'Alan and I might meet for the odd beer, but that's all.' He reached for the double cream, drowned his apple crumble in it and ran his grubby, yellow-stained forefinger around the rim to stop it dripping. 'Cream, anyone?' he asked, popping his finger into his mouth to suck it clean.

'No thanks,' said Mary. Duncan's mouth was again sloping to one side and his chin jutting. 'You mustn't break the lockdown,' Mary said pointedly to Peter. 'You're not meeting Alan for drinks.'

Peter looked up. 'Aren't I now?'

'No, you're not. Show some respect, both for the rules and for Duncan, who's worried about you.'

'Don't try and police me, *Madam*,' he said to Mary. 'We can't all be like your prissy, goody two-shoes parents.' He took a long draught of his beer, before bringing his fist to his mouth and silently hissing a burp into it.

Mary flinched as the odour of Peter's beery belch reached her. She couldn't respond; her kids were already silent, their mouths clamped shut and barely daring to lift their eyes. Plus after this many drinks she knew not to push him too far. She'd put up with fifteen years of this now, *fifteen years* of his bullying and intimidating. She was too scared to let any of her family or friends near Peter any longer, as the stress of waiting until he inevitably leapt on them for making a comment he didn't agree with was too much to bear.

Although Mary considered the bedtime routine for four children to be the stress-level equivalent of a combat mission in Afghanistan, she rushed up the stairs that evening as it spared her more time with Peter. Sometime later as she read to the twins in bed, Duncan called out that his dad was leaving. Given that lockdown was now starting and they might not see Peter for a while, she felt obliged to see him off.

Peter was at the front door hugging Duncan. She kept her distance, to stop him doing likewise with her.

Duncan said, 'Take care, Dad. Oh, and remember we're all clapping for the NHS at 8pm on Thursday, don't forget.'

Peter lit a cigarette as he left and scowled back at them. 'No one clapped me for the thirty years I put in with the council, so why should I clap them?'

'Right, can you pour the flour into the bowl?' said Mary to Annie.

'But I want to do it,' said Chloe, her face crumpling with indignation.

'You can stir in the chocolate chips,' said Mary; Chloe's face instantly recovered.

Mary had gathered all four children in the kitchen to make chocolate chip cookies, an activity guaranteed to bring them together and for everyone a blessed release from the strain of the last two weeks of home schooling. Ben and

Scott were lining oven trays with baking paper, while both secretly tried to steal as many chocolate chips as they could from a bowl, Mary repeatedly slapping their hands to stop them. The twins took turns stirring the ingredients in the large mixing bowl with a wooden spoon.

The children all then reached into the bowl, rolled the moist doughy mixture into small, golf-ball sized balls and placed them carefully onto the baking trays, Mary evenly spacing them knowing they would spread during baking. She rubbed her eyes with the back of her sticky hand; she could barely keep them open she was so exhausted. The sheer logistics of lockdown were defeating her: the early-morning alarm call at 6am, the desperate sorting of documents to ensure she had some control over home schooling, the tears and protestations of the kids during lessons – especially maths – testing her patience to breaking point, *and* of course tending to the basic functions of running a house, all of which had dramatically increased in load, such as washing clothes, cleaning, and cooking for six three times a day.

She placed the baking trays in the oven and keenly anticipated the gorgeous comforting smell of home-cooked cookies that would soon infuse the kitchen. The twins rushed out the back door to bounce on the trampoline while the boys fought over licking the mixing bowl clean.

Mary sat down at the kitchen table and rubbed her forehead; it was clammy, probably the heat from the oven. Her throat was dry and she took a sip from a glass of water. Yes, she knew she was exhausted, but there was something more than tiredness going on; a strip of tenderness was starting towards her tonsils and travelling down the back of her throat and come to think of it, she couldn't smell the cookies baking in the oven…

She stood up and rushed upstairs to the bathroom, opening the cabinet and taking out the thermometer. She turned it on and pushed it into her ear as she'd done so many times with the kids: 38.5 degrees. Shit! She took the paracetamols and throat lozenges down from the cabinet, opened both packets, swallowed two paracetamols with some water from the tap and then popped two lozenges into her mouth and sucked them to soothe her throat. She walked through to the bedroom where Duncan was on his laptop. 'I've just got to pop out to the shops,' she said.

'I thought we got everything in the delivery?'

'We just need some more flour and sugar for baking. Listen, the cookies are in the oven, can you take them out in ten minutes? You mustn't forget or they'll burn and the kids will go mental.'

She went downstairs, grabbed an old plastic bag and got into the car, driving straight to the supermarket. Once there, she was struck by how deserted it was and a security guard had to point out to her that there was now a one-way system along each aisle. She filled her basket with milk, flour, sugar and eggs, but as she walked towards the check-out she stopped, and turned around; she went to the fresh food section and bought three ready meals, then to the alcohol section and bought two four-packs of lager.

Back in the car she drove to Peter's house on the outskirts of town, but had started to cough repeatedly and found the concentration needed for driving exhausting. She pulled up in his driveway and popped two more lozenges under her tongue. She got out, grabbing the shopping bag from the passenger seat, and approached the nineteen-thirties house, admiring its stylish curved bay windows in the lounge and master bedroom above, but then entered his shabby front garden. Grass clippings from a past lawn mowing lay scattered on the ground and had turned to rotting, pale straw, while a dustbin lid lay upturned on the pathway such that the bin's contents were visible: lots of crushed empty lager cans nestling amongst cardboard pizza boxes and aluminium trays from takeaways, all coated in left-over curry and rice and a half-eaten pizza crust with teeth marks. Classic Peter; complete contempt for recycling. Complete contempt for everyone except himself.

She stood outside his front door, admiring its aqua and green art deco stained glass panel before her eyes shifted to the smooth, white, round disc of his doorbell to the side. She stood still, staring at it, conscious of the rasp in her breathing as the fresh spring wind blew puffy clouds past the sun with some speed causing changes in the light, like shifting expressions, to sweep across the front of the house. She rubbed her forehead with her sleeve to wipe away the perspiration and rang the doorbell.

'Hello, Darling, what are you doing here?' asked Peter at the door, standing in a green check shirt and jeans, his hair again greased back. He looked pleased to see her; he tended to forget his drunken arguments, until the next one.

Mary held out the carrier bag. 'I got you some meals, and some refreshment,' she said, picking out a four-pack of lager to show him. He smiled, and as he did so she leant forward to kiss him on the cheek and hug him more keenly than ever before.

He invited her in. 'Okay,' she said, 'but I'll have to be quick, as Duncan doesn't know I'm here. I just popped over because I was worried about you after we couldn't get you any food delivery slots.'

He chuckled in that slightly sinister way of his as he led her though to the lounge and told her they shouldn't worry about him. He offered tea and she accepted, leaving her alone as he went to the kitchen.

There was something dream-like about the stillness and silence in the room where Peter had clearly just been sitting and she had that same light-headedness and stomach cramping she used to get at school before important exams, or the cross-country run, so she sat down on the beige sofa. Despite the lozenges, her throat was drying out fast and already tender, and she struggled to stop herself coughing. The room had that residual stale smell of all smokers' houses and a 1970s feel from the maroon cord carpet and one of those old deep TVs housed in a wooden shell which was playing some awful daytime TV programme about selling junk you find in your attic. A packet of Peter's cigarettes with a red plastic lighter on top lay perched on the arm of the chair directly in front of the TV. A black-and-white photo of her and Duncan on their wedding day stood on the mantelpiece above the fire and various photos of her children punctuated the bookshelf.

Peter returned and placed a tray on the coffee table with two mugs of tea and some Rich Tea biscuits on a saucer, the sight of the dry biscuits almost provoking Mary into a coughing fit. Peter sat down and reached for his cigarettes, but paused and glanced at her. 'It's okay, it's your house,' she said, smiling. 'It's only the kids I don't want inhaling it.'

Peter returned the smile and sparked the fag.

Mary reached for her tea and sipped it, soothing her throat, her mind whirring so fast now she thought she could hear it humming: Peter had confirmed to Duncan on the phone a few days ago that he'd been popping occasionally to the local convenience store for provisions; he was probably secretly meeting Alan for drinks, despite telling Duncan he hadn't; he still received post. Any one of those could result in him catching the virus. *Any* of them. 'Oh,' she said, 'you didn't put any sugar in?'

'You don't take sugar, do you?'

'Yes. Just one.'

'Oh right, sorry, let me get it.' He stood and returned to the kitchen.

She leapt up and reached for his cigarette in the ashtray, licking the stub end and returning it, before reaching for his mug and licking where he would soon be drinking from, making sure it got a decent coating of her saliva. She also licked its handle, knowing he would soon be holding it. In any other circumstances, a younger woman's drool on his fag and mug would no doubt have excited a man like Peter, she thought, before quickly sitting back down.

Peter returned and spooned a sugar into her tea and stirred it in. She immediately brought the mug to her lips to soothe her aching throat and take away the disgusting taste of cigarette. 'Thanks,' she said.

Peter sank back down into his chair and picked up his cigarette, Mary's heart thudding so hard she thought it might work its way loose from its fittings as she watched him closely without blinking; he pouted, inserted the slim stick, and delicately pinched it with his lips before drawing the smoke deep down into his lungs; a small sigh escaped her lips.

They discussed Duncan and his furloughing. She expressed her concern at his mental wellbeing, but Peter just said, 'I wish I got paid to do bugger all,' and followed up with some bitter comments about the council he used to work for, culminating in, 'By the time I left you had to be an overweight, black or Asian lesbian in order to get promoted.' It wasn't long before he took up his mug of tea, Mary's eyes again zeroing in; his lips again parted, his eyes closing momentarily, like a supplicant kneeling before a priest about to receive communion. The coated lip of the mug met his open mouth.

An uncomfortable silence followed, Mary frantically searching for something to say; her eyes alighted on an old black-and-white photo of a man in a soldier's uniform on the mantelpiece. 'May I ask who that is?' she asked, nodding towards it.

'That's my father,' said Peter, his eyes squinting as he looked over. There was a short silence. 'I'm afraid I never really got to know him.'

'No?'

'No. He died in 1952; I was only two.'

She nodded. 'He looks just like Duncan. He died of cancer, didn't he?'

Peter said nothing; he just continued to focus on his father's picture. Eventually, he said, 'He committed suicide actually.'

'Did he?' asked Mary, leaning forward.

'Yes. Actually…' he said, breaking his stare at the photo to return's Mary's eye contact, 'I'm not sure I ever told Duncan that. I was too ashamed.'

'But why?'

'Too ashamed he preferred death to being with me. And because I didn't want to upset Duncan. As you know, he means more to me than anything else in the world.'

There was a short silence. 'I'm sorry, Peter, but I really must be going,' said Mary, standing. She knew she was being unnaturally abrupt, but she had to get out of there. And fast.

'But you've only just arrived,' said Peter.

'I know, I'm sorry, but I've got to get home for the kids.' They walked through to the front door. 'You won't tell

Duncan I was here, will you?' asked Mary. 'He'd be very upset at me breaking the social distancing rules. *Very* upset.'

'It can be our little secret,' said Peter, winking and chuckling as he stepped forward to hug her. She allowed him to hold the hug a little longer than she normally did. 'But you must also promise not to say anything to Duncan about my father?'

'Of course not,' she said. She took a final look at him, at the little hammocks of bruised flesh under his bloodshot eyes and the faint tinge of purple to his nose. 'Goodbye, Peter.'

Duncan was waiting for her by the front door when she arrived home. 'What took you so long?' he said, before bending double and dry coughing into his fist. 'I think I've got this fucking virus.'

'Really?' she said.

'I feel terrible, I'm going to go and lie down. I couldn't find the paracetamol, do you know where they are?'

'I've got some in my handbag. I'll bring them up,' she said, watching him ascend the stairs.

Mary struggled through the rest of the day looking after the kids while Duncan rested upstairs. She slept on the sofa that night after Duncan suggested it to try to protect her from catching the virus from him. The next morning she informed him that she also had coronavirus symptoms.

DUNCAN'S SYMPTOMS TURNED OUT MUCH WORSE THAN Mary's. While he was confined to bed, writhing and groaning in sweat with a hacking cough which eventually brought up a gooey, pale green mucus, she was able to haul herself up each day and just about keep the household going. What choice did she have? However, she sacked off most of the home schooling, allowed the kids plenty of screen time and ordered lots of takeaway pizza. Needs must in an emergency.

On the second day of his illness, Duncan said he should call his father to warn him that they had the virus.

Mary paused momentarily. 'I'll call him,' she said. 'You need to rest.'

She called Peter, but didn't divulge their illness, lest it provoke of flurry of questions about timings and bring her clandestine visit to him out into the open. Instead she just said Duncan was a bit under the weather, hence *her* calling to check how he was. When Duncan later asked her what his father had said, she lied, saying he was obviously worried about them but that fortunately he was social distancing properly so there shouldn't be anything to worry about.

Time grew slower and slower for Mary over the next couple of days as she ticked each passing hour off the clock and stoically endured her illness, her nerves drawn taut by the fear that Peter might call Duncan on his mobile, although he generally always used the landline, or else Duncan might call Peter. If they spoke she would need an excuse as to why she hadn't mentioned their illness to Peter. Perhaps she could say she hadn't wanted to worry him, or maybe that she'd been too devastated to learn that she'd inadvertently put him at risk after discovering she had the disease following her visit to him?

However, all remained quiet until the landline went on the morning of the fifth day after Duncan and Mary first had symptoms. It was Peter, telling her he was feeling dreadful and that he thought he had the symptoms of the virus, especially a fever and terrible sore throat. 'I can't understand where I could have caught it,' he said, in between grim, wrenching coughs. They agreed that Peter should call back if his symptoms got any worse. She didn't tell Duncan that he'd called, but wrestled with her conscience as to when she would *have* to divulge that he'd called.

The next day, Peter called back. 'Mary, I can't breathe,' he said, almost in a whisper, even though he was clearly desperately trying to make himself heard in between panting. 'Help me, Mary, please.'

She called for an ambulance but then waited before telling Duncan. As she sat alone digesting the news, she thought through Peter's catalogue of wrongdoing: bullying his own granddaughter aged four on Christmas Day, threatening her father, his bigotry and racism, their nerves flayed and shredded due to the constant fear of his next unprovoked outburst of aggression. And in any case, Peter had been popping regularly to the local convenience store for provisions; he'd almost certainly been meeting his friend Alan for drinks; he'd definitely still received post. Any one of those could have resulted in him catching the virus. *Any* of them.

She gave it a good half hour before ascending the stairs to Duncan, who was still in bed. 'I've got some terrible news,' she said, causing Duncan to sit upright. She paused, and in that brief moment she realised she *craved* saying the words which followed, delivered with unusually crisp clarity. 'Your dad thinks he has the virus.'

'Oh nooooo…!' he wailed, springing out of bed. He immediately called his dad, but there was no response on his mobile or landline.

'He's probably in the ambulance,' she said.

'But you only just spoke to him.'

'He's probably getting ready, then. We can call him once

he gets there.'

Duncan paced up and down, rubbing his cheeks and forehead with his hand, saying, 'Oh god, oh god,' repeatedly. He kept trying his father's numbers, but still there was no response. He then called the hospital repeatedly and after two or so hours they received a call back from a nurse who confirmed that Peter was in the Intensive Care Unit on a ventilator. 'Can I speak with him?' Duncan asked, but the nurse confirmed that Peter was unconscious, as it was standard practice to anaesthetise patients on ventilators to make them more comfortable and to regularise their breathing so they weren't fighting the operation of the machine.

'Oh my god, this is it,' said Duncan, his face waxy white and slightly ghoulish as he absorbed the news, before his mouth sloped away and his chin jutted as he began to sob.

'I'm so sorry,' said Mary. 'We'll just have to pray for him.' She reminded herself that death comes to all of us sooner or later, coronavirus proving the great accelerator to the elderly and unwell, all of whom were far less deserving of catching it than Peter. And besides, Peter could have caught the virus from many different sources. *Very* many.

The next day the nurse called back and confirmed that unfortunately Peter's condition had deteriorated. He explained how they planned to bring him off the sedation momentarily to wake him up. 'But is that best for him?' Duncan asked.

'It's so you can speak to him. I'm afraid it might be your last chance.'

It was made clear to them that there was no prospect of visiting Peter in person, so a Zoom call was set up for that evening instead.

Mary threw herself into her jobs that afternoon:

energetic and for once productive home-schooling classes, a
determined dinner service catering to each child's distinctive
tastes, a military-style operation with the twins' baths and
bedtime routines; it all helped keep her mind off the later
call.

Once the twins were down and the boys settled in front
of a nature documentary on TV with strict instructions not
to interrupt, Duncan and Jane pulled the kitchen door
closed, turned off the radio and turned on their iPad,
leaning it upright against a stack of cookery books for
stability. Duncan reached out and took hold of Jane's hand;
she feared he would feel the throbbing guilt of her unusually
powerful pulse.

When the call started and the screen flickered, the nurse
came into view like a character from a science-fiction movie,
his full-length visor and bulky white hazmat suit making him
look more like an astronaut than a medic. He explained in a
strangely distant and nasal voice that they only had a short
time, as they wanted to re-sedate Peter and re-apply the
ventilator. When he placed the tablet in front of Peter, the
sight was one of sheer haunting dreadfulness. He was lying
on his front, his face sideways and flat against the bed with a
transparent breathing mask over his mouth, only he wasn't
centred properly such that the screen cut off half his face so
only one eye was visible, which greatly magnified its
twitching restlessness.

'Hi Dad,' said Duncan.

Peter's wrinkled, shaking hand came into view and
pulled the breathing mask clear of his mouth. 'Hi Son,' he
whispered, barely audibly. 'Sorry you have to see me like
this.' They could hear the occasional but regular soft bleep
from some kind of medical monitoring equipment.

'It's okay, Dad. We just want you to know we're all

thinking about you.'

'Thanks,' he said, but was clearly exhausted and returned the mask to his mouth and inhaled deeply, the hoarse hissing Darth Vader sound of his breathing making Mary wince. Duncan spoke about the children and their home schooling, although it was unclear how much Peter could hear above the grating sound of his mask. When he eventually again pulled it clear of his mouth his parted wetted lips reminded Mary of *that day* when his cigarette had nestled there, followed by his mug. 'Tell my grandkids I love them,' he managed to get out.

'We will, Dad, we will,' said Duncan hurriedly. 'Try and be strong, we know you can pull through.'

A tiny upturn took place in the corners of Peter's mouth before he clamped the mask back on and inhaled desperately. After a few frantic breaths, he let the mask fall away and said, very faintly, 'Thank you for visiting me, Mary.'

Duncan turned to Mary who instinctively leant back to ensure she was out of shot, shrugged and scrunched her face.

The screen moved – someone had picked it up – and the large facial visor again came into view; after a few seconds their eyes adjusted and the face of the nurse came into focus behind the visor. 'I'm sorry, we're going to have use the ventilator again. I'll give you a few more seconds. I'm so sorry, but we really must get your dad more air.' He placed the screen back in front of Peter's face.

'I love you, Dad,' said Duncan, his voice breaking.

'I love you too, Son,' he said, the effort of getting out his words seeming to defeat him and his face completely deflated and stilled; it was the first time Mary had ever seen him looking peaceful. The tablet was taken up again by the nurse who said he would update them in the morning, and the screen blanked.

Mary leant sideways and put her arm around Duncan, his head drooping and his body beginning to spasm such was his utter devastation. Mary held him, the man she loved and father of her children, trying to console him. His long-suffering mother had died of cancer ten years earlier, so he was now almost parentless, and she knew he must be feeling utterly bereft and alone. Her mind wandered to assess her own reaction to it all; yes there was sadness as there is when any life draws to an end and particularly at seeing him in such discomfort, but she also forced herself to recall the real Peter: the filthy, grotesque energy drain, *constantly* making their lives more difficult – as if they weren't difficult enough! And his sexism and racism and bigotry and temper. And bullying her parents and her daughter – aged four! – on Christmas day! Despite all they had on their plate with four children, and no money, and Duncan about to lose his job. That couldn't be forgotten. That *wouldn't* be forgotten!

'Well?' asked Duncan.

'Well what?' she asked. She hadn't heard him ask anything.

'What was that my dad said about you visiting?'

She felt a fierce heat erupt in her cheeks, but steeled herself by meeting her husband's gaze straight on and shrugging nonchalantly. 'I really don't know. He must have been imagining it, after all the medication he's been given.'

Duncan looked at her quizzically, before his mouth sloped sideways and downwards, and his chin jutted exposing his lower teeth, as he again began to weep.

Duncan received twice daily calls from the nurse over the next three days, only to be overawed by a series of increasingly bleak prognoses: his immune system was now out of control and causing damage throughout his body, he had septic shock because his blood pressure was dangerously low, his vital organs were at risk because of a lack of oxygen.

The final call came when the family were having breakfast in the kitchen. As Duncan leapt up to answer the phone, she calmly but forcefully told the children to go to their rooms. Duncan stood vacant-eyed and open-mouthed listening intently to the voice on the line, before suddenly his face twisted in hideous contortion. 'My daddy is dead,' he wailed, putting down the phone and again she held him, his arms around her neck, only now there was no stiffness in her neck, and no shooting pains, rather it felt supple and strong and healthy. She reminded herself again: Peter had been popping regularly to the local convenience store for provisions; he'd secretly been meeting Alan for drinks; he'd still received post. Any one of those could have resulted in him catching the virus. *Any* of them.

She stared past Duncan out the window, holding his convulsing body tight as he tried to process the news. In the far distance a long, domed hill of mottled light greens and browns formed a line on the horizon holding up a vast translucent pale blue sky. In their garden the buds on the leafless twigs of the magnolia were swollen and shiny, ready to burst forth, as a long-tailed tit with a blush of pale pink on its belly hopped jerkily along a branch. It desolated her to think of someone dying and never being able to see such things again, but she consoled herself with the knowledge that Peter would never have paid any attention to them anyway. She searched deep within herself for the sadness which she knew should have resulted from his passing and she simply couldn't find it, because her heart and mind were already soaring, lifted by a boundless optimism for the future of her family.

LITTLE REED

'I'm going to have to put a cannula in,' says the portly, kind-faced nurse standing over me.

A *cannula?* The sound of the word makes my stomach knot; anything with a name like that in a hospital is going to hurt like hell, surely?

The nurse shuffles a black fabric tourniquet up my arm and pulls it tight around my bicep – Christ, this is medieval! – and swipes what feels like a wet wipe across the back of my hand. She pulls on a pair of blue medical gloves before lifting into view what looks like a giant needle. 'Best not to look,' she says, seeing my expression. 'Can I have your hand?' It takes an act of will to lift it to her. The nurse shuffles her feet and drives the cannula in with the words, 'Just a sharp scratch—'

'*Jesus!*' I hiss through gritted teeth as the cold thick needle penetrates my vein.

'Sorry about that,' says the nurse, covering where the needle remains inserted with a plaster. 'There's never an easy way to do it, so best to just do it quickly. Do you want me to raise or lower the gurney?'

'The *gurney?*' I ask, sitting upright.

'The gurney is the bed you're on; it's a hospital bed with wheels.'

'Oh, right.' I breathe out. 'It's… it's fine as it is. Thanks.'

'Doctor Shepherd will be with you shortly to discuss the operation. Do you need anything else?'

I shake my head. 'No, thank you.'

Alone again, only now do I take proper note of all the apparatus around me: a tall, thin, silver stand beside me from which hangs a transparent bag of clear liquid; a blank monitor over my head with leads attaching to various unknown electronic boxes; a yellow-topped rectangular metallic bin – I squint to read the sticker on its side – "clinical waste only". Fucking hell. Didn't the nurse just use that bin?

I stare down at the *thing* sticking out my hand, which now aches like hell. What *is* a cannula, anyway? I reach for my phone:

A **cannula** *(from Latin "little reed"; plural cannulae or cannulas) is a tube that can be inserted into the body, often for the delivery or removal of fluid.*

A *little reed* inserted into me to *deliver fluid* or extract my bodily essence. Good god. As if I wasn't fragile enough already, my slim, pale, hairless body protected only by this light blue gown, and now this, this *thing* sticking in me. I'm twenty-seven for fuck's sake, I'm meant to be in the prime of life!

What would Paula think if she could see me now? Oh, Paula… and oh god *that look* she gave Will at the party. It keeps repeating on me, I can't keep it away. The way her chin dipped a little into her shoulder causing her innocent, freckled face to turn slightly, as her long lashed eyes glanced up at him from under her auburn fringe. I put it down to her being shy at the time; only later did it dawn on me that it was a look of longing, of furtive *lust*, a look she'd never given me.

I take a few slow, deep breaths and try to block her out. God, it's so hot in here. And that weird smell. And—

Wait! What's that?! That noise? A mourning sound, like a soft wail or gentle groan, is it close or far off? Christ. They've made this room so warm and still and clean, but those noises give it away. Shortly I'll be wheeled through on the gurney to my fate, my gown raised and my iodine sponged skin opened up by the surgeon's razor-edged scalpel... the flesh easing apart... the crimson ooze... *fucking hell!*

I PICK UP MY PHONE TO CHECK FOR MESSAGES: NOTHING from Paula. It's three days now since I emailed her. I'd kept it positive, and calm, just expressing the hope she was okay and suggesting perhaps we could soon talk. Why hasn't she responded?

I stare at my neatly folded pile of clothes on the chair: the skinny jeans, the fitted ribbed top, the pristine white trainers with my wallet pushed into one shoe and my keys into the other. Fat lot of good they are now. Same with my Instagram photos I agonised over and all that fastidiously watching what I eat. None of it can help me now.

The door opens and a doctor strides in holding a clipboard with the nurse behind him, their entrance allowing a welcome draught of cool air into the room.

Although he's wearing a hairnet and green medical scrubs, I know it's Doctor Shepherd, such is his tall, loose-limbed frame and the peculiar pale intensity of his eyes. 'Are you comfortable?' he asks.

I sit upright. 'Yes, not too bad, thank you.'

'Good,' he says, nodding. 'We're almost ready for you. I'm just going to review your notes.'

Thank god for Shepherd. Having complete confidence in your surgeon makes such a difference, although the first time I met him hadn't started well. 'Tell me what brings you here today?' he'd asked at the consultation in his soothing, slow, baritone voice.

I'd rehearsed my answer for that exact moment, but my mind blanked as the heat of a blush moved into my cheeks. 'I suppose... I suppose I've always worried about certain aspects of my appearance...' Shepherd nodded slowly, '... and I thought perhaps... having this done could help me in some way, I mean with my confidence.'

Shepherd remained still and silent, as if in his mind he was clinically assessing my words with some carefully calibrated precision instrument. On the wall behind him hung half a dozen framed certificates pronouncing his numerous medical qualifications and accomplishments.

I felt compelled to elaborate. 'I... I thought the best approach would be to meet with you to discuss it.' I didn't know what else to say. There was a protracted silence, my discomfort heightened by how cold the room was.

'May I ask you something?' asked Shepherd eventually.

'Of course,' I replied.

'Do you have a partner?'

I felt the blush return and stared down. 'No, I'm afraid she left me,' I replied, barely audibly.

Shepherd waited until I looked up again, then leaned

forward, placed his elbows on the desk and balled his hands together. He fixed me with his stare, his eyes such a clear grey they were almost colourless. 'Roger, you should be proud of yourself.'

'Should I?' I almost sighed with relief.

'Yes, you should. There's not a person alive who's entirely happy with their appearance; the difference is that some are honest about it and brave enough to do something about it. It can't have been easy coming here today?'

'No, it wasn't.'

'But still you came, despite your apprehension. It interests me that you used the word confidence when you said what you thought this procedure could do for you?'

'Yes… well, I think that's it really. I think it could do a lot for my… my self-esteem.'

Shepherd nodded. 'It always amazes me,' he said, 'when I tell people I'm a surgeon, they invariably concentrate on the physical aspects of what I do, it's so rare for people to think about the emotional aspects, and yet that's the first thing you mentioned.' I nodded. 'I would go as far as to say that the *most* important aspect of my job is the emotional and psychological effects, and it's certainly the aspect I find most rewarding. I don't know if you'd find it useful, but I keep a folder of testimonials from previous patients. Would you like to see it?'

'Er… yes, I suppose so,' I said, nodding.

Shepherd leaned down to one side, slid open a drawer and lifted the folder onto the table. He wet a finger and began turning the pages, which were filled with photographs and what looked like letters. 'I'd like to draw your attention to this chap, Johnny.' He spun the folder around and pushed it towards me.

'Thank you,' I said, my eyes drawn immediately to Johnny's before and after photographs. The before showed him slightly stooped and fearful in a somewhat grainy shot; the after showed him straight-backed, healthy and rugged, like he'd filled out a bit and taken a holiday in the sun. On the opposite page was a letter from Johnny. I scanned the words: 'I couldn't be happier', 'marked improvement in my confidence', 'everyone seems to sense something different about me.'

'When Johnny first came to see me,' said Shepherd, 'he was very much like you. His partner had left him for another man. He was short of confidence. But like you he was brave enough to admit he wanted to improve himself. As you can see, the procedure was very successful, but not just the obvious physical results, even more so the emotional side, as you've read. It really is the best thing about being a doctor: the opportunity to improve peoples' lives.' I kept glancing down at Johnny's after shot. 'You see, this is all about quality of life,' continued Shepherd. 'The procedure is relatively straightforward and the risks negligible, but think of the upsides. Renewed self-belief, greater self-assurance, I've even had patients talk about increased poise and charisma, based on the inner confidence they feel. I firmly believe it's a case of feel successful, to be successful.'

The rest of the conversation was a bit of a blur because for the first time since Paula left me I had hope, a route out of the despair, and was already imagining a better future.

'Not long now,' says Shepherd, breaking my reverie. 'Everything's in order with your readings, so we'll get one of the porters to bring you through to theatre shortly. Once there, the anaesthetist will attach a tube to your cannula,' I flinch as Shepherd points at it, 'and you'll be out in a few seconds. The operation should take about an hour and then we'll bring you round in the recovery room. We'll be giving you morphine as you wake up so you shouldn't have any pain. Have you got any final questions?'

I'd asked all my questions at the consultation, but could never have anticipated the fear now upon me of the anaesthetic stripping me of my consciousness. 'Just one more thing,' I say, 'when they give me the anaesthetic, what will I feel?'

Shepherd runs his fingers through his closely cropped beard. 'Well, when the anaesthetic is administered, you'll feel a cold sensation enter your hand and travel up through your arm and then you'll be out. It's really nothing to worry about.' I nod. 'And one more thing,' says Shepherd, handing me the clipboard he's been holding. He pauses, freezing me with those intense, grey eyes of his. 'This is the surgery consent form. I'd be grateful if you could read, sign and date it.'

I stare down at the form as Shepherd and the nurse leave the room.

*R*ARE *AND VERY RARE COMPLICATIONS RESULTING FROM anaesthesia include:*

- *Damage to the eyes*
- *Heart attack or stroke*
- *Adverse reaction to drugs or blood products*
- *Nerve damage*
- *Death**
- *Patient awareness during the surgical procedure*

Deaths caused by anaesthesia are very rare.

Christ. I've had a few shitty days recently, but lying here alone waiting for an operation and signing away the risks is right up there. Isn't it strange how you often hear people talk about the best day of their life, but never the worst? All those grinning lottery winners saying, 'After the birth of my children and my wedding, this is the best day of my life.' I can't think of a best day. Not one. But worst days? Oh sure, I've got plenty of those, mostly recent. Today, right now for instance, waiting for this, this... *procedure* has got to be right up there, but just like those with children having a clear best day of their life, I've got a clear worst one: the day I got the note from Paula. Compared to that, reading a surgery consent form warning me of my potential imminent death is a walk in the park.

I check my mobile, just in case Paula has responded: nothing.

My head's aching from the heat, and the dehydration and hunger, and from that peculiar hospital smell of chemicals trying to mask something... I can't believe how weak I feel, my limbs so heavy I can barely lift them, my skin so loose and clammy under this flimsy gown. Is that why hospitals turn up the heating so high: to get the flesh all soft and malleable and tender for the scalpel?

I stare again at the form. Why weren't all these potential complications mentioned before? How much do I even know about this medical practice anyway? I'd simply found it online and taken their reassurances and testimonials on trust. I'd only skim-read the pack of papers they'd sent through. What sort of due diligence was that? Oh god.

I need to focus on why I'm here. What did Shepherd say? *This is about quality of life and improved self-confidence.*

I reach for the pen.

People will sense something different about me. Maybe Paula will?

I find the place where I'm meant to sign and stare at the dotted line. I imagine again Paula – or any other woman? – suddenly confronted by the new, improved, post-op me: the wide-eyed startled expression, followed by the sharp intake of breath.

I sign the consent form.

Occasional sounds keep reaching me: that soft, plaintive moaning earlier; the odd muffled voice from the corridor – are they lowering their voices on purpose?; intermittent thuds from the next door room; now a series of piercing laughs… at least I think it's laughter. Each noise seems to exist isolated from the other.

All that's left now is for the porter to collect me and take me through to theatre. *Fucking hell.* A disturbing tingling sensation hums throughout my body, as though it's preparing itself somehow for the forthcoming assault. I'm starting to feel like I did when I got Paula's note.

When I'd returned home that night everything had appeared normal at first. Paula wasn't in, but that was no surprise, she often worked late. Soon though I realised something about the atmosphere in the living room wasn't quite right, only it was difficult to pinpoint because it wasn't immediately obvious. I sensed some sort of disturbance, a faint unease in my peripheral vision as I took off my coat.

Suddenly I saw half the books on a bookshelf were missing: adrenalin shot through my veins – had we been burgled?! '*Paula?!*' I shouted, darting through to the kitchen, '*Paula?!*' Two pictures were missing from the walls, evidenced by squares of lighter paint where the pictures had hung. I looked this way and that and back into the living room; the TV was still there and everything neat and tidy, which was odd.

Then I saw it.

An envelope in the centre of the empty kitchen table. The prospect of having been robbed receded, but an even greater fear gathered. I pulled the note carefully from the envelope with trembling fingers, like I was handling some priceless, delicate artefact:

Roger,

I'm sorry I had to do this but I couldn't think of another way. I've moved out and will be staying with friends.

I do love you, Roger, but I am not <u>in</u> love with you anymore. There's no one else, and really it's nothing to do with you. It's me. I need time alone to clear my head and think about what I really want.

As the words sunk in, so I sank to the floor, but in slow motion, in stages; I went down on one knee, then two, then leant to one side and lay on the floor, bringing my knees up to my chest to form a ball. My cheek lay flat against the hard, ice cold kitchen floor tile and I closed my eyes tight to shut out the light.

I stayed that way for some time, not so much thinking as simply existing. I think I just… closed down for a while. My thoughts as I lay there still shame me. My foot touched the bin, and I started to think about what was in there: putrid half-eaten fruit and vegetables, scrapings of slimy congealed fat from the grill, an old damp j-cloth used to wipe up grime and dust, all piled on top of each other in a stinking heap. I started to think about how I belonged in there too amongst all the unwanted filth, because when something reaches the end of its usefulness and no longer has a purpose, it's time to get rid, surely? And the thought didn't disgust me either, it seemed natural for me to be in there, indeed I *wanted* to be in there. There was something comforting in the thought, such a warm resting place, enclosed and dark and safe, somewhere I could rot in peace before eventually being carried off to landfill and covered up for all eternity.

I blink and a tear runs down my cheek.

And then the anguish of the following days lying under my duvet, unable to face the world, not knowing why she'd left me and the tormenting process of rethinking various past incidences in light of my rejection. Those weekends she'd been away 'with the girls' and her overnight stays at work conferences; where had she really been? Who had she really been with? And of course being forced to reassess *that look* she'd furtively given Will at the party, only I kept reminding myself that she specifically said in the note that no one else was involved.

The door opens and the porter enters, a young man who doesn't meet my eye. 'I'm here to take you to theatre,' he says and without waiting for a response presses a button behind the gurney to lower it flat and yanks its sidebars up with surprising force so they click into place. 'You're going to have to leave that,' he says, taking my mobile and placing it on my pile of clothes, but as he does so it flashes.

I sit upright. 'Please, I need to see who that message is from.' I reach out towards my phone.

'I'm sorry, phones aren't allowed in theatre.'

'*PLEASE?!*' I shout, the desperation and anger in my voice surprising both me and the porter, who looks momentarily fearful.

'Okay, okay,' he says, handing me the phone. 'But you'll have to be quick.'

I check my phone: the message is from Paula!

Hi Roger,

Hope you're okay. I'm sorry, there's no easy way to tell you this but I thought you should know before you find out from anyone else. I'm in a relationship with Will. It's early stages, but we have very strong feelings for one another. I promise it hadn't started when we were together.

My hand drops to my side and the porter takes my phone away. I lie flat on the gurney and shortly feel myself being pushed towards the door, staring up at the long, yellow, glaring strip lights on the suspended ceiling as I travel down the corridor. All along I'd hoped that perhaps this, this… *procedure* would help me to win Paula back. What was I thinking?!

I begin to sob. What am I doing here? It's not going to fix me. 'I don't want this,' I say, but the porter doesn't respond. '*Please*,' I say, raising a hand, twisting and grabbing his wrist. 'I'm not sure I want this.'

The porter pulls his arm free. 'You'll need to speak to the doctor.' He presses on and pushes the gurney with increased urgency. Two doors swing open and I feel myself come to a standstill and there's bright lights and a bewildering array of electronic equipment bleeping and winking, and medical staff converging on me with masks covering their noses and mouths. *Dear Christ!*

'I'm… I'm not sure about—'

A hand grips my forearm; leaning over me from inches away is a face covered with a green medical mask, just the eyes visible: they're so pale there's no colour in them. 'Anaesthetist, quickly please,' he says, his eyes flicking towards a colleague then back to me.

'Please, I think I've made a mist—'

An ice-cold sensation deep in my hand startles me to silence, it's travelling up through my forearm, now my bicep, now my shoulder towards my brain and my last memory before nothingness is of my anguished, pleading face reflected in the widening pupils of his colourless eyes.

APPRAISAL

Harry Moore stared into his brightly lit bathroom mirror, confidently slid a razor down his cheek to cut a clean path through the frothy scum, and considered what he had on at work that day: appraisals. Two in particular weren't going to be easy: Neil and Constance. He ran the razor down his neck... fuck! He'd nicked himself. He dabbed the cut with some toilet paper, blood soaking into the tissue. He breathed out deeply. Appraisals were never easy, it was the one time of year when the staff could legitimately raise their grievances. Then again, running a business is *never* easy, he reminded himself. It's those that meet such challenges, those that *relish* them, who get to the top and stay there.

He splashed water on his face, stood tall and appraised himself in the mirror. He looked good, even at forty-nine. He hadn't let himself go like most of his contemporaries, sliding into middle-aged fat and sloth and disillusionment. He pictured them in their tatty semi-detached houses, and driving those horrible ugly people carriers, and their cheap holidays on charter flights... and shuddered.

He reached for his tweezers, leant forward and pulled the mounted, magnified vanity mirror towards him. He couldn't abide stray hairs, particularly any sprouting from his nostrils or ears, which reminded him of his age as he couldn't recall them growing from those places in his youth. He relished the sight of the tweezer pincers closing in on their prey and the satisfying little jab of pain each time one was extracted.

He walked along the corridor to the master bedroom in his heavy, white bathrobe, enjoying the feel of the luxuriant thick cream carpet under his feet. He loved Monday mornings. Loved the feeling of... of *mobilisation*, all his staff striving to get into work in order to power his juggernaut forward. All that energy, all that effort, with him at the vanguard, like a Roman warrior figurehead carved into the bow of a great naval galleon parting the seas... but then he passed the closed door of his wife's bedroom on the landing. His shoulders slumped. It was the one facet of his life that was a failure. Worse still, he couldn't get closure until she left him. She'd promised to leave weeks ago and he in turn had promised to sell the house, yet here she still was, squatting. What was she playing at? She *had* to go soon or else he'd need to think up another strategy to get rid of her. He entered his bedroom and pulled the door shut with a thud.

He selected his day's clothes from the walk-in wardrobe annexing his bedroom and lay them carefully on his bed. He began to dress in front of the floor-to-ceiling mirror, but slowly, savouring the quality and cut of his garments. Expensive clothes were a small indulgence, yes, but his people hardly expected to be led by a CEO dressed in threadbare suits and scuffed shoes, now did they?

The first potentially difficult appraisal today was Constance's. What to do about her? There was a certain inevitability to the progress of their relationship, but timing was crucial given the delicate state of negotiations with his wife. In any case, he loved the delicious tension between them, tension that had been building for months, even years, loved the feeling of being in control of it, loved the feeling that he could do no wrong in her eyes. Trouble was, he suspected that since their little indiscretion at the annual conference she was becoming frustrated with him. She'd recently missed a couple of deadlines, which was highly unusual for her, and queried a couple of his decisions, which was unheard of previously.

He fastened his favourite cufflinks, little blood-red discs which he felt offset the bright white of his freshly dry-cleaned and ironed shirt deliciously. He recalled the days when he'd ironed his own shirts… and grimaced. He pictured instead the outfit Constance might wear today. On appraisal day it was bound to be something fitted, or short, or slightly risqué. She really was a win win, because he'd appointed her on merit too. She was a first-class businesswoman. She got results. Give her a task and she would execute it with dedication and determination. She fully deserved her role as Company Secretary. Good to have a woman on the board as well: showed the company's commitment to equal opportunities and closed up the gender pay gap a little.

Lastly he pulled on his black bespoke fitted suit, flexing his shoulders in little circles so that the jacket settled just right. Would she mention their night together in her appraisal? He wasn't sure. But he needed to be prepared that she might. Could he fib and say his wife had now left him? Risky, but perhaps. He dabbed the cut on his neck with another tissue; it was still bleeding.

He passed the door to his wife's bedroom again as he made for the stairs. As he descended and readied to leave, he reminisced about the twenty-six years they'd spent together. The damp-ridden bottom-floor flat they'd first lived in together in south London. The years of toil as he sweated to build up the courier business, followed by the successes and the transformation of their lifestyle. Two grown-up children. *Twenty-six years.* But now they had nothing left in common: he felt younger than ever; she looked older than ever. He wanted to go to Monaco and Dubai; she to National Trust properties. He wanted to drink champagne and eat Michelin-starred cuisine; she baked cakes and ate comfort food. They'd simply grown apart.

Outside, he climbed up into his huge SUV and settled into the cream leather driving seat. Turning on the ignition, he immediately set the temperature control to cold; he needed a clear head to rehearse the thoughts he'd been putting into order over the weekend about Neil's appraisal. This *was* going to be difficult.

He flicked the switch for the electric gate and felt the purr of the engine power him into the street outside, savouring the contrast to the years he'd spent commuting, all that waiting on freezing platforms, then crammed into a disgusting train with people touching you and coughing and sneezing and their noses running. How fucking demeaning. If there was one thing he would never, *ever* do again, it was travel in cattle class on an airplane or a train. He wouldn't be degraded that way again.

Driving in his little fortress of luxury also afforded him time to think, which was especially important on days like today. Of course an annual appraisal was *meant* to be an assessment of how well someone was performing and how they could improve themselves in the coming year. As if! Hard experience had taught him that no matter how much he tried to make his employees think about their contribution to the company, they always focused instead on two things: their own pay and promotion. The way the troops entered his office proved it, so polite and beseeching, even a bit grovelling most of them. They wouldn't behave like that if it was about skills and development! But their fear was good: it meant they were hungry for success, like him.

And he always kept in mind that it was *his* money they wanted; it was *his* company. How much capital had *they* risked to build up a business? Fuck all, that's how much. That's why he made sure he was armed each year with a detailed knowledge of each appraisee's strengths, and more importantly their weaknesses, because they always conveniently forgot to mention those. He also made sure he was armed with good reasons why pay couldn't be as high as he would like: because of substantial investment needed in the company's infrastructure, because of an imminent change of government, because of increased competition in the market. This year was a cinch: Brexit! What could be more uncertain than that? Better still, there'd been no discernible downturn in profits since the referendum. Win win.

With Neil he had to be clear and precise in his messaging. He did a good job. He worked like a dog. But there was absolutely no way he could promote him just now. Then again, Neil had clearly earned promotion. Worse still, his strong moral sense of right and wrong could be an issue today. Of course, those qualities were why he'd hired him in the first place and championed his career, because they meant he'd be more devoted to the business. Indeed, Neil's zealous commitment to the cause was partially why he himself had been able to ease up a little and concentrate on strategy, the principal one being sounding out potential buyers of his company. Neil had been desperate for a place on the board for a few years now and would ordinarily deserve it, and the life-changing pay rise and company shares that went with it, but these weren't ordinary times, not with an imminent divorce and potential sale of his business. The last thing Harry wanted right now was a further dilution of *his* shareholding in *his* company.

He drew up quickly behind a small car going far too slowly in the fast lane. He reduced the gap between them to a few feet so that he hovered large in their rear-view mirror; moments later they obediently pulled over to the middle lane and he powered past.

Besides, Neil's strengths lay in process and procedure, whereas his board directors had to be *rainmakers* like himself, bringing in new clients and business. Neil had done great things with the couriers, admittedly, but he could have pushed them much harder and needed to understand that leadership often means risking unpopularity. He was no strategist either, evidenced by his mishandling of the discussions with HM Revenue & Customs; he'd provided far too much information. The whole sorry saga proved that Neil was just a capable doer, lacking the dynamism, edge and… *vision* of a board director.

Yes, Neil had plenty to work on. Harry eased on the accelerator, eager to get to work and begin executing his strategies.

≈

HARRY STOOD BEHIND HIS GLASS-TOPPED, STEEL-FRAMED desk which he always kept completely free from clutter, and reminded himself of one of the key lessons he'd learnt as a business leader: the importance of being able to reconcile two mutually exclusive ideas in your head at the same time. Here: Neil clearly deserved promotion; Neil could not possibly be promoted. Once you acknowledged the incompatibility of the ideas, they were somehow easier to deal with.

He saw Neil approach through the glass wall of his office and waved for him to come in and take a seat. 'Good weekend?' asked Harry as Neil sat down.

'Yes, so so…' said Neil, who tried to conjure a smile, but it lacked energy and became instead a slightly pained expression, like someone having difficulty on the toilet. Years of appraisals had taught Harry to pay very close attention to body language. When he didn't owe the appraisee anything, an uncomfortable expression was fine; it just meant they were desperate for whatever they could get. Here it was different; Neil deserved a lot more than he was going to get. 'And how was your weekend?' added Neil eventually.

'Yes, very good thanks. Church yesterday, as usual, after which we had a fundraiser for the hospice.'

Neil nodded and a brief silence followed. The blood appeared to have drained out of him, giving him a ghostly pallor which in turn emphasised the deep bruised bags under his eyes.

'Good,' said Harry, sitting down and taking a sip of water. 'Right, let's get down to business, shall we? Now, how do you think the last year has gone?' Always best to get the appraisee doing the speaking, thus revealing their hopes and fears.

Neil took a deep breath and began the pitch he'd clearly been turning over in his head many times in preparation for this moment. He started by reminding Harry of his Key Performance Indicators for the year, before summarising at length how he'd met each of them: his improvement of the company's governance and controls in order to secure the accreditations so valued by their customers; his oversight of the reconfiguration of the courier booking software producing savings straight to the bottom line; his high levels of commitment leading day-to-day operations resulting in increased turnover and profit. He finished by talking about his hopes for a place on the board and what he would contribute to the future success of the business were he to be a director.

Harry had remained attentive but impassive throughout the long monologue: no nodding, no smiles. Now that Neil had finished, he allowed a long silence to fall, which seemed to increase the distance between them. 'You've had a good year,' said Harry eventually, 'I'm prepared to acknowledge that.' He leaned forward, rested his elbows on his desk and intertwined his fingers. 'Which is why I think you deserve a pay rise.'

Neil's eyes flitted to one side and then back to Harry, almost as if he sensed someone was behind him but didn't want to look. 'Thank you,' he said quietly. 'May I ask how much?'

'Of course,' said Harry, looking down at his papers. 'We're going to raise your salary by five percent, which as you know is well above inflation.'

Neil's shoulders fell a little. His mouth was ever so slightly apart. His eyes flitted sideways again.

'I'm sorry it can't be more,' said Harry, 'but there's terrible uncertainty out there because of Brexit, as you know. In fact, there's virtually no pay increases this year, but I fought hard with the directors to make an exception in your case.'

A frown of concentration settled over Neil's eyes. He took a series of deep breaths, before sitting upright, stiffening and looking at Harry square on. 'Last year we discussed what I had to do to earn a place on the board. I've done everything you've asked of me, so I need to know why my promotion isn't being discussed.'

Harry reminded himself that it was *his* company. And *his* money. He shook his head and spoke very slowly. 'Nobody is going to be promoted to the board this year.'

'*What?!* Why not?'

'Uncertainty. As I've said, there's Brexit to consider; no one knows how that will pan out.'

'But there's been no downturn.'

'Don't be naïve, Neil. Brexit hasn't even started yet and anything could happen. I've always been prudent with my business, which is why I've managed to survive recessions and build us to where we are today. It's also why none of the directors are getting a pay rise this year.'

Neil squinted. 'Really?'

'Yes, really.' Harry allowed a silence to settle. The real reason no one was getting increases was because he wanted to make the business look as profitable as possible to any potential acquirer, but Neil didn't need to know that. It wasn't *his* company. 'There's also the matter of the HMRC inquiry, which I noted you didn't mention in your summary.'

'Dealing with HMRC wasn't one of my original objectives. All I did was tell them the truth about how the couriers operate.'

Harry pursed his lips. Heat gathered under his collar.

'There's answering their questions, and there's helping them. I think your approach flirted with the latter.'

'So you're saying I should have lied to them?'

'I did not say that,' said Harry, emphasising each word. 'My point is that when something new is thrown at you, like this HMRC review, you're not strategic enough.'

Neil shook his head. 'Give me one good reason why I shouldn't quit right now? I'm clearly not going to reach director, so why should I work myself to exhaustion? I've barely seen my wife or children this year.'

Harry sat back in his chair and crossed his arms. He had to make what he'd already decided seem like an on-the-spot decision. He looked out the window. He took his time. After a while he stood up, still looking out the window. Eventually he turned back to Neil, placed his hands on his desk and leaned forward. 'Okay. This is my offer. I'm prepared to officially propose you for promotion to the board next year, assuming no material changes, like a sale of the business.'

'Are you looking to sell?'

'Why would I want to sell? I'm not even fifty.'

Neil pinched his lower lip between forefinger and thumb. There was an alert silence. 'And you're prepared to put this in writing this time?'

Harry nodded.

Neil waited, his eyes flitting again. A faint rasp to his breathing was just audible. 'I need some time to think about this,' he said.

'Of course,' said Harry, nodding.

'The thing is, you know as well as I do that I've worked so hard these last few years and my understanding was that we would be discussing my promotion in *this* meeting. You led me to understand that.'

'I didn't make any promises,' said Harry. 'I merely said I

would consider it. You're almost there, really you are. But I need to be prudent with costs and as I said, there's lots of headwinds out there.'

Neil gazed downward, thinking it through. He began to shake his head, before eventually looking up, his demeanour hard and determined. 'As I said, I'm going to need some time to think about this. This meeting hasn't gone the way I expected, so I'm going to have to reflect on what that means for my career here. I also need to speak to my wife.'

Harry didn't like the idea of him speaking to his wife; it introduced too much risk. 'That's fine, I respect that you need to think about this. However, I'm afraid I'll need a decision today.'

'*Today?*'

'Yes, today. Long experience has taught me that these important issues can fester if not quickly resolved. As I said, I'm prepared to put my proposal to promote you in writing, that sort of commitment deserves a prompt answer.'

'Okay,' said Neil, rubbing his forehead. 'I'll let you know later. But you need to know I don't think the promises I was made last year have been honoured and I'm seriously thinking about resigning.' He stood up to leave.

'Don't do anything rash, Neil. Don't throw it all away. I want you to remember just how much I value you and your contribution here. I realise today has probably fallen a little short of your expectations, but I firmly believe you'll get where you want to be very soon.'

There was a brief silence as Neil looked at Harry quizzically. 'I'll be in touch later,' he said and walked out, shaking his head as he did so.

'Fuck it,' said Harry. He couldn't afford to lose Neil and his talking to his wife was dangerous; the pressures of home could make him re-evaluate his priorities. On the other hand he was within touching distance of making director, surely he wouldn't let that go because of a short delay? Even the most earnest and humble of people like Neil always eventually want the money and status, don't they? He wasn't sure. 'Fuck it,' said Harry again and punched the metal lip of his desk.

HARRY SAT BEHIND HIS DESK, AWAITING CONSTANCE'S arrival, his heart rate still elevated from Neil's appraisal. He focused on Constance; compartmentalising issues was one of his strengths. Two mutually exclusive ideas at once, he reminded himself. Here: he always stressed to Constance that he'd promoted her on merit when he wanted her to feel good about herself; she had to understand that all her promotions had self-evidently been down to him and that she should feel gratitude to him and indebted to him.

There was a knock on the door and he waved her in. 'Please, sit down,' he said, motioning for her to take a seat. She hadn't disappointed. Her lips were painted a deep rouge and a wave of her perfume enveloped him shortly after she sat down. He could see in his peripheral vision that she was wearing a short skirt and high heels, but resisted looking down; there would plenty of opportunities for that during the appraisal. For now, he relaxed a little; her appearance meant she was still eager to please.

They exchanged pleasantries about their respective weekends, Constance expressing frustration with her boyfriend, who preferred wasting his afternoons in front of the telly clutching the TV controller and watching the grand prix rather than paying her any attention. As she spoke, he thought to himself that the fifteen years between them wasn't so much, particularly as he clearly had so much more vigour than her boyfriend. However, as much as he always enjoyed hearing her putting down her boyfriend, he couldn't help noticing the rather strained expression pulling on her face, and a slight defensive edge to the way she spoke.

'Right, let's get down to business, shall we?' he said eventually, taking a sip of water. 'How do you think the last year has gone?'

Constance consulted her notebook and started by summarising her objectives for the year and how she thought she had performed against them, although unusually her summary lacked energy. Each time she looked down to her notebook, Harry stole a glance at her legs, which in turn brought back memories of their recent night together at the annual conference.

'Thank you for that,' said Harry, once she'd finished. 'I agree that you've had a good year, which is why I think you deserve a decent bonus this year.'

'Thank you,' said Constance, but in a voice barely above a whisper. Her lower lip had closed over the top one.

'Is everything okay?'

She didn't look up, but her face was distorted, her mouth slightly twisted. 'No, not really,' she said and made a sobbing sound.

Harry sat forward. 'Why not? What's the matter?'

She lifted her head, eyes forward and bright with determination. 'You, Harry. *You* are the matter.'

'What?'

'Oh, come on, you know what I'm talking about. Us. What happened at the conference. I need to know where I stand.'

'How do you mean, *where you stand*?'

'You *know* what I mean. This thing that's been going on

between us for years. How close we are. How we spend every day together. I can't stand it any longer. I'm thirty-four for god's sake, I need to make some decisions.'

Throughout the ten years he'd known Constance he'd been in total control of their relationship; her last few words wiped that all away and he felt as if he was freewheeling down a steep slope at great speed without brakes or a seatbelt. He put his hands on the lip of his desk to steady himself.

'I'm sorry, Harry, but I came here today to hand in my resignation.' Even before the word *resignation* was fully free from her mouth, she'd started to weep, her head falling forward. 'I just thought it would be best... for both of us,' she said, between sobs.

Harry was worried that someone might see the scene unfolding in his office through its glass wall, but didn't dare deviate from looking straight ahead at Constance. His collar was hot and sticky around his neck and his head dizzy. On top of the Neil situation, he now risked losing the love interest he looked forward to seeing each day. It was intolerable. 'You mustn't resign, Constance. It would be a terrible waste of all that you've achieved here.'

'But it's driving me mad working here. It's killing me.' Her sobbing was now causing her shoulders to shake.

'I'll make it worthwhile for you to stay.'

'Harry!' she said, with surprising ferocity. 'This isn't about money. I need to know where I stand *with you*. You have to make a decision.'

He stood up, walked to the side of the office to pick up a box of tissues and handed them to her. He re-poured his glass with water. All of this allowed him time to think. 'Constance, I have some good news.'

She finished dabbing her eyes with a tissue. 'You have?'

'Kathy is leaving me.'

'Is she?' Her eyes widened and her lips turned upwards a fraction at their corners for the first time since she'd entered his office. 'Are you separated now?'

'She's in the process of leaving me. As you can imagine, there's been lots to discuss and many arrangements to sort out. And of course it hasn't been easy on the children.'

'*In the process* of leaving? Meaning she hasn't left yet?'

'She's leaving,' said Harry firmly.

Constance began shaking her head and glowered at Harry as if, for the first time ever, she disliked him. 'I'm sorry, Harry, I think this conversation just reinforces that it would be best for both of us if I resign.'

Harry pictured his wife bunkered down in her bedroom, refusing to leave. Fucking bitch! 'Look, I'm sorry, okay? I'm sorry it's complicated and I'm sorry I haven't been more transparent with you.' He looked out of the window which took up most of the length of one wall of his office. His breathing was deepening. He turned back to her. 'I was planning on speaking to you about it, but… but things have been difficult. I just need a little bit longer to sort everything. You need to trust me on this.'

'Harry, I can't wait any longer,' said Constance, shaking her head.

'Please, Constance,' said Harry through clenched teeth, such that his words came out in a hissing sound. 'Just give me a bit more time.'

'I don't know, I just don't know anymore.' Her face crumpled as she began to cry again and picked out another tissue from the box. After a short silence, she stood up.

'You're not going to resign are you?' asked Harry.

'I don't know. I need some time alone to think. I'm sorry, I can't guarantee I'm going to stay. I think some sort of…

break might be for the best.' She started to walk to the door, but Harry cut her off by reaching out and taking hold of her upper arm.

'Constance! *Please?* Just give me a day or so.'

Constance looked down to where Harry was holding her by the bicep. Using her other arm, she gently lifted his hand away. 'I'm sorry, Harry. I need some time on my own.' Head down, still clutching a tissue, she left his office.

'Fuck it,' said Harry, returning to his chair and dropping down into it. He couldn't lose Constance, she was the main thing motivating him to come into the office these days. She kept him young and focused. She made him feel good about himself. He pictured his wife still squatting in her bedroom refusing to leave, a smile playing on her lips as her waiting-game plan to ratchet up the pressure on him began to bear fruit. All this despite promising weeks ago that she would find somewhere else to live and they would sell the house. What was delaying her? What was she playing at? Fucking bitch!

LATER THAT DAY THE TYRES OF HARRY'S SUV SCRUNCHED to a halt on the gravel outside his house and he switched off the car's heavy rumbling engine just as the electric gates clicked closed behind him. In the ensuing silence he stared ahead and thought through what a terrible day it had been. 'Fuck it!' he shouted, smashing the underside of his fists against the steering wheel repeatedly until he inadvertently hit the car's loud horn. *Those fucking cunts, don't they know they owe me? Who set the fucking company up, whose money is it, who fucking promoted you all, for Christ's sake?*

Then he remembered: his wife was still in the house. He

thrust open the car door and slammed it shut. *She's going to get it; how dare she try to play fucking games with me, that fucking bitch.*

He ran to the front door, flung it open and ran up the stairs two at a time, his hands clenched into fists.

He ripped open her bedroom door, *ready to fucking kill her,* only to be startled by total darkness. He switched on the light. The room was completely empty. Not only devoid of her, but devoid of all her belongings and possessions.

Harry stood staring and drew a series of deep breaths into his lungs as his panting slowed. He looked around: the wardrobe doors were open showing its empty insides, the dressing table bare of the usual perfume bottles, hairbrushes and jewellery boxes. Harry remained completely still for some time, allowing the desolate atmosphere of the room to seep into the very marrow of his bones. As the full import of the moment registered, a single tear gathered in his right eye... before dribbling down his cheek. A single tear... of joy. She'd finally left!

He strode downstairs to the drinks cabinet and poured himself a tumbler of the ruinously expensive single malt he kept for business entertaining, before sliding down into a dark tan leather armchair and taking a large gulp; it tasted so goddam good mixed with this adrenalin.

They'd both known for a long time that their marriage was over, but it'd been imperative that the final break was initiated by her; if *he'd* done it some weak-willed divorce judge would fall for her sob story and grant her most of his fortune. He'd promised her most of the money from the house in return for him keeping all the company shares; the profits from selling the company would now crystallise post-divorce and to him alone.

He took another generous slurp of his whisky and

allowed himself to imagine the moment when he'd receive the bank transfer for millions of pounds. He deserved it. Selling a company was the time the original founder made good. *He* was the one who'd anticipated the explosion in the courier market in the late nineteen-nineties just as online shopping was becoming all the rage, wasn't he? Well, everyone thought he had, so he must have done. And one thing was for certain: his wife and the likes of Neil certainly fucking hadn't.

His mobile rang and he reached into his inside pocket. Neil's name appeared on the screen. He pressed the button. 'Hi, Neil.'

'Hi, Harry. I'm calling further to my appraisal earlier.'

'Yes?'

There was a brief silence. 'I've spoken to my wife and we've agreed that I should accept your offer regarding promoting me next year. Of course, I'll need it in writing, as we agreed earlier.' His voice was slightly shaky, almost on the verge of breaking.

'Of course, Neil, of course. That's *fantastic* news. I'm so happy, and this is definitely the right decision for you. Listen, how about we set up a meeting tomorrow afternoon, at which I'll put the offer in writing. We can also set out a timetable for your elevation to director next year.'

'That would be great. Thank you, Harry.'

'No, no, thank *you*. Listen, I'm really sorry I couldn't make things happen this year, but I'm so optimistic about the future. Let's talk tomorrow.'

'Okay, we'll talk tomorrow. Thank you, Harry. Bye.'

Fucking hell! Things were looking up! No further dilution of his shareholding. Neil would continue running himself into the ground until he sold the business. He took another gulp of his whisky while still holding his mobile in the other hand. Hang on! Good news often comes in threes! He pressed Constance's number and in the fraction of time between the ringing starting and hearing Constance's voice, he relished the prospect of flicking the switch on their relationship from professional to personal.

'Hello, Harry.'

'Hi, Constance. I wanted you to be the first to hear some positive news I've just received.'

'What's that then?'

'Kathy has finally left me. No ifs or buts, it's completely, one hundred percent over and done with.'

There was a brief silence. 'Really?'

'Yes, really. I'm sorry about earlier. In fact, I'm sorry for lots of what's happened recently, but you have my word that I'll shortly be divorced. I hope you're not going to resign?'

'Of course not, Harry. I never wanted to resign, I just felt I had no other option.'

'That's fantastic, Constance. We need to meet, and I mean now.'

'Now?' said Constance hesitantly.

'Listen, I realise it's quite late and this is a little unexpected, but I really need to see you. Can you meet me?' A brief silence followed, during which Harry thought how the very best questions are those you already know the answer to.

'Well, I guess I could. I'll just need to… to—'

'Just tell him something urgent's come up at work. Tell him the IT system has gone down.'

'Right… okay then. Where shall we meet?'

'The champagne bar in an hour?'

'Okay. I'll see you there.'

'Good. See you soon.'

Harry stood and walked upstairs to his bedroom with his

whisky in order to get changed. He'd need to tread carefully with Constance. Did he intend to embark on a relationship with her? Hell yes! Did he envisage a long-term future with her? Hell no! He'd been imprisoned in a monogamous relationship for twenty-six years and was about to cash in millions, he was hardly going to let someone pin him down again. He'd make sure he made her no promises; that way he couldn't be accused of misleading her.

He calmly tipped back his glass, allowing the last of the single malt to slide down the back of his throat. He placed the empty glass gently down on his dressing table, breathed out a sigh of relief and caught sight of himself in his oval vanity mirror. Finally, everyone was back in their allotted place, each revolving in their correct gravitational orbit, with him at their centre.

THE FAIRER SEX

'Can we build a den, Dad? *Please?*'

'Oh, go on then!' Sam Dixon dropped to his knees to get to the same height as Oliver. He lifted the two seat cushions so they stood upright against the arms of the sofa. 'Grab that blanket,' he said, pointing. Oliver reached for it and together they draped it over the back of the sofa and upright cushions to create a small, dark enclosed space. Sam retrieved the brightly coloured stripy throw from the other sofa and laid it on the floor in front of the den. 'This can be where we eat. Go and get some plates and food.' Oliver ran off to the kitchen, where they had a children's pretend kitchen with plastic vegetables, fruits, plates and cutlery.

Sam lay down on the floor and sighed. He'd had a hard morning, getting Oliver up and dressed, making him runny boiled eggs and fingers of toast, before taking him to football practice, but he'd loved it, because Saturday was *his* day with Oliver. He couldn't understand his friends who were fathers who spent their weekends playing golf or

donning those horrible lycra outfits and going for long rides
on their thousand-pound bicycles. He was just about to close
his eyes when suddenly an image of *her* shot into his head:
standing in high heels, hands on hips, head tilted giving him
that look. No! He mustn't! He just mustn't. He pushed the
image out of his head as Oliver rushed back into the room
carrying the plastic plates and foods.

THAT AFTERNOON, SAM WAS HELPING OLIVER TO 'CLIMB
Everest.' They'd set up a base camp at the foot of the stairs
by erecting their family's small, orange, pop-up beach tent.

'Right, we need to tie ourselves together in case one of
us falls,' said Sam, unravelling a length of string and tying
one end around Oliver's waist and the other around his
own. 'Now remember, we're so high up here that there's
very little oxygen, so you'll have to wear your oxygen mask.'
Sam reached into a small rucksack and handed Oliver his
old snorkelling mask, before helping him by pulling the strap
around the back of his head. 'Ready?'

Oliver nodded.

'Okay, I'll go first as the senior climber.' Sam hauled
himself up a few stairs using only his elbows rather than his
legs, making howling wind noises as he went. Halfway up
the stairs he stopped and turned around, panting. 'We'll rest
here, before the final assault on the summit. Climb up.
Remember, no legs, you can only use your arms.'

Oliver pushed himself up each stair using only his hands
while Sam again made blustering gale noises. When Oliver
reached him, Sam pulled a packet of Maltesers from the
backpack, causing Oliver's face to light up; Maltesers were
his favourite. 'It's important we have enough energy,' said

Sam, smiling. Once the pack was done, he said, 'You go for the summit, because I'm tired and you're younger and fitter. I'll follow.'

Oliver pulled himself up the last few steps to the top landing. 'I've made it!' he cried out, arms aloft.

'Help me up, then,' said Sam, reaching up. Oliver grabbed his dad's arm and leant back to haul him up, until they both stood on the landing together. They embraced, before Sam reached into the rucksack and pulled out a small Union Jack tied to a twig. 'We must plant the flag,' said Sam, handing it to Oliver, who propped it upright against the wall. Sam took a photo with his phone of Oliver standing on the summit next to the flag with his snorkelling mask on and sent it to his wife Heidi.

'Can I play on the Kindle now?' asked Oliver.

Sam checked his watch: it was 4pm, and Oliver had had no screen time yet that day. 'Sure,' said Sam, 'I think it's charging in the kitchen.' Oliver dropped the snorkelling mask to the floor and ran off.

Sam walked to his bedroom and slumped on the bed. He closed his eyes. He was knackered, and wondered what he'd done with all his free time before becoming a father. A memory flashed up in his mind: his mum pulling a rope attached to a plastic sledge outside their house in freshly fallen snow, dragging him down the road to the café, where they stumbled inside for hot chocolates with whipped cream and marshmallows to warm themselves up. He pictured her clearly in her bobble hat, her cheeks glowing red from the cold and her glassy blue eyes sparkling in reflection of the snow outside. How many other memories had he been denied? His chest rose as he took in a deep breath, before blowing it out; it just made it even more important that he created as many memories of his own with Oliver, when suddenly *another* image of *her* fired into his mind: wearing an embroidered balconette black bra and legs encased in fishnet black stockings. *Jesus!* More images flooded his mind: the undulation of her hips under the sheer fabric of a fitted dress, the flare of her calves curving down to feet skewered into five-inch-tall high heels. *Fucking hell.*

He drew deep breaths into his lungs. He had to resist this. He *had* to. After all, she'd almost cost him his family. He recalled the moment of shattering confrontation with his wife: when he'd returned from work that day she'd been waiting just the other side of the front door with her arms folded across her chest, her face wearing an expression he'd never seen before, one of unfathomable loathing. 'You bastard,' she'd said.

'What?' he asked, although already deep down he realized she *knew*.

'I found your bank statement. Why have you been transferring £100 every couple of weeks to a Natasha Bates? Tell me the truth or I swear to god you'll never see me or your son ever again.'

He whimpered and fell to his knees at her feet. 'I'm sorry. Please, I can explain.'

'Have you been paying to see a woman?'

He hesitated.

'Well?!'

'Yes, but it's not—'

'Get out!' Heidi shrieked. 'Just get out!'

He kept trying to explain but each time she just screamed at him to get out, so he packed a bag and left, heading to a cheap hotel where he stayed for the next five nights. He spent those days chain smoking Benson & Hedges cigarettes and drinking neat vodka, while sending Heidi a series of emails begging for forgiveness and telling her just how much he loved her, despite what he'd done. When she subsequently allowed him back into the flat she made him sleep on the sofa for the next few days while deciding whether to leave him and take Oliver with her. Those had been the darkest days of his life. When occasionally Heidi appeared, she did so with swollen, puffy eyes and a blotched face, and would look at him as he imagined she would a psychopath or paedophile, a mixture of disgust, horror and incomprehension. It was a look which said she wouldn't be taking him back, and that they were merely now playing out an agonising end game and he would soon be alone, the sole author of his own demise.

It was during those days that he'd made *that* journey to the train station. He'd tried not to think about it since. He'd originally left the flat that evening just to get away from the suffocating atmosphere of hostility and to think through his options if Heidi left him. Head down, collar up, he'd not known where he was going, just wandering the streets aimlessly, traipsing on, splatting through puddles. He couldn't remember consciously deciding to go to the station, it was more a case of him eventually running out of options of places to go, or else being pulled there by an answer that somehow lay in wait for him. Once there, he sat down on a hard, metal bench on the empty platform, staring ahead, the pink luminescent sky slowly extinguishing and the branches of the dark trees crowding the station throwing increasingly suggestive shadows around him. He spent a long time thinking about his childhood and about what his mother would make of her son on the platform about to lose the two people he loved most in the world. In his unbearable sadness he felt himself drawn to the tracks in front of him.

He stood up.

He took a series of small steps to the edge of the platform.

He waited. The deep drop in front of him to the tracks unsettled his balance and as he swayed slightly he felt he might simply fold forward onto the line.

He looked down the track and shortly the lights in the nose of an Intercity appeared in the far distance on the horizon. It seemed to close the distance to him slowly at first, just a slight increase in the brightness of its lights as it wormed closer, but then the tracks below him started to hum and vibrate causing him to glance down at their shiny scraped smoothness and when he looked back down the line the train cut the final gap to him with terrifying velocity, like liquid sucked through a straw, and he lifted his foot, but froze – an image of his mother's anguished face appearing in his mind's eye – and with a thunderous explosion of noise the train detonated through the station.

He fled, deciding to dull his mind entirely from such thoughts, buying a cheap bottle of vodka from the off-licence and swigging it until empty while sitting on a swing in a deserted, dark and menacingly cold children's playground, the temperate falling so fast and far that the neat alcohol coursing his veins felt like anti-freeze being the only thing keeping his blood from turning to ice. He stumbled home at two in the morning.

Slowly, ever so slowly, a sort of silent truce had descended on the flat in the days that followed and he'd offered to do his usual stint with Oliver on the Saturday and Heidi had agreed. A conversation had started later that day about what he'd been up to with Oliver and thus began the thawing of their relationship.

In time they'd had a discussion and Heidi had laid down the new law if she were to accept him back. As well as never seeing Natasha or any other woman again, Heidi insisted that all money would now go through their joint bank account, over which she had visibility, and that he would close down his personal account. All his expenditure would be jointly agreed henceforth: his haircuts, any new clothes or shoes, drinks with work colleagues, music downloads, everything.

He was in no position to resist. After all, the total had come to £2,100. £2,100 they didn't have. After the oversized mortgage on their two-bedroom ground floor flat and the cost of utilities and food there was nothing left over each month. To finance his habit he'd spent months preaching financial prudence, querying whether she really needed any new item of clothing, imploring her to make savings on the weekly shop, even insisting she buy a cheaper brand of shoes for Oliver. All so he could blow £100 every fortnight for an hour with *her*.

'What's for dinner, Dad?' shouted Oliver from the kitchen, breaking Sam from his memories. As he rose from the bed one of his wife's floral-print dresses on a coat hanger on the front of her wardrobe caught his eye. No! No, no, no! He pushed such thoughts from his mind, or else he'd start imagining *her* in it rather than Heidi.

A FEW DAYS LATER, SAM WALKED INTO TOWN ON HIS LUNCH break. It was an unusually hot and humid summer's day, the hazy air viscous, the sun beating down on him with a fierce intensity causing his brow to bead with perspiration. He removed his jacket but still felt the damp sweat building under his arms and on his lower back.

An attractive young woman in a bright summer dress

crossed in front of him and accidentally met his eye but immediately looked away. Women always did with him. Her long, tanned legs moved with a supple litheness which was precisely the opposite of his own shuffling gait. He admired her choice of dress, the way it fitted snugly to her waist before flaring sensually over the curve of her hips, but it was a sight he really didn't need. His senses had become so finely tuned recently, such that images, sounds, sensations, even smells of *her* kept jumping into his head no matter how much he tried to suppress them. Each sensory trigger was then rapidly crushed underneath an avalanche of debauched and vulgar thoughts and cravings.

He tried to think instead of what to buy for lunch. He took a packed lunch to work most days now – one of his many reparations – but was allowed to buy lunch occasionally, with a strict £10 per day limit to cover the cost of food and any extras such as coffees or chocolate. Jacket potatoes piled high with cheese and coleslaw were his favourite, so he joined the short queue at the baked potato stall. As he waited, the weight of the sun bore down on the top of his head, particularly as he tended to burn there more easily since losing his hair. He looked down at the small black island of shadow he was standing in and a thought occurred: what if he *didn't* buy lunch? He would then have money *for her* and no one would know…

No! He mustn't do that. He mustn't. He enjoyed potatoes smothered in cheese and coleslaw, it was an innocent vice. But he *could* make do with a cereal bar instead? And some of the free fruit in the office?

'What can I get you?' asked the man in the stall, bending and looking down at Sam from the hatch.

'Er… actually, I've forgotten my money. Sorry.' He

walked into the nearest newsagents, bought a cereal bar and scuttled back to work.

Sam was the only person in the office, having worked late. He hadn't noticed either the passage of time, or the automatic sensor lights turn off, so that the soft, hazy glow from his PC monitor was the only illumination in the room. He dragged a formula down a line of numbers in the spreadsheet he was working on and watched the cells blink and reveal their new contents. He rubbed his eyes; his tiredness was slowing him up.

Almost without thought, more as a reflex, he stretched down and slid open his desk drawer. Reaching in, he drew out the little pile of notes he'd been accumulating, held together by a paperclip, handling it with extreme care. He licked a finger and counted them slowly and methodically: £70. It was the third time that day he'd counted them.

He replaced the notes in his drawer, closed and locked it, and returned his attention to his PC, logging into his personal email account and clicking the icon for 'new message'.

He was just testing himself.

He could draw back at any time.

Besides, sending a message wasn't a crime, was it?

He moved the cursor to the 'To' field and pressed the letter N on his keyboard: her email address loaded automatically. Even after eighteen months of no contact, it refused to forget her; or had been programmed not to.

What would he say to her? She may no longer be in the same line of work. Would she even remember him? Of course she would! How could she not? After all, he'd bared his soul to her in a way he'd never done to anyone else; surely that meant something? He began to type:

Hi Natasha, just wondering how you are?

He stared at the words. The sort of thing you'd write to your granny. He deleted them and typed some more:

Hi Natasha, sorry it's been so long. Would it be possible to arrange a meeting?

He stared again at the words. He pictured her reading them and throwing her head back in laughter at his capitulation. God, he wanted to see her! He re-typed the message again:

Dear Natasha, I've never stopped thinking about what we shared. I can't cope without it. Please let me see you again, I implore you.

His mouth dry and gummy, he re-read the words. His heart throbbed thickly behind his ribcage. Heat radiated off his tingling fingers as they hovered over the keyboard. He took hold of his mouse and moved the curser until the little arrow hovered over the "send" sign, his forefinger just above the button on the mouse, twitching.

In his mind he heard her lovely, softly spoken, clipped voice and then pictured her bright, painted lips as she smiled at his complete inability to resist her: he pressed his finger down affirmatively and with a click the email was sent.

Shit shit shit! It was wrong.

But wait! It was just an email. No final decision had been made. He'd committed no crime, only perhaps a thought crime, and there was no sanction for that, surely?

He quickly closed down his email, hoping that would block out further thoughts of her and, suddenly realising how dark it was, turned off his PC and hurriedly left the office to return home.

A LONG, SHRILL BLAST OF THE REFEREE'S WHISTLE AND THE game of football was over. Oliver ran over and hugged Sam's leg. 'Did you see my goal?' he asked, face alight looking up at him.

'Yes, it was brilliant!' said Sam, lifting Oliver high into the air. 'You're the new Harry Kane! Come on, let's get you back home.'

They returned to the flat to find Sam's wife Heidi buzzing around the kitchen putting away the week's food shopping from various plastic bags scattered on the floor. Oliver launched into another animated match summary for his mother's benefit as Sam made himself a cup of tea.

'Now, Sam?' said Heidi once Oliver had wandered off to get changed. 'I'm taking Oliver out for lunch with my dad but then at 3pm you've got to take him to Joshua's birthday party. Okay?'

'Sure,' said Sam.

'Thanks for letting me have a lie-in this morning,' said Heidi, kissing him on the cheek and walking out to the hallway. 'Come on, Oliver, we've got to go to Grandpa's.' After a short while of Heidi cajoling Oliver to hurry up and Oliver complaining, the front door thudded closed and Sam was alone.

He sat down with his cup of tea at the small, cream-coloured Formica kitchen table and savoured the quiet, just the occasional sounds of the flat's breathing audible: the dishwasher gurgling lightly, the faint voices from the radio still on in the bedroom. Just as he brought his mug to his mouth, Natasha leapt into his mind. Unbeknown to him, his temperature began to rise, his pupils dilated. He pulled out his mobile and logged into his email account. The screen blanked fleetingly as his username and password were processed and his inbox appeared: there, in bold type, was an email from her! Fucking hell! His throat constricted, causing his breathing to shorten. His first contact from her in over eighteen months. He clicked on her message, purposefully slowing his eyes to ensure he fully digested and processed every word first time:

Sam,

I thought you'd make contact eventually and glad you did. I have a slot on Monday at 6pm. I'm on holiday for two weeks after Monday, so let me know what you want to do. I assume your needs are the same as before?

Natasha

Monday? Shit. He closed his eyes and imagined her standing in front of him: her flawless, polished white teeth exposed as she smiled enigmatically; her coy, giggling laughter; the way her long eyelashes made it appear like she blinked in slow motion. *Fucking hell!* He hurriedly typed a response:

Dear Natasha,

I will be there at 6pm on Monday. Needs exactly as before. I need to pay cash this time, rather than transfer money. Hope this is okay?

Sam

As he pressed send a thought struck him: he didn't have the money. How much did he have? £70. He could take out £20 for next week's lunches but that still left him £10 short. His eyes skimmed left and right without seeing anything. Suddenly he turned and hurried up the stairs to his son's bedroom. Where was it? He swung around, scanning the surfaces… there! On the shelf, a large plastic Thomas the Tank Engine with a slot in the roof of the driver's cabin for coins. He grabbed it and turned it over, his fingers beavering busily to loosen the round plastic stopper. He prodded his fingers inside hungrily and touched what he needed: a note. He pulled it free: £10 deposited there last Christmas, a present from relatives. He put it in his pocket with a mental note to replace it, before easing the stopper back and returning the piggy bank to the shelf.

HE SLIPPED HIS FINGERS INTO THE INSIDE POCKET OF HIS rucksack and touched the three £10 notes. He peered inside: he needed to *see* them as well as touch them. Satisfied, he turned to Heidi. 'Right, I best be off,' he said.

'Have you packed your gym stuff?' she asked.

'Shit, no!' said Sam. 'I'll get it.' He berated himself as he ran upstairs to get his shorts, t-shirt and trainers. How could he be so stupid? He'd told Heidi last night that he was going to the gym after work, his excuse for why he'd be late home. Returning downstairs, he pushed his kit into his rucksack, struggling to force the zip closed.

As he unlocked the front door, Heidi approached. 'Sam?' she asked, looking at him in a peculiar way, a slight cocking of her head and a smile suggesting itself on her mouth.

'What?' he asked, a little defensively.

Heidi put her hands on his shoulders and looked at him closely. 'Thanks for all your help over the weekend.'

'No problem.'

'It's really good all the effort you put in with Oliver and now with the exercise. I'm proud of you.' She kissed him on the cheek as he left.

With his footsteps crunching on the gravel drive he heard the front window being tapped. He turned. Oliver was peering over the bottom of the window pane and waving furiously. Sam waved back, but the sight of such pure devotion and love caused him to choke up and as he rounded the corner tears welled in his eyes.

As he walked to the train station, he consoled himself that he still hadn't made the final decision. He could still back out. Indeed, perhaps his steps so far *weren't* such a bad thing; after all, if he could *still* pull out after coming this far, perhaps he could say he'd conquered it?

In any case, it was hardly his fault he'd been born at the unlucky end of the looks scale. Take his build. He'd once read an article saying the ideal shape for a man to be attractive to women is tall with broad shoulders tapering down to a slim waist. He was the precise opposite: small, with a large midriff tapering *up* to thin shoulders. Then there was his lifelong battle with his weight. He just couldn't reduce. He couldn't resist crisps and chocolate and biscuits and cake, and his use of the gym was so sporadic that the subscription was a total waste of money. The heavier he got, the less he wanted to go to the gym, and the less he exercised, the more he consoled himself with comfort food.

He reached the station and joined a little posse of commuters huddled together where they anticipated the train doors would open. It struck him that he'd never once in his whole life experienced a woman looking at him in a way which contained any element of desire. Even Heidi often said, 'I hadn't been sure about you to begin with, but you grew on me.' Wasn't he allowed, just momentarily, to experience being desirable? Was that really such a crime?

∼

AT 5.40PM HE REACHED INTO HIS DESK DRAWER AGAIN AND drew out his little wad of cash. He licked his finger and counted each note in turn: ten £10 notes made it a round £100. He carefully folded them, slipped the wad into his trouser pocket and prepared to leave. Strangely, he'd got quite a lot done that afternoon, as though his mind didn't need to wander off to dark places because it knew it would later get its fill. That didn't mean he'd finally decided to go through with it. No. There was still a choice to be made. He could still pull back from the edge, but now needed to be fully confronted with the temptation to make that final choice.

He walked briskly to her street, but as he neared, realising he was early, slowed down, finding himself just fifty feet from her premises. He stopped and stared: it looked so innocuous standing in the middle of the long, Georgian, dark brick terrace. The properties were all two-storey with a lower ground floor, with short flights of steps flanked by iron railings leading up to their front doors, most of which had small, discreet plaques in brass or silver to one side: a dentist, a solicitor, a consultant.

He walked forward until he was just a few feet away and again stopped. He stared at the burgundy coloured door. This was the moment of choice. He could still turn around. He'd committed no crime.

Suddenly he sensed some people walking up behind him and instinctively pulled his mobile from his jacket, held it to his ear and said too loudly, 'Oh hi! Thanks for calling, mmmm, mmmm, that's right,' while nodding and turning his back on them to shield his face. It was ludicrous, making fake calls in the street. But it was what she'd reduced him to. It was what *she* wanted. He patted the wad of notes in his trouser pocket to reassure himself it was still there. Just once. Maybe if he went just this once it didn't necessarily mean he'd come again. He checked his watch – 6.01pm – looked both ways, walked up the stairs and pressed the intercom with his head down: the buzzer's quick response startled him, the lock releasing with a heavy click and he pushed the door to enter.

His eyes had to adjust from the late afternoon sunshine to the darkness of the empty waiting room, lit only by the meagre yellow glow thrown from a large, round, bronze bottomed lamp. The room came into focus as he remembered it: rich crimson walls, dark wood plantation blinds closed shut, a brown studded leather armchair and a large, squat antique coffee table on which stood a black vase holding a single white orchid, its petals flecked with purple and yellow. The warmth of the room matched the heat radiating from his skin and seemed to hold the delicate fragrance of the orchid in suspension. He remained standing, perfectly still, knowing she'd call him through any second, those final moments dreamy and hazy and a dull ache in the pit of his stomach.

The far door opened a few inches, then her quiet, composed, disembodied voice floated to him, 'Undress and come through in one minute with your money.' The door closed. *Jesus, this was it!*

He undressed hurriedly, each discarded garment heightening his sense of vulnerability, placing his clothes in a pile on the armchair. Once naked, he reached into his trouser pocket and pulled out the money. He approached the door, gently pushed it open and gasped: there, on a mannequin, was the outfit: a short pastel blue dress and cream high heels underneath.

Natasha approached in a short, pale pink dress and put her arm around his shoulder. 'Now then,' she said, 'we're going to make you look *so* pretty.'

'Oh, thank you,' said Sam in a prim, falsetto voice.

'Let's get you started,' said Natasha, lifting the dress from the mannequin and holding it over Sam's head. He pushed his arms up through the short sleeves and when Natasha let the material fall, Sam again gasped at the feel of the soft, silky material against his goose bumped skin.

Natasha stood back to admire him and smiled. 'Oh, Jenny, you look beautiful. Let's get you made up. Then we'll call through Norman.'

WHEN SAM RETURNED HOME AND ENTERED THE KITCHEN, Heidi was holding the wok with one hand and pouring sauce into it from a packet with the other. 'Can you lay the table?' she asked. 'It's almost ready. How was the gym?'

'Tiring,' said Sam, opening the cutlery drawer. Heidi leaned over to kiss him on the cheek, but he instantly recoiled, conscious that perhaps some of the... the *essence* of earlier had somehow seeped into his clothing, or imprinted his skin, and she'd smell it. 'Sorry,' said Sam. 'I'm still sweating.'

'Didn't you shower at the gym?'

'I did, but I'm still hot.'

'Your face is very red.'

Heidi brought the plates to the table, followed by wine glasses and a bottle of Pinot Grigio. 'Oh, shit,' she said, sitting down, 'can you *please* check your emails to see if they've processed Oliver's new passport? Apparently they email you if they've started it.'

'I'll check later.'

'No, you'll forget. Please, Sam, I've been worrying about it all day. I don't want anything to ruin our holiday.' She reached out and grabbed the iPad from along the table and thrust it in front of him.

'Can I just have my dinner?' he asked, his voice whiney. He reached for the wine bottle and filled their glasses; perhaps that would distract her?

'Please, Sam, you know how much this holiday means to me. I don't understand why you can't just check. And besides, who forgot to send in the application for so long?'

'Okay, okay, I'll do it,' he said, spinning the iPad round and logging on. Had he deleted Natasha's email? He couldn't be sure. He thought he had. He glanced up furtively to ensure Heidi wasn't watching him.

He entered his log-in details and the screen flickered: his inbox appeared, with an email from *her* at the top! His hand jerked forward, striking his wine glass, which fell and shattered, glass and liquid shooting across the iPad and table. 'Shit!' said Sam, standing and rushing to grab a tea towel.

'Are you okay?' asked Heidi, reaching for the iPad and tilting it to allow the wine to run off; she stilled as the message at the top of her husband's emails came into focus and the implications registered.

Sam approached with the dishcloth, only to find his wife staring at the iPad; so he too immediately recognized that the fuse was lit, and his life about to change forever.

'Why is there an email from Natasha in your inbox?'

Sam couldn't find any words; they could make no difference now.

Heidi placed the iPad down and touched the message to bring it up.

'No!' cried out Sam, reaching for the iPad.

Heidi snatched it away. 'Don't you *dare*. I have a right to know what's going on.' She stared at the screen and Sam looked over her shoulder as they both read the message at the same time:

Sam,

I hope you enjoyed our session earlier. I must say, you looked extremely pretty – a real head-turner! I'm on holiday now until 22nd. Please feel free to contact me after that and we can have another session with Norman. I know he'll be keen!

Natasha

x

The spark reached the dynamite: Heidi stood, face knotted by hate and revulsion, 'You fucking bastard!' and threw the iPad at Sam, who backed away and ducked, causing it to smash into the top of his head; he staggered backwards but heard Heidi shouting, 'That's it, it's over between us. Get out you fucking pervert!'

Sam stood up, holding his head where the blow had struck. When his senses cleared he saw Heidi staring at him just as she'd done the last time, with a look of uncomprehending disgust. He desperately wanted to apologise for again destroying the woman he loved, but deep down he knew it was hopeless saying anything at all. 'I'm sorry,' he said, the words sounding so utterly pitiful and inadequate.

'This will destroy Oliver, you know that, don't you?' said Heidi. 'Now he's not going to have a daddy to grow up with, and it'll be *you* who has to explain to him why. Get out.'

Sam hesitated.

'GET OUT!'

～

A FEW MINUTES LATER SAM WAS OUTSIDE, WALKING AWAY from the flat for what he presumed was the last time,

holding a hurriedly packed overnight bag. He had no idea
where he was going. Head down, collar up, he wandered the
streets aimlessly, traipsing on, splatting through puddles, but
eventually found himself heading to the train station. He
hadn't consciously decided to go there, it was more a case of
him eventually running out of options of places to go, or
else of being pulled there by an answer that somehow lay in
wait for him.

Once there, he sat down on a hard steel bench on the
platform, the cold of the metal seeping up through his
trousers. He stared down between his legs at the cold, grey,
coarse concrete, spending a long time thinking about his
childhood and about what his mother would make of her
son so desolate and alone, having now lost the two people he
loved most in the world. In his unbearable sadness he felt
himself drawn to the tracks in front of him.

He stood up.

He took a series of small steps to the edge of the
platform.

He waited. His mind blanked such that his only
conscious thought was how bitterly cold the wind was
against his cheeks, which seemed a fitting last will and
testament.

He looked down the track and shortly the nose of an
Intercity appeared in the far distance on the horizon. It
seemed to close the distance to him slowly at first, just a
slight increase in size as it wormed closer, but then the
tracks below him started to hum and vibrate causing him
to glance down at their shiny scraped smoothness and
when he looked back down the line the train cut the final
gap to him with terrifying velocity, like an arrow in the
eye, and he lifted his foot, but froze – an image of his
son's face appearing in his mind's eye – and with a

thunderous explosion of noise the train detonated through the station.

TWO WEEKS LATER, SAM WAS AGAIN SITTING IN A WAITING room, anxiously anticipating the forthcoming session. He leant forward on his hard, plastic seat, resting his elbows on his thighs and gazing expressionless across the empty room with its scuffed wood parquet flooring, the only sight before him a low, square table with some ancient, falling apart copies of *Reader's Digest* flung on it.

He dropped his head down into his hands. He'd been dreading coming here, dreading having to confess his crimes, not only the emails and visits to Natasha, but also presumably his thought crimes. Would he really have to describe them in all their gory detail? Christ, every man alive would be strung up as guilty if his innermost thoughts and desires were laid bare for all to see, surely?

He tried to think of something, anything, else, but all he could think of was his vastly changed domestic circumstances. He was now living back in his old bedroom at his dad's house and had only seen Oliver once, for one hour, since leaving the flat. Communications with Heidi were purely practical and functional.

In the days following his ejection by Heidi, he'd wondered what to do. Visiting a sex therapist had brought to mind a procession of freaks alongside him in the waiting room: the swivel-eyed letch constantly on the lookout for the slightest opening, the drooling pervert with the sinister smile, the dirty old man in a soiled raincoat sweating and twitching in the corner. And him. But he'd had to do something, so had researched online for counsellors specialising in addictions and picked one whose site mentioned bringing compulsive behaviours under control. They'd had a brief initial chat on the phone to organize today's first session.

The door to the waiting room opened and in stepped a short, bearded and balding man in his fifties wearing brown cords and a moss green jumper, who confirmed he was Robert. He took Sam through to his consulting room, where everything had been designed to induce a sense of calm: the blinds tilted half shut to soften the light; Sam seated on his own on a long, low settee which compelled him to recline; the bookshelf behind Robert meticulously neat and ordered with rows of books whose spines bolstered his authority and credentials with words like 'Therapies' and 'Behaviours' and 'Psychology'.

'So,' said Robert, once they were settled, peering at him over his tortoiseshell reading glasses. 'Shall we get started? Perhaps you can begin by talking me through the events which have brought you here today. Needless to say, everything is totally confidential. I'll only ever mention any aspect of what we discuss to another person if I think you are a risk to yourself. Once you've brought me up to date, we can talk through how I may be able to help.'

Sam nodded. Rigid and taut, he consciously breathed deeply to release some of his inner tension as he considered how to begin. Into the silence dropped the sound of a bus's brakes hissing in the distance. It seemed to Sam that this wasn't so bad after all, just facing one other person, and a person who could potentially help. Besides, he had nothing left to lose. He started, describing how his use of online porn some years earlier had progressed to chat-lines, before finally to Natasha. He went through his recent relapse and the shattering discovery by his wife for the second time. Robert paid close attention, nodding occasionally and making notes in a moleskin notebook, but said little other than clarifying a few facts.

Once Sam finished a short silence settled while Robert completed his notes. 'Right, well, the first thing I want you to know is that your experience is by no means unusual,' said Robert.

'It isn't?' said Sam, pushing his hands down onto the settee to adjust his seating position; he felt like some giant, industrial-sized lever had just been unlocked and lowered, allowing a great weight to be discharged.

'No, it isn't. There're lots of people in your situation, men *and* women.'

Sam shook his head; for so long he'd thought of his secret world as unique, but it made perfect sense that it wasn't, it had just needed an outsider to confirm it.

'But my help alone won't fix it,' said Robert. 'You've got a lot of hard work to do to address this.'

Sam nodded. 'I'll do whatever's needed.'

Robert smiled. 'Good. Now, I've been through the questionnaires I asked you to complete. The first didn't show anything which concerns me. It shows you're perhaps a little bit dismissive of support, but there's nothing which suggests you can't build strong, secure relationships.'

Sam nodded. The last thing he'd wanted was to be labelled with an underlying condition beyond the reach of therapy.

'The other questionnaire did show something interesting, however,' said Robert, looking up.

Some saliva collected in the back of Sam's throat.

'You've got a very high score for emotional deprivation in childhood,' said Robert, 'which of course is a period in our lives when we're almost entirely dependent on others.

Can you think of anything in your childhood which might explain that?'

His mother's death in a car accident when he was six had been an issue buried so deep that it had never been properly exhumed and examined. Sure, he'd discussed it with his dad and with Heidi a number of times, but generally fleetingly and without any real depth of analysis, for it was simply too heavy a subject to dwell on for any length of time. Here though, sitting in the calming, slightly anaesthetised setting of the consulting room, talking to an understanding stranger, he felt able to articulate some of his real feelings more clearly. He told Robert about his surprise the day his dad picked him up from school and how he'd realised something was terribly wrong even before being taken home in silence to have the news broken. The words 'passed away' had seemed so gentle and unthreatening at the time. Afterwards the confusion and shock, followed by unbearable sadness, and finally the anger. That was it, the anger. The unjustness of being the only person he knew without a mother. The constant feelings of isolation and disorientation. The anger at being so scared and alone, and the wretched grief of not having his mother to hold him and console him whenever he was upset or afraid. By the time he'd finished, he'd been talking for some time.

'Well done, Sam,' said Robert. 'We'll need to examine all this in more detail in future sessions. For now, I want you to know that the behaviours you've been exhibiting, the acting out, isn't because you've got a high sex drive or for pleasure, it's likely because you've got unresolved trauma which you're subconsciously trying to disperse through your actions. Worse than that, each time you act out, the brain gets a rush of dopamine, which like any drug needs ever greater amounts to replicate the high you crave. That's why you progressed from online porn to eventually visiting this lady.'

'So you really think my mother's death could explain what's happened?'

'Sam, if I had ten therapists in here, all ten would unquestionably link what happened to your mother to your recent issues.'

During the remaining part of the session Robert explained how he would try to wean Sam off his dopamine dependency through a ninety-day period of abstinence, followed by a longer period in therapy examining the underlying trauma caused by his mother's death.

When the session ended, Sam left the building and sat outside on a low brick wall bordering a car park. He breathed in and out deeply a number of times. One or two isolated figures walked promptly to their cars and drove off to get home after a hard day's work, although Sam didn't notice them. His eyes were trained on the horizon. The sun had slipped low as dusk fell and appeared as a red ball, like the eye of Jupiter, suspended in layers of stratus clouds in a radiant atomic sky of purples and pinks and oranges bleeding into one another. He was deeply flawed, yes. He'd betrayed those closest to him in the most terrible way imaginable, yes. But if all else in his life failed, he would always retain control of one positive thing: to be a good father to Oliver.

Two months later, Sam was unpacking clothes from a suitcase laid on the bed of his new one-bedroom flat. Leaning over it, he spotted some grains of sand nestling along the seam at the bottom of the case; the last time he'd used the case was last year's holiday to Turkey with Heidi and Oliver. He quickly continued unpacking, desperate not to break down and cry again. As he took out his boxer shorts and placed them in the top drawer of the chest of drawers, he smiled ruefully to himself at how he could dress in as many women's clothes as he liked now, only it was the very last thing he wanted.

His thoughts cut again to Heidi and a wave of emptiness crashed through him, a sensation of being entirely stripped of light or life, which in turn made him feel faint and he sat down on the bed. He'd met with her recently for the first time since *that day* to discuss practicalities, the chosen venue a neutral one, a Starbucks coffee shop a short walk from his office. He'd still been clinging to the possibility that perhaps she'd take him back, once she understood, and so after they'd discussed their joint care of Oliver and their finances, he'd described to her the therapy he was going through and the theory behind what had led to his damaging behaviours. He'd known straightaway from the pained and strained expressions pulling on her face as he spoke that there was little chance of a reconciliation. After hearing him out, she'd said, 'I'm sorry for what you've been through, Sam, really I am, but I can *never* take you back. I'd be constantly living in fear of what you might be up to, just like I've been these last two years since the first incident. I'm sorry, Sam, but I want a divorce.'

He'd tried to persuade her otherwise, but her resolve had been absolute. It wasn't her words he recalled now as he sat on the bed with his head bowed, but rather her cold and distant demeanor, and the way she spoke to him with such certainty and formality and without a trace of warmth or feeling. He'd known then it was over.

Tears coated his eyes and he wiped them away with his

fingers. He glanced around; his new flat was so bare and empty, devoid of all the toys and books and clothes and clutter that had been the backdrop to his old home. The sterile environment seemed to mirror the sense of melancholy underpinning his new life, but worse than that were the frequent lightning strikes of grief which smashed into him whenever he remembered that henceforth he wouldn't be able to see Oliver every day, or read him his bedtime story at night, or see him at breakfast, or share the pivotal moments of his young life. Sam wept uncontrollably, his whole body shaking with utter wretchedness.

After some time, he stood up and continued his unpacking.

REVENGE PORN

'Would you like a cup of tea?' asks her mother.

'Yes, thanks,' replies Audrey, while thinking, isn't it strange, how we often fall back on the most mundane of habits, such as drinking tea, at times of most stress.

She takes a seat at the long, elm kitchen table, its pale, uneven surface scarred with the ruts, scratches and pen marks from her and her sister's early years. Although the children's magnets are no longer on the fridge door and the floor-to-ceiling world map no longer on the wall, it's still the kitchen she grew up in, drenched in childhood memories: the Sunday roasts and Christmas dinners shared at this very table, struggling through homework tantrums with her parents' patient encouragement, lying on the flagstone floor cuddling the family dog, Hector. The room retains the perpetual comforting warmth of the imposing AGA range in the corner.

Her dad enters and greets her, bending down to kiss her cheek, his day's growth of beard like sandpaper against her skin; she's never known him not shave in the morning. He inquires about her journey before helping her mother with the tea.

The atmosphere in the kitchen is dense and heavy, amplified by an extended wordlessness, the only noise that of the kettle rumbling to a crescendo in the background. Playing on Audrey's mind is her father's description of Virginia's deterioration over the phone a few days ago: refusing to leave her room by day, the collapse of her personal hygiene, caught in the middle of the night standing in her nightgown in front of the open fridge scooping peanut butter from the jar with two fingers and smearing it onto her tongue to eat it.

Her parents sit down at the table with the cups of tea, both momentarily silent and staring vacantly downwards, each marshalling their own thoughts. The skin on her mother's face appears thinner than before and stretched across her cheeks like a thread has been drawn tight at the back of her head; it's as though she's ageing in real time.

'We're sorry to ask you to come home, we're just so worried about Ginny,' says her father. 'We thought perhaps you might be able to get through to her... given how close you've always been.' Her father strokes the table nervously with the tips of his fingers, a scattering of dark liver spots covering the leathery skin on the back of his hand.

'Is she in her room?' asks Audrey.

'She's always in her room,' says her mother. 'She hasn't left it for days now, except sometimes at night. It's as though we've... we've lost her.' Her voice falters and she begins to sob. Her father leans over and puts his arm around her, she in turn resting her head on his shoulder.

Audrey looks back and forth between her parents' haunted faces; they're not so much diminished, as destroyed, and it dawns on her for the first time just how serious Ginny's condition might be. At nine years her senior, she's always looked up to her sister, considering her impossibly worldly and knowledgeable, and indestructible; now all those ideals are falling away.

Seeing her parents comforting each other, it occurs to her that although she'd always considered them a bit staid when she was growing up – her father a mechanical engineer at a car components' factory, her mother a teaching assistant at the local primary – they are in fact simply kind and humble people who'd never wanted for much, other than the safety and happiness of their daughters. Now that one aspiration was being stripped away.

'We can't get through to her,' says her mother. 'She doesn't leave her room, doesn't see or speak to anyone. She doesn't *do* anything.'

'I tried texting and calling her, but she never responds,' says Audrey.

'Her phone's been sitting over there for days,' says her dad, pointing to the counter. 'As far as I can tell, she has no contact with the outside world at all.'

'So, what happened exactly?' asks Audrey.

Her father and mother exchange a glance, causing her mother's head to fall forward as she begins to sob again.

'It's all because of this man she worked for,' says her father, shaking his head. 'The way he's behaved is absolutely disgraceful. I presume you knew he was married?'

Audrey sits back in her chair. 'I *eventually* found out he was married, yes, and then tried to persuade her to finish with him.' She glares back at her father, refusing to take any blame for a situation she always knew would end badly, and more so for her sister than for her boss. 'I said to her repeatedly that she was wasting the best years of her life on that man.'

'And do you know how it ended?' asks her father.

'No. As I said, she's not answering my calls.'

Her father and mother exchange another glance.

'What?' asks Audrey.

'When Ginny came home, she was clearly unwell,' says her father. 'Her mood swings were dreadful and then she retreated to her bedroom and we saw less and less of her. Eventually, after much prompting, she told us what had happened.'

There's a brief silence. 'What? What was it?' asks Audrey.

Her father's face scrunches in anguish, or is it disgust? 'Your sister had a miscarriage.' Her mother emits a loud, animal-like wail.

'Jesus,' says Audrey.

'Only your sister also had bruises on her face when she came home, but refuses to discuss how she got them.' Her father stares out the window, his chin uplifted but the corners of his lips turned down. His chin begins to tremble.

Unable to bear the sight of her distraught parents, she stares down at her cup of tea, the kitchen window opposite reflected as a white rectangle on its shimmering surface. Such unassuming people, and once so contented. They'd never wanted for much. What sort of man does this to other people? What sort of sicko? What sort of psycho? Her hands and shoulders begin to tingle with rage, she feels the need to *do* something rather than just sit here. 'I'm going upstairs to see Ginny,' she says.

As she slowly ascends the stairs, her thoughts turn to another psycho content to casually inflict life-changing and permanent damage on wholly innocent people, her ex, Dan.

Six months have passed since their break-up, but *that moment* still haunts her: he'd left their flat to pop to the corner shop to buy bin liners and a bottle of wine, leaving his laptop unguarded, and there, in plain sight, in bold, sitting proudly at the top of his inbox, an email from *her*, from Laura, their mutual friend from university. She experiences now the same light-headedness and shortness of breath as she did then trying to work out why she was emailing him, yet somehow knowing the answer even as she moved the cursor to the email and clicked; followed by that exquisite agony, like a fine needle sliding into and right through her heart, as she read Laura's words referring to their three-year affair, and her life's journey jolted violently onto a different set of tracks.

As she tops the stairs and reaches her sister's door she recalls how Ginny had coaxed her through her break-up with Dan, giving her comfort and strength when she most needed it. She knocks on Ginny's door.

No response.

She knocks again.

Still no response.

She slowly turns the handle, which squeaks a little, and pushes open the door.

Ginny is sitting stone still at her dressing table in a pale pink nightie looking out the window. A bright shaft of white light falls into the room behind her, tiny particles of dust and fluff floating in suspension in its warming beam, almost as if they've been undisturbed for days, or weeks. The bed is unmade and clothes strewn on the floor.

She steps into the room; it's unnaturally hot, but even worse is the fetid odour, musky and dense, with an alarming slightly sweet edge to it. 'Ginny?'

No response.

She walks slowly forward until she's alongside her sister; still she stares out the window, although there's a hollowness in her eyes suggesting she's not really seeing anything.

'Ginny, are you okay?' She daren't put her arm around her sister as she wants to, for fear it might startle her from her reverie. She feels the tears welling in her eyes as she squats down next to her sister, so she's looking slightly up at her. 'It's me, it's Audrey.'

Slowly, her sister's head revolves from the neck, like it's mechanised, until she's facing Audrey; her hazel eyes twitch a little from side to side, as though she's dragging thoughts back from some faraway place. Her lips open silently as if in slow motion, then close again, like a fish, until eventually a little bead of drool dribbles down her chin. Her dynamic, worldly, vivacious older sister, reduced to... a vegetable.

Audrey clenches her teeth so hard she might break the big molars at the back clean in half and thinks again; what sort of fucking sick psycho does this to people?

GRAHAM POKES HIS HEAD OUT HIS OFFICE DOOR. 'AUDREY, you couldn't get me my usual could you?' As has become the norm, his eyes curtsy quickly down and up, taking in the contours of her legs.

He can't help himself, she thinks, especially not today, their *special* day as Graham refers to it, and certainly not when she's dressed like this. Forget the usual three-inch heels of the typical female corporate striver; hers today are five inches tall and patent black, the heel coming to a point like the tip of a sabre. They're so indecent she thinks of them as something a drag queen might wear, but since they make Graham drool like an out of breath puppy, she considers them money well spent. And then there's her black stockings with a seam running up the back, shown off by the short skirt she's wearing. 'I'll just get it for you,' she says, flashing her eyes at him, before standing and pulling on her coat to fetch his *usual*, a two-shot skinny latte.

The freezing dry winter air slaps her cheeks as she steps outside but she's already invigorated, her senses pin sharp. Her limbs are all loose and supple and strong. She has no appetite. Her throat is raspy dry. The last three months have all been leading up to tonight. Their *special* night. No matter how many times she's run through the plan in her mind, she's petrified something might go wrong at this final stage.

She joins the queue at Starbucks. Routinely fetching someone's coffee is demeaning, but she's come to realise that the key to being a successful PA to a CEO is essentially wiping his arse all day long. Sure she had to do the usual typing and printing and organising and cajoling, but even more important was thinking ahead to make sure his personal life stayed on track: the wife and children's birthdays remembered and gifts bought and wrapped, the dry cleaners instructed to pick up and deliver his suits and shirts, the taxi ordered to take his family to the airport at the start of their holiday. It seems to her that senior executives are far from the peak of sophistication they consider themselves to be, rightly sitting at the top of the tree of meritocracy. Rather she considers them to be in advanced stages of regression to babyhood: every need catered for, every whim indulged, everyone fawning on them and nodding approvingly without question.

Back at work she hands Graham his coffee. 'Thanks,' he says, 'and Audrey…'

'Yes?' she asks, knowing from the yearning expression

distorting his face that he's about to blurt out something amorous.

'I… I can't stop thinking about tonight, our *special* night.' The way his eyes travel as he says this is such that it might as well be his hands resting now on her legs, her waist, her chest.

She pauses, holding a smile, until he makes eye contact again. She lets the silence lengthen. Silences always make him squirm. 'You remember the golden rule for tonight?'

'Yes, of course.'

'What is it?' She knows he knows but likes to make him say it out loud.

'I have to do whatever you say.'

'Good boy,' she says and has left his office almost before the words have left her lips. On returning to her desk she's panting; Christ, the consummation is so close now she can almost taste it.

As their *special* night approaches, Audrey considers just how much her life has changed these last few months. Moving to London following her break-up with Dan to start afresh. Establishing a new social life, which hadn't been easy but at least helped her try to forget about Dan, although thoughts and feelings about him still regularly leap into her mind, amplified by her revulsion and dismay at the reason for the break-up. Fucking psycho. Finding a flat share in Clapham and eventually, after dozens of applications, being accepted on the graduate programme of a national media group, which starts in the autumn.

The day she opened the email from the agency offering her current temping job also keeps coming to mind.

Reading the name of the business, her whole body had spasmed like sometimes happens when you've just fallen asleep and you shudder so hard it startles you awake. She'd flung her laptop onto her bed and paced her bedroom, energy pumping her limbs, shaking her head repeatedly. What were the chances? She'd spent that night considering it, barely sleeping, thinking about what the doctor had recently said about Ginny's recovery, how 'it might be a case of years, not months, if ever.' By morning she knew she had to take it.

Once she'd started at the company, it hadn't taken long to get Graham's attention. She really did take pride in the way she'd executed her carefully formulated plan. First few weeks: chatting to Graham by the water dispenser, smiling liberally at him, always showing a keen interest in whatever he had to say. Thereafter she began ratcheting up the pressure: pretending her break-up with Dan happened just last week, jokingly asking Graham if he knew which dating sites she should join, wearing high heels and makeup whenever he was around. Shortly afterwards she was promoted to being his PA. Then the attack phase: laughing at his jokes, shorter skirts, a little innuendo, but always maintaining her professionalism. She'd wanted him to think perhaps she was in reach, or wasn't she? A woman twenty-five years his junior wouldn't be interested in him, would she? He was very rich and powerful though, so perhaps? She knew the ambiguity would be fertile ground for his lust to be nourished and thus grow.

She'd also been determined to make sure his amorous feelings for her were unique, feelings he'd never before and would never again have for another woman. After all, the more powerful his cravings, the more he'd risk all to taste their fruit. So she'd wondered what fantasies seeped into his secret mind in the very quietest moments of his life? What proclivities could he never admit to his wife and had thus far remained just thoughts fermenting inside his head, seemingly destined never to be shown the light of day? There must be plenty now, having solidified these last few months.

Occasionally dressing provocatively hadn't been enough, though. She'd had to be direct, had to tempt him outright, but thought it prudent for her first attempt to be when Graham had been drinking, just in case she didn't get the reaction she wanted and needed to blame the booze. Her opportunity came at a client seminar at their offices, followed by drinks to encourage all that ghastly networking business people do. She'd kept Graham's glass of red wine topped up throughout the evening and made sure she was always holding a glass of her own, though she barely sipped it. She'd worn suitably revealing attire and made sure she'd flirted with both Graham and whichever boring businessman he'd been speaking to.

They'd returned to Graham's office at the end of the evening to get their belongings and, much to her encouragement, Graham brought a half empty bottle of wine with him and two glasses. 'One for the road?' he'd asked, his eyes wet with alcohol. She nodded. He poured as they both sat perched on the edge of his desk, his half-lit office and the stilled, expectant atmosphere contrasting starkly with the bustling place of industry it was by day.

He spoke about the event and some of the clients in attendance, Audrey trying to work out what women saw in him as she listened. He was certainly very confident in the work environment, which gave the impression there was nothing he couldn't master if he put his mind to it, although she guessed people wouldn't have been quite so easily impressed had they known just how much he leaned on his PA to keep his personal life on track. He was also conventionally attractive: tall, which added to his natural authority, reasonably slim although all his business lunches had caused him to grow a little protruding paunch, full head of salt and pepper hair, but it was an exterior in her view devoid of real character or personality, as though all that had been subsumed into his all-consuming role of CEO. Perhaps that was the point, she thought, perhaps people read into his blank canvas appearance the competence, control and confidence they so longed for in themselves. Or else he cultivated his impeccably professional appearance because it gave him the greatest cover to operate with impunity.

At the next pause in the conversation, she let the silence linger between them and smiled. He took a glug of wine and breathed in deeply. 'By the way, thank you for all your help tonight.' He was slurring his words a little and a light film of sweat shone high on his forehead. 'I hope you don't mind me saying this, but you look fabulous tonight.'

She paused. 'Well, I'd quite like to dress like this more often, only such clothes are very expensive.' She gave him one of her widest smiles.

He took a sip of his wine, his eyes shifting to one side, before cutting back at her. 'I'd love for you to dress like this *every* day at work.'

She allowed her eyes to flash at him. 'Every day? I wouldn't want to over excite you, Graham. Could your heart handle me dressing like this *every* day?'

Graham's delivery suddenly became noticeably slower, deeper and very earnest. 'I would do anything, *anything* to have you dress like this every day.'

She cocked her head to one side. 'Really?'

'Yes, really. I could... I could even help out?'

'And how would you do that?'

'Well, I was thinking, I could...' his words trailed off.

'Say it, Graham. Tell me what you're thinking.'

He glanced towards the door to ensure they were alone, even though everyone else had long gone home. He reduced his words to a whisper. 'If I can get you a decent pay rise, would you promise to spend the money on... well, you know, would you promise to dress... er...'

'Like a slut?'

'Well, I didn't mean—'

'Oh come on, that's exactly what you mean. Go on, admit it.' There was a brief silence. 'I said admit it.'

'Yes, yes, I admit it, I'm desperate for you to dress like a slut for me.'

She giggled at him. 'How much will you pay me?'

He looked down. 'Er... I don't know... a hundred pounds a month?'

She laughed out loud. 'A hundred?'

He looked wounded. 'One hundred and fifty?'

She paused, the protracted silence having the benefit of making him look slightly afraid, for once shorn of his confidence. 'Make it two fifty and I'll wear clothing guaranteed to make you slobber every time you see me.'

Graham's Adam's apple bobbed as he gulped. 'Okay, I'm pretty sure I can get you that.'

'What, three thousand pounds a year?'

'I think so.' He grinned, baring his wine-stained teeth as he leant towards her, a smog of his hot booze breath enveloping her. 'The key to getting people to agree to it is to benchmark your pay against other CEO PAs. I have a few friends who can vouch that their PAs get more than you.

Once I get that evidence and present it to HR, they'll do as they're told.'

She held out her hand and Graham shook it. 'Okay, you've got yourself a deal,' she said, before having to yank her hand free from his grasp when he tried to pull her towards him. 'Don't plan on getting much work done tomorrow,' she said, standing. 'I think you're going to be a little preoccupied.' Rather than wait for his reply she made for the door, turning to look back at him as she walked out. 'Sweet dreams, Graham.'

She heard his pleading voice reaching after her as was leaving, saying, 'Audrey? Audrey? Please wait.' She ignored him.

The next day was the first day she wore the five-inch heels and seamed stockings.

❧

THEY'VE JUST BEEN SEATED AT THE MICHELIN-STARRED restaurant chosen by Graham, the crockery and cutlery arranged immaculately atop the starched white pressed tablecloth, the wine glasses so pristine they catch the light, glinting and sparkling. He's made a lot of effort with his appearance too: his best sapphire blue fitted suit, plum shirt with black onyx cufflinks, fresh aftershave perhaps a little too liberally applied. Is there a glimpse here of what others found so attractive? She can't see it herself.

They make small talk about the wine and menu, but throughout her mind is preoccupied with her family. She'd been home last weekend, but her sister remained in solitary confinement in her bedroom, still barely washing or eating. The doctor had recently upped her medication, which just condemned her to retreat further into herself. Her parents' deterioration also continued, both thinner, greyer and frailer than ever, and increasingly desperate, clinging to anything for hope: a support group in town who organised days out for those with poor mental health, something called Cognitive Behavioural Therapy, purchasing various self-help books and leaving them out for Ginny. The trouble was, they couldn't persuade her to engage with any of it.

A tiny dish of fish is placed in front of each of them and Graham hurriedly says, 'Ah, a palate cleansing amuse-bouche,' before the waiter can speak to prove how knowledgeable he is. The waiter waits his turn, bends from the waist with an arm in front of his midriff like he's addressing royalty and explains that it's the chef's personal, Japanese-inspired amuse bouche of hamachi, salmon roe and basil flower. Imagine being a waiter in a place like this, all that toadying and bowing and mincing about, to make it just right, just so, for the pretentious prats being served. She understands perfectly well that idiots are drawn from all strata of society, it's just that a special type of twat can clearly be found being served in first-class lounges and Michelin-starred restaurants.

Graham is in ebullient form throughout the meal, talking about how the company has flourished under his stewardship. The rich smells of the food and wine seem to saturate his words. Like all successful businessmen, he's most comfortable talking about himself. He mentions his 'legacy' a number of times. After a few glasses of wine that yearning expression returns to his slightly reddened face, which means he's beginning to think about what happens after the meal. He holds up his wine glass by its stem without realising how effeminate he looks, before gushing out, 'I can't tell you just how stunning you look tonight.'

'Thank you.'

'I must say, you've been looking sensational every day since your pay rise.' He winks at her, his lips curling up at their sides.

'I was wondering…' she replies, 'if there were any other items of clothing you had in mind…?'

'Oh god,' he says, closing his eyes. 'There are so many outfits I long to see you in.'

'Describe them.'

Now the words come tumbling. Thigh-high boots, a latex catsuit, a police uniform.

'Those outfits are prohibitively expensive,' she says.

He leans forward. 'I was thinking perhaps we could get you another pay rise to finance them, like we did last time?'

She nods. She asks Graham for his views on the other senior individuals in the business and he doesn't disappoint: Matt, the Client Services Director, is 'solid, but essentially characterless' and 'living in fantasyland if he thinks he's got what it takes to be the next CEO'; Stuart, the Director of Operations, is 'a hard bastard, but lacks the diplomacy required to keep all the stakeholders onside and probably has a drink problem'; Julie, the Head of Digital, 'is a workaholic because she's never found love and has nothing else in her miserable life to focus on other than work.' It must be tiring leading a double life, pretending to respect these people by day, but secretly having nothing but contempt for them, but she now knows that psychopathy and narcissism are the key qualities of those who reach the top. Her thoughts turn to her ex, Dan, another sicko psycho double-crosser, and how every memory of every romantic occasion they spent together is corrupted in hindsight, knowing that all along he was living a double life with that slut Laura. In all the long period leading up to tonight, she has never felt so convinced that she's doing absolutely the right thing.

'Can I ask you a question?' she asks him later during the dessert course.

'Of course, anything,' he says, wiping the corner of his lips with his napkin.

She pauses long enough for him to realise it's important. 'Have you ever done this before? I mean, had an affair? I won't hold it against you if you have, I'd just like to know, that's all.'

Graham becomes pensive, his mouth narrowing to a thin slot. He picks up his teaspoon by its end between thumb and forefinger and slowly revolves it in his coffee. 'I know we haven't properly discussed it before, but I think I should tell you a little about my wife.' He looks up. 'The thing is, my wife has been unwell for years. I mean her mental health has always been very bad, and she has to take a lot of drugs to stay on top of it. I know there's no excuse for me having an affair, but I hope this information at least puts it in context.'

Audrey doesn't know how to respond. She'd sensed from occasional calls from his wife and the odd email she'd seen that things weren't quite right, but this new information is still a surprise. 'But what happens if she finds out about us? Won't it destroy her, or push her over the edge?'

He grimaces and brings a hand to his face, rubbing his forehead. 'Obviously, I'm hoping she *doesn't* find out,' he says, staring intensely at her. 'The thing is, we haven't had any sort of physical relationship for years. I know I shouldn't seek comfort from another woman, but I hope you won't judge me too harshly.'

She stares at him, gauging if he's telling the truth. 'You still haven't answered my question about any other affairs.'

He pauses, a pained expression drawing down on his face. 'There was someone else, yes, just one other person, but I can assure you it's in the past. I realise this must make me seem like a serial adulterer, but I can promise you that's simply not the case.'

'May I ask when this was?'

He reaches across the table and squeezes her hand. 'Let's not ruin tonight by talking about the past. Please? Tonight means so much to me.'

She wishes he'd never mentioned his wife and denied any previous affairs. It would have be easier. Cleaner. But she hasn't invested the last three months of her life to fall short now. 'You're right,' she says, 'let's not ruin tonight. Do you think it's time for us to…?'

Graham nods and turns to catch the waiter's eye; when he does he mimes signing his signature in the air to get him to bring the bill.

They're inside their suite at the five-star hotel. The décor is predominantly dark wood offset by lilac and purple furnishings, soothed by recessed soft lighting. The double bed has a wrought-iron frame and is monstrously large, the perfect smoothness of its sheets and bedspread seeming to emphasise its vast size. 'You remember the rule?' she asks.

'Yes, of course,' he says, his voice wavering upwards. 'I have to do whatever you say.'

She looks him up and down. 'Get undressed,' she says sharply. 'I'll be out in a moment to deal with you.' She takes her holdall with her into the bathroom, which is brightly lit by spotlights, with alternate black and white floor tiles and Victorian-style fittings.

She takes off her dress, standing in heels, stockings and suspenders, and all is momentarily still, silent and expectant. Graham's words at the end of dinner have unnerved her; had she got him wrong? She pictures again her parents, all hollowed out and haunted, and her sister, unwashed, unloved and broken in her bedroom, that little droplet of drool dribbling down her chin. Justice *would* be done.

She unzips the holdall, lifts the leather corset with five buckles up its front out and pulls it on, followed by long black silk gloves which come up past her elbows. She studies herself in the broad, high mirror above the basin; she reminds herself of a gladiator about to enter the arena, all her training now ready to be put to the ultimate test, and failure unthinkable.

She opens the door, steps into the bedroom and Graham gasps. He's sitting naked on the edge of the bed. 'Lie on your back, hands above your head,' she commands. She's holding two pairs of handcuffs.

'But—'

'NO BUTS! You know the rule.' Graham shuffles back up the bed and lies down. She clips one end of each pair of handcuffs around his wrists and the other ends to the wrought-iron headboard.

'I can't believe this is finally happening,' says Graham.

'Oh, it's happening alright,' she replies, carefully checking the handcuffs to ensure they're absolutely secure.

'Oh god, Audrey, I've wanted this for so long. I've been thinking about it every day. I'm… I'm in love with you.'

She stares down at his helpless, naked, soft fleshed body. 'Did you say you *love* me?'

'Oh god, yes. Yes, I do. I love you.'

'You mean like you loved my sister?'

'*What?*'

'Virginia Jones is my sister.'

The ensuing silence is so pure, it's like a soundless, motionless nuclear detonation has taken place, with this hotel room at its epicentre.

'She can't be,' he says, lifting his head off the pillow with bewildered eyes. 'She isn't.'

'Yes, she is.' She reaches for her mobile and takes a photograph of him.

'What are you doing?' His voice is now laced with fear. 'Audrey, what are you doing?' She ignores him. '*Audrey!*' he shouts, pulling hard against the handcuffs, causing the headboard to rattle.

She looks at him. 'Don't shout at me. The days of me taking orders from you are over. You're about to pay for ruining my sister's life.'

'I didn't ruin it, she was completely unreasonable. She tried to destroy my family.'

'*She* tried to destroy *your* family?!' Audrey shakes her head. 'The only person hurting *your* family is *you*, with all the affairs you have.'

'I told you, there's only been one other woman other than you; it was your sister I was talking about. I loved her.'

'You said you loved me a minute ago! Now it's my sister. I bet you also claim to love your wife. How many women can one man love?'

'It's not like that. Please, Audrey, it's not like that.' He begins to weep, loud and pitiful, like a distressed, helpless child.

'Ginny gave you three years of her life. She miscarried because of you, you bastard, after you hit her.'

'I did *not* hit her. Is that what she told you? She fell. That was all, she fell; it was an accident.'

'That's utter bullshit. And what about her breakdown afterwards? You've never even contacted her. You used her and discarded her like a broken… toy.'

'I *have* contacted her. I've sent her lots of emails but she never replies. Why do you think I'm transferring money to her every month? I've been trying to make amends.'

'You can't possibly expect me to believe you.'

'Check my phone. Please, check my phone. It's just there. I can give you my pin and you can check I've been transferring money every month. Check the emails I've sent her.'

Audrey sits down in the chair by the bed, her head slumped forward. Now the moment has arrived it's nothing like how she imagined. It's all so much more… complicated, but then the memory returns of her sister sitting alone in her bedroom, smelling of decay and decomposition, and the anguished sounds of her mother's distraught weeping at each mention of Ginny… she stands and turns her attention back to her phone.

'What are you're doing?' says Graham, his face puffy from the alcohol and purple spidery veins on his cheeks.

'What do you think I'm doing, I'm sending this picture to your wife—'

'NO!' he shouts, eyes ablaze, his forehead coated in sweat. He yanks again at the handcuffs. 'It'll kill her. Please, it'll send over the edge. I told you, she's not well.'

She holds out her mobile towards him with one hand, the forefinger of her other hand pointed and hovering over the send button. 'You should have thought about that before trying to fuck all the women in the office.'

'NO!' he screams, pulling so hard on the handcuffs that

the bed shifts. He begins emitting deep, guttural moans before saying, 'I'll pay you, I'll do anything!'

'That's the trouble with people like you, you think everyone's for sale. Even more reason why your wife needs to know precisely who you are.' She leans even further forward over him and lowers her forefinger to just a centimetre above the send button.

'NOOOO, SHE'LL DIE!' he shouts, his body jerking and juddering uncontrollably like an electric current is being passed through it, the bed jolting under his erratic movements, the air filled with a cacophony of appalling grunting noises she can never unhear. She stares transfixed at the sickening sight of twitching pale flesh, his arm and chest muscles spasming under his skin, his bulbous crimson head coated in sweat and his grotesquely contorted face, as his grunting suddenly turns to high pitched squeals, like a pig in the abattoir being funnelled to its fate. Eventually he collapses, lying still but panting fiercely. He turns his haunted face to her.

'This is for Virginia…' she says, lowering her finger to the send button while staring so hard into his horrified eyes that she hopes the image of her face will be forever etched onto his retina. As her finger touches the screen he sucks in a sharp breath, like someone startled, before emitting a long, drawn out groan and falls silent.

She stands and retreats to the bathroom.

SHE   DRESSES   HURRIEDLY   AND   PACKS   HER   BAG,   HER breathing heavy and her mind buzzing off fragments of thoughts and words and feelings. He's a sicko, a psycho, he deserved what he got. When she returns to the room

Graham is still silent, thankfully. 'I'm going to leave the handcuff keys here on the side,' she says. 'I'll call room service now and tell them to come up in five minutes.'

As she reaches for the phone she glances at Graham; his face is stone still, eyes wide open. He doesn't blink. She leans over and looks down at him; his bloodshot eyes look right through her before one pupil drifts off a little to the side as if its slipped its anchor, while the other continues to stare straight ahead. She leans down; he's barely breathing.

Shit! Shit! Shit! Adrenalin shoots through her body. 'Graham, Graham, are you alright?' She reaches down and shakes his body, but it's just a heavy, lifeless, clammy lump and he doesn't respond.

She picks up the phone and presses 0 for reception. As soon as she hears a voice, she says, 'Please, send for an ambulance. Room, room...' Shit, what room is it?! She sees the room number written on a sticker on the top of the phone. 'Room four one seven. He's had a heart attack, or a stroke, or something... I don't know. He's barely breathing. Please, please, come quickly.'

She racks her mind for the CPR procedure she once learnt in a First Aid class: hands in the middle of his chest, interlock the fingers and push firmly down – what was it?! – five times? Tilt the head back, pinch the nose, breathe into the open mouth? She approaches his motionless body and reaches towards his heart... but what if pushing on it makes it worse? Shit! Shit! Shit! She doesn't know what to do and stands paralysed, weeping, making strange snivelling noises.

The door to the room opens and a lady and a man in hotel uniforms enter. The woman attends to Graham and uses a walkie-talkie to ask someone to call for an ambulance. The man ushers Audrey to a seat and asks her what happened.

She cannot respond, for her sight is fastened to Graham on the bed, his skin so white though his face retains a strange, eerie mauve colouration.

She thinks of her parents. Such unassuming people, and once so contented. They'd never wanted for much, other than the safety and happiness of their daughters. But what had they got instead? One daughter broken and the other? A sicko, a psycho. She experiences again the exquisite agony, like a fine needle sliding into and right through her heart, as her life's journey jolts violently onto a different set of tracks.

MANY HAPPY RETURNS

Jake took a window seat on the train and immediately checked Twitter: Donald Trump had tweeted for various women of colour in Congress to 'go back' to the corrupt countries they came from! Fucking racist! Another tweet told how Boris Johnson was now inevitably going to become Prime Minister; couldn't people see Boris was so clearly the UK's Donald Trump?! He was about to add a comment to the cauldron of online spleen and hatred when he was distracted by a disturbing thought: his mother was a Boris fan.

As the train slowly pulled out of the station, the clickety clack rhythm of its wheels on the tracks had a soporific affect, causing Jake to sit back and stare out the window: a deep orange blush of late setting sun came into view to the west of London. Many of the apartment buildings, shops and offices hugging the railway had lights on inside as dusk fell and in their illuminated windows silhouetted figures could be seen busying themselves with their routines and personal business. There's no better place to live than

London, Jake reassured himself. The energy and purpose, creativity and innovation. A melting pot of peoples, races and cultures so much greater than the sum of its parts. It baffled him why anyone chose to live anywhere else.

It had been over six months since he'd seen his mother, the long delay a result of their falling out the last time they'd met. Many times since he'd played their argument over in his mind, the way you do when you feel you've lost a battle you should have won and only in hindsight can you find the words you wish you'd been able to deploy at the time.

He had little reason to travel home these days in any case, as he was too busy enjoying himself in London. His last few years in the capital since graduating had lived up to all his expectations, indeed they'd exceeded them. He loved his job at the charity, loved the dynamic and principled people he worked with, and of course there was his colleague Marjorie. Although the events of last night weren't entirely clear through the smog of his hangover, the first kiss they'd shared was a fact, and although he'd failed to persuade her to return to his flat, there'd surely be plenty more opportunities… but an image of his mother again intruded on his daydream, leaning forward at him, jabbing her finger at him and dementedly hectoring him with comments about how the country had changed so much for the worse. He wanted to avoid a confrontation with her this weekend. All he had to do was get through two nights: the small family gathering tonight, followed by the larger event tomorrow in the private room of a local pub with wider friends. Then again, he also refused to be pushed around by her any longer, because their last argument was just the culmination of years of her undermining and belittling him: his school grades had never been satisfactory, especially when compared to his sister's sustained academic excellence; he'd only managed to squeeze into a second-rate university, which she kept reminding him had once been a polytechnic; now his career as a charity fundraiser was forever worrying his mother because of its lack of career progression and proper financial reward, and she'd taken to casually referring to him occasionally as a 'charity case'.

Jake shook his head at these injustices and with a faraway look in his eyes recalled their argument in the Chinese restaurant. The catalyst had been immigration – what else? – in particular his mother commenting, 'It's unusual to hear an English voice in London these days.'

'And what's wrong with that?' asked Jake.

His mother sat back. 'Nothing. There's nothing wrong with it. After all, we now have a Pakistani in charge of the Home Office, so nothing surprises me anymore.'

'It's interesting how you comment on his race rather than his qualifications for the job.'

'Oh come on, you have to admit, it's a bit much. It's like putting a fox in charge of the chicken coop.'

Jake shook his head.

'And I assume you've seen the news about all these Muslim gangs grooming young white girls in northern towns? Apparently the police were too afraid to tackle it for fear of being accused racist. If that's not political correctness gone mad, I don't know what is.'

Jake thought quickly, and carefully. 'Jimmy Savile was English… and white,' he said.

'What's that got to do with it?' asked his mother.

'I just don't recall you mentioning Jimmy's ethnicity when his crimes were exposed, that's all.'

It had soon escalated, as always seemed to happen when such matters were discussed, despite his sister and dad trying to diffuse it. His mother had drunk too much as usual, so the argument had been fought more on instinct than intellect. He'd even tried to end it when he'd seen the dread gripping his dad's ashen face. 'I don't want to get into an argument. We're all as qualified to hold an opinion as you are.'

'You? As qualified? Since when have *you* had to suffer? Since when did *you* know what it feels like to be poor?'

'Oh, pleeease,' he'd said, knowing where this was all headed. He couldn't bear hearing again her worn-out monologue about her impoverished childhood in Liverpool with which she'd beaten him over the head for as long as he could remember. 'Spare us your sob stor—'

'SHUT UP!' she said, her nostrils flaring so wide it was a wonder flames and smoke didn't start pouring forth from them. 'The trouble with you is that you've been too *privileged* your whole life.' Some spittle had arced forth from her lips as she spat out the word *privileged* and people from the neighbouring tables turned to glare at them.

As he sat there too afraid to respond, something began swelling inside him, a great injustice inflated by years of being put down by her. How dare she say he was too privileged. How *privileged* is it to be sent to boarding school at the age of seven and cry yourself to sleep every night in a dormitory of eighteen boys because you're so utterly petrified and alone? How wonderfully privileged spending your childhood in a state of constant vigilance trying to avoid being the next victim of the casual cruelty and brutality that pervaded the place. How delightfully privileged to be abandoned by your parents, aged seven. *Seven!* But he hadn't responded. He'd swallowed his words as usual. But every day since when he'd recalled her shouting at him and insulting him, the injustice of it had eaten up his insides like some vile bile corroding the very core of his being, and he'd vowed never to back down again.

He was breathing deeply now and tried to calm himself by looking out the train window. The scenes turning in the large rectangular pane began to change in character as the last of the sun's light drained from the evening sky and everything became engulfed in a peculiar, stilling half-light: first came glimpses of dreary suburban housing – hunched and grubby – which always made Jake melancholy; then a uniformly tired and grey industrial estate abandoned for the weekend; finally dark empty fields and hedgerows stretching into the distance, backed on the horizon by looming sombre grey silhouettes of hills rising up like earthen fortresses. He would be at his parents' station soon.

His sister Joy and her boyfriend Martin would be at home too on account of it being his mother's sixtieth birthday. He'd drifted apart from his sister since their university days. For him, university had been a blessed release from school and once there he'd gravitated to the artistic and bohemian types so different from the arrogant, entitled toffs he'd endured for so many years. His sister by contrast had socialised with the very same types she'd schooled with, a sort of country set favouring dinner parties and skiing trips and whose idea of fun was attending a horse trial or a black-tie ball.

After university he'd travelled to London and joined the charity, while his sister had moved to London three years earlier, but joined an investment bank, where she'd met Martin. God he resented the way his mother fawned and salivated over Joy and Martin's material success, constantly applauding their taste and refinement, which of course was simply based on cost, not discernment. And good god, the way she became so glistening eyed and animated when talking to family and friends about Joy, whereas his own circumstances and career choice were always communicated so much more flatly and with an expression of quiet resignation.

As his train neared the station, he quickly checked his Twitter account again, clicking a link to an article about how Brexit was deterring foreign doctors and nurses coming to the UK, resulting in NHS staffing shortages. The hate-soaked adrenalin began pumping through his veins again and without knowing it all the muscles in his face tensed, pulling his skin taut. Fucking scum! Fucking racists! Another article told how Brexit was designed to secure a trade deal with the US, accompanied by a bonfire of food standards and being swamped by chlorinated chicken! Fucking Frankenstein freak show! He scrolled again, subconsciously craving more and more confirmations of their evil wrongdoings to fuel his sense of injustice. Thank god he'd discovered Twitter last year; how else would all this wickedness be exposed so quickly and comprehensively? He was just about to add his outrage to the visceral disgust expressed in the comments field when unfortunately his train slowed as it entered his parents' station.

In the station carpark a pair of headlights flashed him and he walked over and lowered himself into the passenger seat of his dad's car. 'You mustn't leave it so long next time,' said his dad. 'I've missed you. We've *both* missed you.'

The effortless hum of the car's acceleration pushed Jake gently but firmly back into the leather upholstered, heated passenger seat. The car's headlight beam cut through the night darkness, picking out snapshots of the provincial town of his youth: the run-down local newsagent where he'd once bought sweets, its front window emblazoned with adverts for cheap booze and fags; a cold empty bus shelter with an empty can of lager on its bench, he just knew if he was standing shivering inside it would stink sharply of piss – it was all so depressingly tired and small. Small places for small minds. He was relieved when the car left town.

Halfway home his dad said, 'I need to speak to you about something.'

'What?'

'It's about your mother—'

'If this is about the restaurant argum—'

'No, it's not about then, it's about now. The thing is, your mother's quite delicate at the moment. She gets very out of breath and she's been a bit... emotional. I really don't want anything upsetting her this weekend, if you don't mind. Please we can avoid discussing Brexit, for instance?'

'Upsetting *her?*' asked Jake. 'It's normally her upsetting everyone else, isn't it?'

'Please, Jake, it's complicated.'

There was a brief silence. Here he was again, defending her and trying to smooth things over. He knew his dad must have suffered at her hands even more than him, but he resented the way he just absorbed it all and never fought back. 'Okay, I'll try... but if she attacks me again I intend to defend myself.'

His father stared straight ahead without saying a word.

As he entered his parents' house, he was speared by his mother's shrill laughter shooting out from the living room. That was the thing about her, she was always somehow upon you even before you met her, be it her oversized voice reaching along corridors and up through floors, or her dense lavender perfume fogging up the place, or her forthright demeanour as she approached you with a back as straight as a broom handle.

As he opened the door to the living room he heard her say, 'Well, they have a much more sensible approach to these things in Australia,' before the room cut to silence at his entrance. 'Ah, the return of the prodigal!' his mother declared, throwing an outstretched arm bejeweled with rattling bracelets around his shoulders and pulling him into a pillowy embrace, all the while holding her other arm aside so as not to spill her gin and tonic. 'Let me get you a drink.'

'It's alright, Dad's getting me a beer. Happy birthday.' He shook hands with Martin and hugged his sister, both of whom were also holding gin and tonics. The living room had a festive feel: a large white candle scented by cinnamon and clove sparkled on the mantelpiece above the fire, two helium balloons – one a large figure of a six and the other a large nought – were attached by string to a weight on the floor and floated mid-air, while Radio 2 played a familiar song from the nineteen eighties in the background.

His mother began a lengthy soliloquy about her past week of birthday lunches and drinks, which Jake conceded was testimony to her popularity and wide circle of friends. As she spoke, he observed how his sister, who he hadn't seen in a while, was gradually becoming a smaller replica of their mother. She preferred tweed trousers to jeans these days, and suede loafers to trainers. Martin as usual was sporting the classic uniform of the clueless upper middle class: brown brogues, pressed tan chinos, check shirt tucked in. You almost had to admire a man with so little interest in fashion, thought Jake, smiling to himself as he imagined introducing Martin and Joy to his colleagues at the charity and the jarring clash between their stiff, conformist attire and the sea of tattoos, facial piercings and urban streetwear.

'Now then, shall we tell Jake the exciting news?' said his mother, looking back and forth between Martin and his sister. Jake immediately pictured a lavish wedding reception at an imposing, seventeenth-century manor house with extensive gardens followed by an inordinately expensive honeymoon in the Maldives, all lovingly photographed so his mother could force her friends to envy their gluttonous success. 'Martin and Joy are moving to Australia, to Sydney.'

'*What?!*' said Jake, before checking himself as all eyes turned to him. 'Sorry, I mean… congratulations. When are you going?'

'In six weeks,' said Joy.

'Six *weeks?!*' said Jake.

'We've been thinking about it for a while,' said Joy. 'We thought it would be nice to experience a different culture. Plus Martin's been offered a really good opportunity out there by the bank.'

'The emerging markets are so dynamic,' said Martin, sinking the last of his gin and tonic. 'There's going to be some really interesting opportunities out there in the next few years.' He took Jake's mother's empty glass and his own to the sideboard to refill them.

'Well… I'm pleased for you,' said Jake to his sister. 'Have you been offered a job by the bank out there too?'

'Of course she has,' said his mother, wrapping an arm around Joy's shoulders. 'She's just too modest to mention it. They've not only offered her a job, they've also given her a promotion.'

As Jake listened to Joy describing her new job, he knew he should be pleased for her, it was just that he couldn't help dreading his mother assaulting all their family friends for months on end with further news of Joy's success. There was something else too, a more hidden, subconscious disturbance; Joy's relocation overseas nudged memories of his parents' seven-year posting to the Middle East, sent there by the multinational petrochemical company his dad had worked for. That was when he'd first been sent to boarding school.

'Right, more G and Ts,' announced Martin, returning with a glass for Jake's mother and one for himself.

Jake's mother tipped back a healthy measure, before turning to Jake. 'I was in London the other day. It's changed so much. And I kept being accosted on the street by charity workers begging and pleading for money. I hope your charity doesn't do that?'

Jake's charity did exactly that. It was proven as an effective way to raise money and make people like his mother face up to the world's problems rather than living in their own personal bubbles of ignorance. 'Occasionally we do it,' Jake replied, not wanting to engage. 'If you'll just excuse me, I'm going to put my bags in my room and freshen up for dinner.'

'Oh, Jake?' said his mother as he made for the door. 'Martin and Joy are in your old room. You're in the spare.'

'INDIAN IS MY FAVOURITE, I LOVE THE FLAVOURS,' SAID Jake's mother, reaching forward to pick up the aluminum foil tray of chicken korma, 'but I don't like it too hot.'

The family were eating in the dining room, an austere room which tended to lie fallow for most of the year and was only brought into use at Christmas and the odd birthday or anniversary. Such sporadic use made it a depressing place in Jake's view, augmented by its dark, severe, polished mahogany dining table and the matching ornate, glass-fronted display cabinet with its hideous dated plates and china trinkets on display.

As they tucked into the takeaway, Jake's thoughts turned to Marjorie and the previous evening's encounter. A drunken kiss was still a kiss, and proved that she must have some feelings for him? He allowed himself to imagine his relationship with Marjorie deepening and growing into something more… permanent. He pictured bringing her home to meet his parents and the look on his mother's face as she was forced to accept the reality of his generation's attitude to race. Another bonus was that Marjorie's stories of her poor upbringing in Sierra Leonne would make his mother's stories of her working-class childhood in Liverpool seem like sheer indulgence.

He lost the thread of his daydream when he realised his mother was whispering to Martin; rather than deterring him from listening, the whispering made him more determined to hear what was so secret. 'It's the same with airport security,' his mother said, leaning in on Martin, 'you're hardly going to conduct searches on the passengers arriving from New York when the passengers from Lagos are picking up their suitcases from the next carousel along.' Martin had a slightly pained expression. 'It's just common sense,' continued his mother, 'it makes me so cross when our police and security forces are accused of racism simply for doing their jobs properly.'

'Well, I see your point,' said Martin, 'but one does have to be rather careful about the optics of such things.'

Jake tensed at his mother's words and noted her finishing yet another glass of her favourite South African white wine, which she was very particular about having served ice cold.

'Just remember, we'll support you as much as you need

in Australia,' said his mother to Martin, this time forgetting to whisper. 'We've already helped out Jake with his flat in London, so I feel we owe you and Joy.'

Jake felt himself redden. He'd thought his parents' assistance with the flat deposit was a private matter, and what's more he'd promised to pay them back, so he considered it more of a loan than a gift. Besides, whose fault was it that property prices were so exorbitant? Whose generation had leveraged themselves up on ridiculous amounts of cheap money, only to now be dumping the biggest IOU in history on *his* generation?

'I think we should be alright,' said Martin. 'The bank is sourcing us a flat.'

'I know you and Joy earn a lot more than Jake,' said his mother, tapping Martin on his forearm, 'but still, it's only fair we help you too if you need it.'

Once again the pressure began building inside him, the injustice inflating and expanding and needing an outlet. He took a few deep breaths and turned to his dad, starting a conversation about the football results and refreshing himself with some long draughts of his beer now that last night's hangover had finally abated. Conversation with his dad was a pleasure compared to the tightrope of talking to his mother, but it occurred to Jake as they spoke just how much his dad had aged recently, his face pinched and worried, and his eyes, once bright blue and searching, now dulled and dilatory. Jake knew it hadn't been easy for him all these years, shackled to such an overbearing wife.

As dinner finished, Jake thought he could probably ride out the evening without engaging further with his mother, perhaps even get an early night and text Marjorie once upstairs, but a disturbance in his peripheral vision then caught his attention: his mother, head bowed, with Joy's arm around her shoulders. She was crying. 'I've given my children everything,' she said, dabbing the streaks of tears on her cheeks with a napkin, 'and now one of them is going to the other side of the world. Where did I go wrong?'

'You haven't gone wrong,' said Joy. 'We just want to try a different culture. You'll have Dad here, and Jake.'

His mother looked up briefly and met his eye, before dropping her head back down and weeping even more forcefully. 'I had nothing when I left Liverpool all those years ago and soon I'll have nothing left again.'

Martin leant over and lifted the wine bottle from its cooler, causing it to drip on the table, and poured Jake's mother another glass.

'I don't know where this country has gone so wrong that decent, hardworking people want to leave it,' said his mother to Joy.

A wounded expression drew down across his sister's face. 'We just want to try something different while we're young,' she said, her voice taking on a whiny, almost pleading, tone.

'You're probably leaving because of all those terror attacks. London's not safe anymore.'

'What?' said Jake. 'London's perfectly safe.'

His mother turned to him, her face set hard. 'Being mowed down by a van and then macheted to death is hardly what I call safe.'

Jake rolled his eyes and tutted. 'You'll be blaming it on immigration next.'

His mother pulled a face as though she thought him stupid. 'What would *you* blame it on?' she asked. 'They *were* all immigrants, weren't they?'

'They were all born *here*, they were second and third generation. Perhaps you should question what drove them to do it.'

'Oh, come on, what could possibly justify butchering innocent people? In case you've forgotten, they favour *beheading* people. It's medieval, just like their religion.'

'If you really want to educate yourself, you should put down *The Telegraph* and read some of the articles I've seen on Twitter – news which isn't controlled by millionaire media moguls.'

'I wouldn't believe everything you read on social media,' said Joy. 'Thankfully Martin and I never use it.'

Jake struggled to comprehend how an intelligent person could get by without using social media to keep themselves up-to-date and informed, but then a thought struck him, and an ever so slight upturn occurred at the borders of his mouth. 'Perhaps the Australians should resist *immigrants* like Joy and Martin gatecrashing their country.'

Jake's dad sighed in frustration and said, 'Why don't we—'

A thud cut the room to silence and all eyes turned to its source: Jake's mother had banged her hands down on the table to lift herself into a more upright position. In the candlelight, her lowered brow and the thrust of her jaw made her face appear chiseled from coarse, weathered granite and a dreadful expectancy settled on the table as they all waited for her to speak. 'I just want my country back,' she said slowly, 'and we can't keep letting them all in.'

'Letting who in?' Jake asked, knowing exactly who, but wanting to hear his mother vocalise her prejudice for all to hear.

'The immigrants. The Eastern Europeans and now the Syrians and anyone else who wants to come here.'

'The thing about immigration, and Brexit for that matter,' said Martin, 'is less whether you're for or against it, and more whether you acknowledge there's two reasonable sides to the argument or not.'

'I agree with that,' said Jake's dad.

'You can't reason with prejudice and hatred,' said Jake, shaking his head.

'Please, Jake,' said his dad, 'we discussed this. Just drop it.'

'But we're not *letting them all in*, as Mum says,' replied Jake. 'Many of them are drowning in the Mediterranean before getting here.'

'Then they shouldn't be trying to get here if it's unsafe,' said his mother. 'The irresponsibility of pushing your family onto an overloaded dingy is disgusting.'

Jake shook his head. 'Have you ever questioned why someone would *push their family* onto an overloaded dingy? Can you possibly begin to imagine how desperate you have to be to do that?'

'They're not desperate, most of them are economic migrants,' said his mother.

'And what's wrong with that? Why did *you* leave Liverpool? Why did Dad go to work in the Middle East? Why are Joy and Martin going to Australia? What's the difference between you and them?'

'It's completely different,' said his mother.

'What, because they're a different colour? The only real difference is that you all *chose* to move. *You* were the economic migrants, not them. Many of them are escaping wars, or famine, or disease, what choice do *they* have? Why don't we all just admit this comes down to one thing: you're a racist.'

'Jake!' said his dad. 'What's got into you?'

'Dad's right, Jake,' said Joy. 'You can't say that.'

'Well what would *you* lot call someone who detests people solely on account of their race?'

'I… am… not… a… racist,' said his mother slowly, emphasising each word. Her cheeks had taken on a fierce, radioactive red complexion, like someone about to suffer a stroke.

'So why do you hate them all so much?'

'I don't hate them. I've given to your charity's projects in Africa. I sent money to that project last year, didn't I?'

Jake stared so hard at his mother he hoped his gaze would melt right through her eyeballs and burn away all the ignorance and prejudice infecting her brain like a virulent cancer. 'So we sold millions of their ancestors into slavery and have plundered their natural resources ever since, but you buying them a water pump makes up for it?'

'THERE'S TOO MANY OF THEM!' shouted his mother. 'They don't belong here! You can sit there spouting your stupid liberal views all you like, but you've not got the faintest clue. People are losing their jobs because of immigrants working for next to nothing and living ten to a room like rats in a sewer. People can't see a doctor because they're clogging up the hospitals and surgeries, and you dare to sit there and tell us about the realities of life? You, who've known nothing but *privilege* your whole life?' She turned away from him and knocked back the last of her wine. 'Pass me the bottle,' she ordered and Martin hurriedly poured her a glass.

Jake stared at his mother, the injustice welling inside him, expanding until the fibres in his muscles tingled with rage. In his mind's eye he saw clearly the photograph of the small Syrian boy that had been in all the newspapers, the lifeless and still body of that innocent child lying face down on the beach in Greece having drowned on the journey from North Africa. His death could not be in vain. 'How *dare* you judge people fleeing war and natural disasters,' said Jake, causing everyone to turn to him. 'These are peoples whose backgrounds make *your* childhood sound like a royal upbringing. How can you not admire these people, if what you say is true about your own suffering? But you don't, do you? You hate them because you're a fucking racist Tory snob without a shred of compassion, and it's no wonder Joy is fleeing to the other side of the world to get away from you and a mystery why Dad ever married you in the first place.'

Silence.

His mother's eyes now appeared idly focused at a great distance, the way a boxer's do when he can no longer defend himself and the referee is forced to step in and wave off the bout. Eventually, her head dropped and she began to cry again.

'Jacob, you need to apologise to your mother,' said his father eventually.

Jake turned to him. 'Never,' he said.

'Apologise,' repeated his father.

'Please, Jake,' said Joy. 'You were totally out of line. It's one thing having an opinion; it's quite another abusing someone for daring to disagree with you. Just apologise and we can all move on.'

Another silence ensued as all eyes focused on Jake, imploring him to diffuse the situation. The tension again began building inside him, like a long handle being turned, winding the thread ever tighter. This was how it always started, he'd been reading about it on Twitter. The demonization of minorities. Everyone turning a blind eye. He wouldn't be one of those who failed to stand up to prejudice and hatred. He wouldn't do that to Marjorie. He wouldn't do that to the little Syrian boy lying face down dead on the beach. 'I will *never* apologise,' said Jake, staring straight at his mother.

'Then I must ask you to leave,' said his father.

'Are you kidding me? You're actually going to side with these bigots?'

'I'm sorry, son, but this has nothing to do with taking sides. It's to do with basic human decency and respect.'

'I can't believe you're actually siding with Mum on this. Perhaps I should have expected it; you both abandoned me all those years ago at boarding school and now history is repeating itself.'

'It isn't like that,' said his father. 'Your mother and I did what we thought was best when we sent you to boarding school. This is different. This is about whether you accept someone else's right to have a different opinion to yours. If you can't accept that right, then you need to leave.'

All the facts Jake had digested at work and on social media recently now came rushing back to him, all the weight of evidence so clearly articulating the evil now closing in on liberalism. He pictured the crowd of Trump devotees repeatedly shouting 'Send her back!' about the Democratic congresswoman of colour. He visualised his family dressed uniformly in buttoned-up brown shirts, slotted into symmetrical rows of devotees at the rally, right arms extended skyward in salute, carried away on a controlled tidal wave of all-consuming hate. *He*, however, would *never* surrender. 'Fine,' said Jake. 'I'll leave.' He pushed back his chair and stood, taking one final glance around the table; Joy, Martin and his father all had their heads bowed, only his mother met his eye. He walked out, went upstairs to fetch his belongings and promptly left the house.

Jake sat unwashed and unshaven on the bed in his North London bedsit, staring into his phone and trembling with rage, like the angry water in a kettle at boiling point. Donald Trump had again referred to Covid-19 as the 'Chinese virus'! Fucking racist! Same as the Tories trying to deflect blame for all the pandemic deaths caused by their tragic underfunding of health services for years. Fascists!

Jake was on lockdown at home like the rest of the country, and meant to be drafting letters to the charity's former donors begging for funding, but had become distracted by Facebook. Post after post confirmed the unprecedented government spending required to cope with the policy of social distancing. Funny how it took the greatest world disaster since the Second World War to prove socialism right and expose the electorate as idiots for voting Boris over Corbyn. Funny how they're all clapping for the NHS every Thursday night now!

He clicked on Twitter, desperate not to miss out on the latest news; tweet after tweet confirmed everything he already knew about Trump and the Tories: they were liars, narcissists, men capable of anything to get their way. *Anything!* They had to be stopped!

Jake hurriedly added his livid comments, his thumb jabbing down quick-fire, like a man urgently sending a Morse code message. 'Just like Hitler!'; 'He should be strung up from the nearest tree like all dictators'; 'The shortage of PPE is a Tory *choice* – they're murderers!' The outraged energy pulsated throughout his body. He felt alive! Mobilised! Ready for the fight! Ready to kill!

An email popped up in his inbox from Marjorie to the office, inviting them to a Zoom social later that week. Fuck off! He wouldn't have anything to do with *her* now she was having an affair with the boss. Funny how she'd dumped all her principles as soon as an older, more senior and richer suitor had come knocking. And to think she'd accused *him* of needing to *lighten up.*

Suddenly his mobile started vibrating, his father's name on the screen; he sat upright as his pulse quickened even further. His father kept calling and texting these last few days but he refused to read his texts, let alone answer his calls; why should he? He hadn't spoken to any of his family since his mother's birthday six months ago and wasn't going to start now, not with so much at stake. After all, they probably also called it the 'Chinese virus', just like they'd voted Brexit leaving the NHS understaffed and exposed.

He clicked back on Twitter, desperate to feel the all-consuming revulsion and hatred again. By the time he started adding more comments of outrage, he'd already forgotten that his father had called.

After an hour typing vitriolic abuse into Twitter, he inadvertently clicked on the latest text message from his father:

Jake – I've tried calling but clearly you don't want to answer. I'm sorry to have to tell you this, but your mother has coronavirus and is in intensive care in hospital. Please can you call me? I love you. Dad x

Jake stared at the screen of his phone digesting his father's words. One little Syrian boy dies of drowning in the Mediterranean Sea because his family *pushed him* onto a dinghy; one sixty-year-old woman in the Home Counties dies because she's overweight and drinks too much and has caught coronavirus. What's the difference? He clicked back on Twitter.

A distracting beam of sunlight from outside caught in his eye, so he stood and pulled the blinds shut, causing the

room to fall dark. The sounds of voices conversing on Radio
5 Live from his clock radio by the bed could be heard, so he
reached over to switch it off. In the past if he'd been at a
loose end like this with time on his hands, he'd have listened
to music or caught up with a film he'd been meaning to see,
but such matters did not enter his busy mind.

He picked up his phone again and stared at Twitter.
There was no use in writing to the charity's donors anyway,
they were all freaked out by Covid and saving their money.
He doubted he'd have any work to do tomorrow either, or
even for the next few weeks or months. He had no social
engagements planned and refused to join those dreadful,
forced Zoom socials. He wouldn't be talking to his family
anytime soon either, not after they'd conspired against him
simply for standing up to evil.

He lay back on his bed and settled by breathing in and
out deeply a number of times, feeling his chest cavity
expand and deflate. He lifted his mobile closer to his face, its
bright screen the only thing clearly visible in his bedroom.
He clicked on the first tweet and once again felt the hate-
soaked adrenalin begin to pump through his veins. He
scrolled to the comments and began to think of the vilest
abuse imaginable, something to make the recipient feel the
most acute pain conceivable, something they could never,
ever forget and would haunt them and hurt them and hit
them and fucking *kill* them! *Nothing* could now stand in the
way of him distilling all his earthly energy into the purest,
sharpest and most vicious form of hatred with which to
defeat all those who dared to question the truth.

CAREER OPPORTUNITIES

She woke, her mind shifting instantly into overdrive like it had every night for months now. Her body was coated in a slick sweat, like from a fever, but when she threw the duvet back to cool off she immediately shivered from the cold. She pulled the duvet back up to warm herself, but it just returned the clinging dampness of the cotton to her skin and so she rolled over to the dry side of her bed. She stared out into the jet-black void of her bedroom: precisely nothing was visible, such that she might as well have been staring into the depths of outer space, and momentarily she experienced a feeling of weightlessness and disorientation. She leaned over and pressed her mobile; it showed 03:46am.

She needn't have bothered to check the time, for each night was the same, she'd always wake at 3 or 4am. There was no grogginess or disorientation either when she came to, rather she straightaway began thinking with total clarity, carefully calibrating the chances of success and the reasons behind those chances.

Despite the darkness, her eyes remained open, fluttering all around the room even though there was nothing visible for them to land on. She reminded herself, as she always did at these moments, of the key point: she deserved the promotion. She deserved it because she'd earned it. She'd worked as Financial Controller for nine years now and had started with the company seventeen years ago. And this was her second go at the job. Three years ago she'd applied to be Finance Director, but the private equity backers had wanted someone more experienced. Now the current Finance Director was leaving to take up a new opportunity. Perhaps they should have better tested his commitment when they'd appointed him? She'd made a big play about trust and commitment in her two recent presentations to the board.

As usual, for every positive which came to mind, so there was an equal and balancing negative, the first being that there was serious competition for the job. Jeremy, the CEO, had brought in a policy that all senior vacancies had to be subject to an open and transparent process including outside applicants. It was all part of his drive to sweep away the rampant nepotism of the old owners, the Reynolds family. She supported the policy, even if she resented going up against an outsider who knew nothing about the company. The trouble was, the other shortlisted candidate was already a Finance Director, which meant he could always play the experience card. The other issue was that he was a man. If appointed, she would be the first woman to serve on the board. What did that tell you? He'd probably just refer to his love of golf or cricket, or his passion for single malts, and that would sway it his way. After all, discrimination was everywhere you looked. Why else did so few women reach board level?

The beginnings of pins and needles tingled in her arm as it lost feeling due to her weight on it, and she rolled over onto her other side. She closed her eyes, despite knowing it wouldn't help her get to sleep. She didn't know what she'd do if she didn't get the job; she stiffened at the thought. If they passed her over again she might slap a discrimination claim on the bastards. Who cared? She'd be leaving anyway if she didn't get it. But by god she didn't want to leave, she'd invested so much there. Seventeen years. *Seventeen!* She might never get this chance again.

And she had faith in Jeremy's judgement. Three years ago, when the company had still been in the ownership of the Reynolds, it had been run like a medieval court, patronage bestowed on those who flattered the egos of the owners and who never dared question their authority. Jeremy's appointment as CEO had been a breath of fresh air; he'd completely overhauled the company's strategic direction and updated all its governance and policies to bring the business into the twenty-first century. Jeremy was progressive. He was young (what? mid-forties?), handsome, but more importantly for her chances, he was committed to change. He'd recently made announcements about the company tackling its gender pay gap, and was completely dedicated to diversity and inclusion. *Surely* he could see the advantages of a young, female FD with fresh ideas, as opposed to yet another pale, stale and male in a grey pin-stripe suit. *Surely?*

Jeremy had that, that… *sheen* of all successful people. He radiated confidence and natural authority and gravitas. He had a lustre to him, a glow she knew was within her too, if only she got this job. Plus there was a slight *frisson* between her and Jeremy. Just a slight one. In fact, so slight she suspected he missed it entirely, but she couldn't deny she would enjoy working closely with him. They were alike. Both young and ambitious. Both modernisers and forward thinkers. Of course, he was married. All the best ones were. But that didn't mean they couldn't have a strong working relationship and enjoy each other's company. Once again she allowed her thoughts about him to wander a while: what it would be like to spend more time with him, get to know him better, see how their friendship progressed. Her thoughts drifted off towards fantasy, as they often did with authority figures, their command and control, their poise and purpose... but then she remembered he was married.

Which reminded her of the other reason she was so preoccupied with today's decision... and even before her thoughts coalesced about it a sense of dread moved into her core, accentuated by the silence, stillness and complete absence of light in her bedroom. She pulled her legs up to her chest and adopted a foetal position. She didn't like to think about it, but how could she not? How many women reach thirty-nine years of age and still don't have a husband or kids? But there was still time... wasn't there? The trouble was, even if she met someone tomorrow, there'd presumably have to be a dating phase, then a period of engagement before marriage. Even then, how quickly would she get pregnant at her age? She sighed; she'd been through this all so many times in her head. But there were so few single, successful men...

Almost all her friends had families now, many with two or even three kids. She hated the way they patronised her with phrases like, 'my priorities have changed', and 'my career is no longer as important.' How was she meant to react to that? She couldn't afford to be single and childless *and* stuck in middle management. No. *No!* She had to have something to show for her life.

But did she *really* want kids? She wasn't sure. Besides, it wasn't a possibility without a stable relationship. She'd once had one of those, but Simon was now married with kids, as he constantly reminded everyone on Facebook. Do happy people really post on Facebook? Or just the unhappy ones trying to convince everyone including themselves?

Had she got it wrong with Simon? He'd kept pressurising her about family but she hadn't been ready. Plus he lacked ambition in his career. They had different priorities. Surely that meant they were best apart? She sifted back through various recollections of their time together, but eventually began to wonder whether her memory of him had become more flattering with the passage of time. In any case, what was the point in thinking like this? He'd gone now and that was that.

She rolled onto her back again and opened her eyes; a thin edge of faint orange from the streetlight outside was just visible to the side of the curtain. Her thoughts turned again to the promotion. That at least she had some control of. In a few hours she would be meeting Jeremy for the final decision.

She deserved it.

She'd earned it.

She knew the company better than anyone.

Her presentations to the board had gone precisely according to plan.

She was up against a white, middle-class, middle-aged stale male.

Jeremy was progressive and an ally.

She leaned over and pressed her mobile; it showed 05:06 am. She had almost an hour to get some rest, so closed her eyes and tried to forget about everything.

'PLEASE, SOPHIE, TAKE A SEAT,' SAID JEREMY, EXTENDING A hand towards the chair the other side of his desk. He reached forward and pressed a button on the phone on his desk. 'Penny, it's really very important I'm not interrupted during this meeting, so no calls or visitors please until I come out. Thank you.' He looked up at Sophie. 'Now then, can I get you a drink?'

'Just a water, please,' said Sophie. As Jeremy went to the sideboard she couldn't help but notice again how handsome he was, with that strong jawline and powerful shoulders. His tailored suits helped, too. And the way he spoke slowly and deliberately, with an even gaze, it all oozed authority. He had that *sheen*.

His office was located on the top floor of their building, with only the boardroom next door and Jeremy's secretary sitting along the corridor. As such, the trip upstairs to Jeremy's office always had something of the feel of visiting the Headmaster's office at school, the precious and rare inner sanctum of the whole operation.

As Jeremy returned with her water she looked down on herself and hoped she hadn't overdone it with her appearance. She had on her power uniform: a salmon pink two-piece business suit consisting of a fitted jacket over a tight black shirt, skirt cut to just above the knee and high heels. It was an outfit that always got her noticed. She'd also applied lipstick and eye shadow, but hopefully not too much, and a tiny burst of her favourite perfume.

'Right, shall we get started?' said Jeremy, sitting down. 'I would guess you're a little nervous?'

She gave Jeremy a half smile. 'Yes, a little.'

'Would it be helpful for me to explain a little more about the decision process?'

She nodded. 'Yes, please.'

'As you know, it's come down to two applicants, yourself and Bob. After your final presentations there was a meeting of the board and we consider you both excellent candidates. The board therefore decided to delegate the final decision to me as CEO. In some ways it comes down to who I think I can work best with.'

Her heart leapt. This surely played to her advantage. She'd worked with Jeremy for the last three years, they were alike, they had personal chemistry.

'The board were universally impressed with your presentations. You've got some very good ideas and I have no doubt that the company will be looking to implement many of them over the coming months and years.'

She sipped her water; why wasn't he just confirming it?

'Now, to be clear, nothing is final until I confirm my decision to the board this afternoon. Also, I haven't spoken to Bob yet, my meeting with him is immediately after this one.' He paused, and she felt herself nodding. 'After much consideration, I've decided to appoint Bob as our new Finance Director.'

There was a silence. Her eyes dropped from Jeremy to his desk, her sight fixing on a glass paperweight with some inscription describing Jeremy as "Businessman of the Year". As she stared she experienced a sensation of slowly descending. She'd failed: husbandless, childless, stuck in perpetual middle management. It was as if every last drop of her confidence was draining down through her body and out through her feet, and collecting in a puddle on the floor.

Her head fell forward as tears flooded her eyes. She brought her hand to her face. She just wanted to hide. 'I'm sorry,' she said, but the pitiful quietness of her words seemed to trigger a deeper sadness and she started crying.

Jeremy walked to the front of his desk and handed her a tissue. 'There's no shame in being upset, Sophie,' he said. 'It shows me how much you care about this company.'

She blew her running nose and wiped her wet eyes, but it couldn't hold back the tide, and soon great waves of misery swept through her as her failure seeped deep into every last cell in her body. All those wasted years. All that wasted effort. She'd never now be a success. She had nothing. Nothing. Her shoulders juddered as she wept forcefully, head bowed.

Jeremy's hand rested on her shoulder. Oh god, what would he make of her crying like this? 'I'm sorry, Jeremy. I'm so sorry.'

'It's okay,' he said. 'It's okay.'

When she finally recomposed herself a little, she looked up at him. 'Where did I go wrong? Surely I know this business better than Bob? I *know* I can do a better job than him, I just wish you could have given me the chance.'

Jeremy looked down at her and shook his head. 'I'm sorry, Sophie.' He paused. 'Look, I confess, it's been a very difficult decision and although nothing is final until I confirm it to the board this afternoon, I really couldn't change my mind now.'

There was a silence as Sophie digested his words. Then there *was* a chance? There was still hope? 'Just tell me what you think he can do that I can't. Why is he the preferred choice?'

'My reason for choosing Bob is he's got a lot of experience dealing with private equity backers and I could do with someone taking that burden away from me.'

'But I can do that,' said Sophie. 'You must know I can do that. Please?'

Jeremy again shook his head, but slowly, pensively, as if in deep thought. 'I don't know, Sophie. I really should stick with my original decision.'

There *was* a chance. *'Please?'* said Sophie. 'Just give me a chance. I promise I won't let you down.' Jeremy didn't speak, just his eyes moved, roaming her face in little circles. She reached up and grabbed one of his hands. 'Please, Jeremy. I *need* this. I need it more than you can ever know.' Still he didn't speak. Still his eyes roamed her face. In the ensuing silence she became very conscious of the heat being generated where the sensitive skin on the palms of their hands met.

'Sophie?' he asked eventually.

'Yes?' she said, craning her neck backwards to look up at him, which had a slightly dizzying and disorientating effect on her, as did holding his hand and his standing so close, close enough for her to smell notes of cedar and pepper in his aftershave.

'I admire you *so much*,' said Jeremy, his eyes flaring in intensity, like a dimmer switch had been turned up inside. 'Do you really think you can do this job?'

Tears were still running down her cheeks. 'I know I can. I just need the chance.' A little sob escaped her lips as she recalled all the recent sleepless nights, all the agonising over the meaning of her life.

Jeremy reached down and took both her tear-stained cheeks in his strong, but gentle, hands. What was he doing? He wasn't saying anything; just staring at her with his penetrating gaze. It was a moment she'd thought about… but never really believed would actually happen. 'Sophie, you're the new Finance Director.'

She drew in a sharp breath.

He leant down and kissed her on the lips; her face tilted upwards compliantly, open-mouthed, she accepted the thrust of his tongue, all the while a maelstrom of competing thoughts and emotions swirling inside her head causing confusion, but also rising arousal. It had been so long since she'd been kissed. So long since someone cared.

After some time – she didn't know how long – one of his hands reached down and cupped her breast over her shirt, its nipple immediately hardening in response. With his other hand he reached down; she heard the buzz of a zip. Her brain couldn't process it, too much was happening, her excitement, her body's reactions, the realisation that she'd achieved her dream, that she *was* a success.

'Please, Sophie,' whispered Jeremy and she felt her hand guided to his monstrously erect manhood. She involuntarily gripped it and Jeremy moaned long and loud. His kissing became more passionate, pouring his tongue into her mouth, and shortly she sensed his hips thrusting. Some part of her knew she should resist, and she pulled clear of his kiss.

'*Please*, Sophie,' hissed Jeremy; in automatic response to his desperate voice she kept stroking, while he also reached back to make sure her hand stayed on him. 'Look into my eyes,' he said.

She couldn't do otherwise; their faces were inches apart. She kept stroking him on instinct. He bent at the knees, building a quickening rhythm. His hands came either side of her face again, holding her head still. 'Keep looking at me!' he implored, even though she hadn't looked away. He began grunting and his face agonised, the noises and facial expressions combining in agitated synchronicity. A sense of alarm rushed through her as his climax neared but she daren't let go… 'Keep looking!' he cried, his eyes as frenzied as a wild beast, followed by a deep guttural moan.

They both stared down; long strings of semen spurted onto the skirt of her salmon pink suit and across the tops of her stockinged legs.

Jeremy keeled over, panting, before placing himself back inside his trousers and zipping himself up. He reached for the tissues and handed Sophie a clutch of them. 'I'm sorry, I'm so sorry,' he said.

She was too stunned to say anything, her brain jetting out so many thoughts she couldn't settle on any single one of them. She dabbed the tissues onto his semen to soak it up.

'My god, that was amazing. *You're* amazing. I can't believe that just happened.' He leant forward and kissed her softly on the forehead. On occasions over the last couple of years she'd flirted with the idea of her relationship with Jeremy progressing beyond the professional, but they'd mostly been just vague, throwaway, schoolgirl-like daydreams, she'd never entertained thoughts of anything like *this*.

Jeremy returned to his side of the desk and sat down. 'I'm sorry, Sophie, that was *very* unexpected and I can assure you it's *never* happened before.' He looked downwards and shook his head; it was the first time she'd seen him anything less than supremely composed. He gathered himself and looked up. 'But it *is* clear to me that you and I will make a great team leading this company.' He leant forward and stared at her very directly. 'I intend to make your career *soar.* Your promotion will be confirmed shortly, Sophie. Congratulations.' He smiled at her.

She didn't know what to say. This was the moment that she'd thought about for so long, the moment she'd wanted so much, the moment she *became someone*, but instead she found the image of Jeremy's fiercely contorted face and frenzied eyes at the moment of climax lodged into her mental hard drive and she wondered when she could get to the shops to get her suit dry-cleaned.

'I'm sorry, Sophie, but I really have to prepare for my meeting with Bob. He'll be here shortly.' Jeremy stood up.

Automatically, she also stood. 'Don't you think we need to discuss what just happened?'

'Of course, Sophie, of course. But let's just get today out of the way first and get your promotion confirmed, shall we? It goes without saying that this promotion will change your life. We have plenty of time to discuss everything. We *have* to discuss everything.'

'Okay,' she said, nodding. Jeremy walked to the front of his desk and with an arm around her waist gently ushered her towards the door. As she left the room all she could think about was how, how... empty she felt.

She returned to her desk and sat staring at her screen for some time. She couldn't fix her mind onto a single solid thought; each time she tried the substance of each eluded her. And every time she began to experience a sensation of buoyancy and excitement, something tugged her backwards, like a heavy chain was tethering her to the ground. She didn't know how much time passed. Was it an hour, two hours? Eventually an email from Jeremy arrived; she clicked on it but it was a companywide email, not just to her. It read:

Dear Colleagues,

I am very pleased to announce that Sophie Hill has today been confirmed as our new Finance Director. I am sure all of you will join with me in congratulating Sophie on this fantastic and well deserved achievement.

As most of you know, Sophie joined us as a graduate and has spent the last nine years as our Financial Controller. While Sophie was up against some stiff competition for the role, the board felt that her tremendous knowledge of, and commitment to, the company meant she was best placed to take on this important position. Sophie has lots of fantastic ideas for driving the business forward and I am sure she will be announcing some of her initiatives soon.

If anyone has any questions, please let me know.

Kind regards,

Jeremy

≈

SOPHIE SAT FEET UP ON HER SUEDE, DUCK EGG BLUE, CORNER sofa and glanced out of the vertigo inducing floor to ceiling window of her thirty-second-floor apartment at the city below: the galaxy of sparkling lights, the cluster of skyscrapers in the distance reaching upwards like the searching fingers of a hand, the glassy flat river sliding through and reflecting it all. It was a view still able to send a shiver through her even after six months of living here, and reminded her why she'd been right to move into the city centre just as all her contemporaries were retreating to the dreary suburbs.

She was catching up with some work on her laptop, but as it was a Sunday night, she decided to click on the news. An article caught her eye and as she read it she shook her head in disbelief. It was incredible that such things were still happening in 2017. She'd heard of Harvey Weinstein, but hadn't realised exactly how important and influential he was in Hollywood. But these allegations, my god, *so many* women had come forward, it was a wonder he had any time to make any movies. It was another of these 'hiding in plain sight' situations, like Jimmy Savile, or even Harold Shipman, they always adopt such high profile and powerful positions, ironically to *hide* their crimes. And all the while they pretend to be helping their victims...

The incident in Jeremy's office two years earlier came back to mind when... well, when *that* had happened. She'd erased the memory of it, as though for self-preservation reasons, like mothers forgetting the pain of childbirth. Shortly after her appointment as Finance Director, she'd pushed him for another meeting, to discuss what had happened and to make sense of it. He'd asked her to meet him in his office at 7pm, which he explained was the only time he could do because his diary was full.

Entering his office for that meeting, she still hadn't known where she stood with Jeremy on a personal level. He'd started off with his usual pleasantries and queried how she felt about her promotion. There was something about the way his questions were framed which made her feel unsettled and then nauseous, particularly after he stood and sat on the lip of his desk in front of her and mentioned the two of them forming a 'great team' and being a 'perfect fit'.

'I really think we need to discuss what happened the last time I was in here,' she'd said eventually. She asked him directly about the state of his marriage and what his feelings were about the incident, but as soon as his marriage and feelings were mentioned he'd closed up completely, and when pushed he eventually conceded it had been a 'mistake' and that he'd 'been under a lot of pressure' and 'going through a rough patch' with his wife. He was sorry, and kept repeating that the incident had no bearing on her promotion.

She'd accepted his explanation, even though she was livid with him, but then at the next board meeting which involved an overnight stay in a hotel he'd tried it on again when they'd found themselves alone together at the bar at the end of the night. He'd asked her to come to his room for a final drink and when she'd refused, pointing out he was married, he'd said, 'Oh come on, Sophie, I've championed your career, the least you can do is share a little drink.' She'd promptly walked off to her own room; he didn't want a relationship, all he wanted was… a receptacle.

She stared again at the Weinstein article. How many other women had Jeremy tried it on with? How many other women's careers had he 'championed'?

Did she owe her position as Finance Director to *that* incident? No. She'd earned it through the years of hard work she'd put in. Or had she? God, she hated Jeremy for making her feel like she hadn't fully deserved the promotion. And then there was the way he kept looking at her in meetings, his eyes burrowing into her soul like they'd done *that day.* And the way he ever so slightly talked down to her, so subtly no one else would notice, but which inferred so many, many things.

It hadn't been easy being Finance Director and, at times, she admitted, she'd struggled. Then again, she hadn't expected it to be easy, it was just that the circumstances of her promotion meant she couldn't be sure to begin with that she was entirely up to the job. Thankfully, over time, her confidence and competence had increased and she'd learned to love the role. She loved the power, loved the way she could control so many aspects of the business and make people take action, loved the financial security for life. She now had that *sheen* of all successful people, she sensed it in the way that the juniors in the office and her friends in dead-end jobs reacted to her. Everyone had treated her differently since she became a director. Everyone *deferred* to her. Everyone except Jeremy.

Her personal life hadn't improved, but that was at least partly down to the heavy workload. There'd been a brief affair with a senior businessmen she'd met on the business conference circuit, a man recently divorced. Initially it had been wonderful to enjoy the intimacy of a rich, powerful man who understood the demands of her job, but it wasn't long before he'd started wanting her to play a role with his kids, as though all he really wanted was a like-for-like replacement for his ex-wife, and she'd called it off.

She thought again about Weinstein and his casting couch. And about Jeremy's eyes always somehow on her in every meeting, mentally undressing her, working out ways to open up opportunities to violate her again. The way he stared at her was unsettling, like he was trying to relive the very moment she'd tried to banish from her mind. Now it came flooding back: 'Keep looking at me!' She shuddered as she recalled the words but then it hit her: an idea to make it stop. By god, it could just work. And she would be entirely justified.

THE NEXT TIME SHE MET JEREMY, SHE MADE SURE IT WAS IN *her* office, not his.

'So, what was it you wanted to show me?' asked Jeremy, standing at her door with his shoulder leant casually against its frame.

'Take a seat,' she said, motioning to the chair on the opposite side of her desk. Jeremy's slightly uncomfortable expression at being ushered in like a guest was a bonus; she wanted him to feel that he wasn't in control for once. Her throat was dry and nerves prickled her skin; she'd been building herself up for this meeting for days now.

As Jeremy sat down, she walked over and closed the door before returning to her desk. 'Actually, before we look at the spreadsheets, I'd like to raise another important matter with you.'

'Oh, yes? What's that then?'

She paused; she wanted this to be a moment he would never forget. In preparation for this meeting she'd been on a recent night out with the girls from the office; normally she avoided such nights like the plague, all that talking drivel and drinking Prosecco, but she knew the girls often discussed the men in the office after a few glasses. The information she'd managed to extract was utterly damning of Jeremy. He'd clearly slept with at least two colleagues, but there were also tales of him trying it on with others. Sophie had felt herself redden during one particularly uncomfortable conversation concerning speculation as to whether Kirsty in Human Resources owed her recent promotion to her close friendship with Jeremy. Interestingly, one pretty young colleague confirmed she now avoided being alone with Jeremy, to avoid any misunderstandings.

'So, Jeremy,' she said. 'I've been thinking a lot about what happened two years ago in your office.'

Jeremy's face set hard. 'What about it?' he asked.

'It's just that you said at the time it was a one-off. You said it had never happened before and was because you had difficulties in your marriage.'

Jeremy reached down to the sides of his seat with both hands and shifted his position a little.

'I thought now might be an opportune time to discuss the company's succession planning,' she said.

Jeremy sat motionless and expressionless, digesting her words. 'What are you talking about?'

'Well, it's just that you've been CEO for… what is it, five years now? I think it's time for some fresh ideas and new thinking, don't you think?'

'I don't know what you're talking about, Sophie. I think you'd better spit out precisely what you mean.' His voice had taken on an edge of hostility.

Again she paused, looking deep into his eyes the same way he'd made her *that day*, adrenalin coursing through her body. This was it. 'If you don't resign within the next two weeks and appoint me as your successor as CEO, I'm going to expose you as another Harvey Weinstein. I'll blow the whistle on what you made me do in your office that day, as well as all your other grubby little adventures with all the other women in the office.'

Jeremy's lips parted but no words were immediately forthcoming; his gravitas and sheen were falling away completely. 'I didn't *make* you do anything in my office; what happened that day was entirely consensual. You never complained once about it.'

'You abused your position in the most disgraceful way imaginable.'

'And *you* as I recall were only too happy to oblige and take your current position.'

Her teeth ground, causing a scraping noise to sound in her head. Not only was he a sick pervert, he was a fiendishly clever sick pervert who knew exactly how to make his victims complicit in his crimes. 'You must realise the game is up,' she said. 'All these stories in the press about men abusing their power shows the world has moved on. No one will believe anything you say. As soon as I expose you there'll be a great rush of other women coming forward to corroborate what I'm saying. You know it, and I know it.'

'I'll bring you down with me.'

'How? *I'm* the victim here.'

'Because you never said anything two years ago. You took the promotion. You stood by when you allege I've done more things wrong, even though everything has always been consensual.' As she thought this through, Jeremy's back straightened, he began to gather himself and some of his old confidence and assurance returned. 'Not only that, but I have plenty of information about your competence as FD. Or should I say incompetence. I have more than enough to make sure you're discredited.'

'How dare you talk to me like that. You're a bully. A bully and a pervert.'

'Everything was consensual. Not a single serious complaint has been raised against me.'

'That's because you're the CEO! It's the same as Weinstein, people thought you'd ruin their careers. You bullied them into silence!'

He paused and she thought she detected the beginnings of a smirk at the very boundaries of his mouth. 'It's their word against mine,' he said.

She thought this through, before deciding on a different tack, adopting a casual and slightly sarcastic tone. 'Does your wife know about all your extra-curricular activities?'

He sprung from his seat and leant forward over her desk, anger lighting up his eyes. 'How *dare* you threaten me. Who the hell do you think you are? Just because you've never found anyone to love you, you now want to ruin everyone else's happiness, you spiteful little bitch.'

She leaned back, her heart pounding hard and fast. 'Sit

down, Jeremy,' she said firmly and deliberately, while gripping the arms of her chair.

He slowly did so, his head trembling almost imperceptibly, his eyes dementedly ajar and unblinking. A short silence followed.

'You have a simple choice,' she said, consciously slowing her words to help calm herself. 'You either resign and appoint me as your successor as CEO, or else I'll expose you both here at work and to your wife.'

The muscles in Jeremy's jaws flexed visibly. She heard him breathe out through his nose repeatedly, like an agitated bull contemplating whether to charge. He appeared so stiff and tense she feared what he might do next. 'No, the choice is *yours*, not mine,' he said, jabbing his finger at her as he spoke. 'Either you let me leave this company in a dignified manner, or else I'll bring you down with me.' He stood up. 'I want your decision tomorrow.' With that, he walked out.

She woke, her mind shifting instantly into overdrive, an image of Jeremy clear in her head, leaning over her desk threateningly, his face snarling in anger.

The duvet was clinging to her clammy body, so she threw it back and immediately shivered from the cold. She rolled over to the dry side of the bed and lifted the duvet back up to her chin. Precisely nothing was visible in the jet-black void of her bedroom, such that she may as well have been staring into the depths of outer space. She leaned over and pressed her mobile; it showed 04:17am.

She shuffled her upper body to try to get comfortable, but as she did so an image of Jeremy's taut face reappeared, rage simmering just under the surface of his skin, almost as if it might start cracking and blistering right in front of her. Her heart beat harder and her breathing shallowed. How *dare* he try to intimidate me like that, she thought, but her anger was tempered by the fear of what it all meant for her. What would she do later this morning at the meeting with Human Resources and Jeremy? What *should* she do?

She needed to be prepared. She mustn't be intimidated by Jeremy. She needed to keep reminding herself that he *had* to be exposed. There could be no doubt about that. He was a repulsive pervert hiding in plain sight as a charismatic business leader. She rehearsed in her head various opening sentences: 'Jeremy has continually abused his position as CEO to bully woman into granting him sexual favours.' 'Jeremy made my promotion conditional on performing a sex act on him.' 'I'm speaking out on behalf of many of the women in the office because Jeremy has sexually harassed us.'

She kept repeating to herself: he *had* to be exposed. Christ, if she had anything to do with it, she'd want his wife to know as well; there she was at home lovingly looking after his children and looking up to him as a caring protector and provider, meanwhile he was using his seniority and power to wheedle into as many female orifices as he could prise open.

And yet, and yet. She rolled onto her back, hands at her sides, slowing her breathing to try to help with the analysis as to how events could play out at the meeting. Exposing him meant her own position being called into question. The last two years had completely transformed her life: the luxury, city-centre apartment; five-star holidays in Mauritius and Fiji; tens of thousands building up in her bank account, her investments, her pension. All of it at risk! *Christ.* As Jeremy had said, she'd have to divulge what happened on the day she became Finance Director and why she hadn't said anything since, despite now making such serious allegations. The passage of time made her complicit. She could lose it all.

But how could *she* be accused of wrongdoing when *she* was the victim?

She rolled onto her front, the sound of her face sliding against the satin pillowcase bringing to mind his hissed commands *that day*, 'Keep looking at me!' My god, what women had to put up with! Being objectified and leered at, and underpaid and discriminated against, and groped and fondled like possessions or pets. All the while forced to endure it, passive and helpless and vulnerable and scared while *they* did everything humanly possible to get their disgusting, revolting kicks from them. That was the trouble; if she didn't expose him, he'd be free to find another senior role and start again in another company. A whole new ignorant flock to work his way through.

Her hand moved down to her stomach as a queasy feeling cramped it. She took a series of deep breaths and pictured sitting behind Jeremy's desk as various subordinates were called into her office so she could dispense knowledge and strategy and wisdom as CEO... the summit was within reach; all she had to do was let Jeremy leave without exposing him. Was it even her job to expose him? Surely any women who'd suffered at his hands should have complained to HR themselves? Perhaps all his encounters with them had been consensual, if a little unsavoury?

What was she thinking?! He'd manipulated all his encounters to make sure they appeared consensual. She needed to remember precisely what he'd done! And the casualness of it! He hadn't even asked! You could forgive someone in the office borrowing your stapler without asking, or perhaps using your favourite coffee mug without asking, but putting their big fucking cock in your hand?! And spunking all over you! Without asking?! My god! Who was to say what he was capable of? He could be a rapist or serial killer for all she knew.

She couldn't bear thinking about it, so leaned over and pressed her mobile; it showed 04:49 am. Just over an hour before her alarm.

SHE OPENED THE DOOR AND ENTERED THE MEETING ROOM; before her a white laminate table for six, with Sally from Human Resources seated at its head and Jeremy on the far side. All three exchanged tense and terse pleasantries as Sophie sat down opposite Jeremy and Sally poured each a glass of water.

'Right, I suggest we begin,' said Sally in a formal tone and with the deadly earnest expression of a pallbearer at a funeral; it wasn't every day she was summoned to a meeting with the CEO and FD without knowing in advance what it related to. 'I received an email yesterday from Sophie saying she needed an urgent and important meeting to be organised with Jeremy to discuss an extremely sensitive matter. I know no further details at this stage, so perhaps Sophie you could begin by explaining what you'd like to raise?'

Sophie sat forward. This was it. Her throat engorged and constricted, such that she worried about her ability to articulate herself clearly. Jeremy sat erect and upright opposite her, arms folded, his face disdainful but resolved. 'Thank you, Sally,' Sophie said hesitantly. 'The matter I wanted to discuss today… relates to Jeremy.'

He now leaned forward with his forearms on the table,

poised, alert and focused. There was a moment of silence, only the faint ticking of the second hand of the white-faced clock on the wall audible. Sally held her biro between thumb and forefinger an inch above the fresh page of her notepad, poised to document the imminent revelation. Sophie tried to conjure a memory of *that day* in Jeremy's office, tried to recall the revolting nature of Jeremy's sex act in order to propel her to make him pay for his crimes.

'Sophie?' prompted Sally, looking quizzically at her. Each time Sophie tried to summon the memories they eluded her. She couldn't recall the feelings, or the actions, or the smell or taste of him, rather she imagined herself seated behind Jeremy's desk, hosting a series of earnest employees, dispensing orders and edicts for the successful running of the company.

'The point I wanted to make is… is that Jeremy here… and I… have decided to tell you that Jeremy is standing down as CEO and he's proposing me to replace him.'

Sally looked back and forth between Sophie and Jeremy, her eyebrows drawing downwards and inwards.

'That's right,' interjected Jeremy. 'I've decided the time is right for me to pursue new opportunities after five very successful years. We wanted to meet with you today to discuss how we can make the transition as orderly as possible.'

Sophie could not make eye contact with Jeremy. She stared at the empty centre of the table as Jeremy listed the points which would needed actioning over the following days: communications to stakeholders, settling of his final remuneration and share options, the exact timing of his departure. As he spoke she briefly experienced the same disorientation as she'd done *that day*, that unique blend of confusion, excitement and disgust. If the last two years as a director had taught her anything however, it was how to compartmentalise such thoughts and feelings. She was about to become CEO because she'd earned it. Anything Jeremy had done was his affair. She would work tirelessly to make the company a success under her stewardship.

After some time they all agreed to meet again next week, by which point Jeremy would have spoken to the board and proposed Sophie to replace him.

'Right, well then, thank you for your time,' said Sally.

As they all stood, Jeremy smirked at Sophie, causing her to flinch. The sick pervert! She was about to say something when her inner voice said, *keep calm, the ultimate prize is almost yours.* Compartmentalise, she told herself, it's what leaders do. You're about to become CEO, about to have everything that was once his.

She smiled back at Jeremy and walked out.

SOPHIE LEANT BACK IN HER CHAIR BEHIND THE IMPOSING desk in her new office, clasped her hands behind her head and allowed herself a brief moment during her hectic schedule to savour what she'd achieved. She cast her eyes at the chair on the opposite side of her desk in which she'd sat two years earlier; her subordinates would be occupants of that chair soon…

And to think she'd once been stuck in middle management! And now… now *she* was in charge of the whole enterprise. That sheen and lustre which she'd once seen on Jeremy was now hers. People looked up to her. They deferred to her. God, how she'd loved updating her LinkedIn profile and Facebook with her new CEO status. Beat that, you bastards!

She leant forward and pressed 'Send' and the companywide email was sent:

Dear Colleagues,

As most of you know, today is my first day as CEO of Reynolds. I started with the company as a 22-year-old graduate at the end of the last century (!) and could never have imagined then that I would one day be leading the business. I am very proud to be the first woman to rise to CEO and hope my personal story shows that everyone here can achieve their professional ambitions with this great company.

The most important asset of any organisation is its people, and having worked here for almost twenty years, I know what a truly exceptional group you are. It really is an honour to lead you.

Over the coming days I will be announcing some changes to the senior management team and will also be refreshing the company's strategy to ensure we stay ahead of the competition. More details to follow shortly.

Finally, I'd like to express my sincere gratitude to my predecessor Jeremy Hyde, who after leading the company through a period of sustained growth, is leaving to pursue fresh opportunities. I know all of you will join with me in saying a big thank you to Jeremy for his exceptional leadership and counsel. Jeremy leaves the company in a much stronger place than when he took over five years ago, in particular his foresight in setting our new strategic direction. He leaves with our very best wishes and I am sure he will be successful in his new endeavours.

If anyone has any immediate questions, please do not hesitate to contact me. I very much look forward to working with you all on the next leg of our collective journey.

Kind regards,

Sophie Hill

JUST ONE MORE THING

Colin gripped his cold, hard, metal fork but could only manage to push the fish around his plate.

Andrea glanced at him, then at his plate, then back up at him. 'You not hungry?'

It took a moment for Colin to register that she'd spoken, after which he shook his head. 'Sorry, I've had a really hard day at work. I've lost my appetite.' He began to drift off again into his own thoughts, but some part of him knew he needed to remain present for his wife and he managed to wrestle himself back. 'How's Robin?' he asked. As usual, he'd returned home after Robin had gone to bed. That morning, he'd promised him he'd get home before his bedtime, but work had become so, so… *intense* these last few months that once again it hadn't happened.

'He's… okay,' said Andrea. 'Although…' Her face twisted into a pained expression.

'What?'

'Mr Fletcher said Robin was disruptive in class again.'

Colin slowly and carefully placed his fork down beside

his plate and closed his eyes. He allowed the worry and pressure implicit in his wife's words to be fully absorbed into the depths of his mind and body, like a sponge slowly immersed in water. 'I'll speak to Robin about it again tomorrow.'

The meal continued in near silence. How had it come to this? He couldn't think of a single aspect of his own upbringing which could have given his parents cause for concern. Just the opposite, in fact. He'd applied himself diligently at school, securing good grades. After A-Levels in Maths, Physics and Biology, he'd studied Law at university and was now twenty years into his career as a solicitor. He attended church every Sunday. He led a clean life. Surely all this meant he should have been rewarded with a relatively stress-free existence?

Instead he had countless concerns on his mind. Indeed, there were so many of them, he'd lost track of some. That was part of the problem, he didn't have a handle on things. How can you begin to untangle the strangling web of worry when you're continually firefighting each emergency that needs dealing with every day?

'I'm hoping you're going to be a bit more lively tomorrow night?' said Andrea, looking at him out of the corner of her eye.

He paused; this meant there was some sort of social engagement he'd forgotten about. 'Remind me what we're doing again?'

Andrea tutted under her breath. 'We're going to Kirsty and Bill's for dinner. I reminded you about it yesterday.'

'Oh yeah,' said Colin, nodding. Only he couldn't remember her mentioning it before. He slumped in his seat, his face not much above the level of the table. The last thing he wanted was a night out. He was visiting his mother in her care home tomorrow, an outing guaranteed to suck out the last of his residual energy. Now he'd have to then sit through Kirsty inevitably banging on and on about her wunderkind daughter; how gifted she was, how clever, how she's not being stretched sufficiently at school. His shoulders tensed and hunched at the thought of it. 'I'll do my best,' he said.

'I know you're seeing your mother tomorrow, but you haven't forgotten about what else you promised to do, have you?'

Colin didn't look up. Why did she ask it this way, forcing him to prove he could remember what she'd said? Why couldn't she just tell him? Some part of him in a perverse way hoped it was something really challenging and difficult and unreasonable, just to see if he could handle it on top of everything else which was dragging him down. Indeed, the bigger and harder her ask, the higher the likelihood that it would provide the final weight to snap him in two. *Then* perhaps she and everyone else would think twice before loading him up with more tasks and obligations. 'Remind me what it is again?'

Andrea rolled her eyes. 'You said you'd pick up Robin's medicine from the chemist. After seeing your mum of course, but remember the chemist closes at 1pm.'

He closed his eyes while nodding. 'Okay, okay. I'll get it.'

After dinner, Colin didn't have the energy to watch TV so they both retired upstairs. After brushing his teeth and putting on his pyjamas, he climbed into bed, but without consciously thinking reached for his phone and pressed the icon for his work email. There, top of the list, timed just a few minutes earlier, was an email from his boss, Sebastian. The long, gradual process of unwinding after work immediately wrenched into reverse as his heart rate sped up and his mind started whirring:

Colin,

I'm surprised still not to have received your ideas for margin improvement, which I requested by the end of the week. As you know, margin improvement has been identified as a key strategic priority by the Board.

As you know, this matter is the first item on the agenda for Monday's meeting, so please come prepared to share your proposed actions.

Thanks, Seb

Colin slowly placed his mobile down on his bedside table, lay back and stared at the ceiling above, his eyes travelling along the jerky path of a hairline crack in the corner of the room he'd noticed recently; was it his imagination, or had it lengthened and widened since he last saw it? As he contemplated Seb's email, his temperature began to rise and all the muscles along his back stiffened.

'Is everything okay?' asked Andrea.

'Er… yeah. Sort of. Just an email from work.' He didn't want to elaborate on it, because talking about it would just amplify his worries. What he badly needed was some rest, but that wouldn't be possible now, because his mind was already preoccupied, thinking through what he would say at Monday morning's meeting.

What sort of person emails his staff last thing on a Friday night to remind them of a work matter? Forcing just one more thing, just one more task, squeezing just a little bit more profit. Colin's hand balled into a fist.

Sending emails last thing at night, knowing full well the stress they would cause. Forcing him to think about work during his tiny amount of downtime. Colin's breathing was now audible.

Trying to *control* people. To *own* them. Trying to infiltrate his very mind and soul in order to reduce him to a simple, efficient cog in his money-making machine. Money was Seb's god. Money to spend, money to count, money to crow about, money to consume and show off, money, money, money, these people were barely human, they were fucking machines, they had to be stopped!

'Are you okay?' said Andrea, sitting up and looking at him, eyes wide with alarm. 'You look like you're about to kill someone. And you're panting.'

'Sorry, sorry,' said Colin, slowing his breathing as the shame ran through him. Just recently he'd started having these hot flushes of rage each time Seb micromanaged him with another order or edict. 'I've just got a lot on my mind. I'll be okay.'

'I think you should get some rest,' said his wife, lying back down and switching off the lamp on her bedside table.

Colin did likewise, said his evening prayer, but then lay awake in the darkness, eyes open, his heart still throbbing up against his ribcage. He knew that every hour, awake or asleep, between now and Monday morning, he'd be worrying.

Colin's car drew to a halt behind the car in front in the tunnel. He leaned one way, then the other, to work out what was causing the delay up ahead, but couldn't see anything. He looked at the clock on the dashboard: 11.19am. He wouldn't now get to the care home until at least 11.45am, which meant how long with his mother to ensure he got back to the chemist to get Robin's prescription? He sighed and sat back in his seat, closing his tired eyes to protect them from the harsh, unnatural glare of the tunnel's overhead lights.

He hadn't slept well for worrying about work. All night he'd kept thinking about Seb's email and trying to list ways in which he could improve his team's profitability. His colleagues were already working flat out, he couldn't think of anything innovative to squeeze more out of them. If the company wanted more profit then they should just be honest about it and tell everyone to work longer hours. But they didn't like to put it like that, did they? It was always about working *smarter*, or *understanding the value of what we do*, or whatever other euphemism they could think up for sucking up more money through their greedy, twitching, shining with saliva snouts. Colin cupped his left hand in his right and cracked his knuckles.

He wondered whether to fight back against Seb. He'd never liked confrontation, preferring instead to simply get on with his work quietly and without fuss, but he'd become sick to death of Seb's obsession with targets and billing and margins and costs. Of course those things are important in business, Colin understood that, but surely there was more to it than that? What about quality of service? What about the overall purpose of the business? In any case, surely Seb had enough money to last a lifetime? An image appeared in his mind of Seb staring lasciviously at his bank statement with his little pig-slit eyes, counting the zeroes after the numbers and grinning to himself, before turning his attention to his laptop and tapping in an email about margin improvement with his piggy, bristly cloven hoof. Colin's chest tightened.

Now he pictured *all* the bosses at work, all wriggling slippery on all fours in their business suits in the stinky, sticky mud, all snorting and groaning and grunting and wallowing, shoving each other out of the way and rooting for their turn to hungrily suck up more of the rancid swill from the trough…

The harsh blare of a car's horn startled him upright. The traffic was now moving but he hadn't noticed. Flustered, he grabbed the gear stick but struggled to get the car into gear. Another blast of the horn from the car behind. 'Alright, alright,' said Colin.

Once at the care home, he pressed the intercom and said who he was. A short silence followed, before a female voice said, 'Can you pop along to the nurse's office before seeing your mother please?'

'Sure,' said Colin and they buzzed him in.

The stuffy heat inside the care home and his tread sticking slightly with each step on the pastel green linoleum floor made him feel slightly nauseous, not helped by a faint scent of antiseptic, or by the fact that whatever he was about to be told by the nurse could only be bad news.

The nurse was waiting for him in the doorway to her office and asked him to come in. 'I just wanted to let you know that there's been some deterioration with your mother.' She paused, which had the effect of adding pressure and weight onto her words. 'She's had difficulty recognising me and the other nurses recently. A lot of difficulty.' Again she paused; time seemed to slow and become denser as he absorbed the information deep within the tissues and fibres of his body. 'I just thought you should know,' she added.

'Thank you,' said Colin. 'I appreciate you telling me.'

'Oh, and one more thing?'

'Yes?'

'Your last invoice is outstanding.' She smiled nervously as she said it. 'I'm sorry to have to ask you, it's just that my boss asked me to say something.'

'No, it's me who should be sorry,' said Colin. 'You did send it through, I'd just forgotten about it. I'll pay it as soon as I'm home this afternoon.'

'Thank you,' said the nurse.

Colin pictured the nurse holding a warm, damp flannel, and reaching out to begin the process of full bodily washing his mother… and flinched. For that she probably only earned Minimum Wage, yet he'd been paying two and a half thousand pounds a month to the care home for over two years now, so it was clear someone was making a lot of money. 'I hope they pay you well for the work you do here,' he said.

She laughed. 'I wish! One doesn't do a job like this for the money.'

He walked to his mother's room, mulling over what the nurse had said about her *deterioration*. He paused momentarily outside her room and said a little prayer hoping that perhaps her condition wouldn't be as bad as he feared and that his mother wasn't in any distress, before knocking on the door and letting himself in.

The heat and stuffiness inside was up a notch even from the corridor outside, supplemented by the unnaturally sweet, lavender flavoured odour being pumped out of the plug-in air freshener. He had to pull more deeply with his breathing in order to get sufficient air into his lungs. His mum was in her lilac dressing gown, sitting in a chair looking out the window. Colin had recently hung a birdfeeder from a nearby tree and was pleased to see a colourful goldfinch perched on its little stand, jabbing its red-faced beak at the sunflower seeds with surprising carelessness, causing many to fall to the ground.

'Hi, Mum,' he said, kissing her on the cheek and sitting down on the bed.

She kept looking out the window and showed no sign of registering his presence. The last time he'd visited a week earlier she managed a half smile at him and a faint squeeze of his hand as he talked to her. He'd certainly felt she was attentive and comprehending of what he said, despite her silence. But today she appeared unmoored and adrift.

'How are you?'

She continued to look out of the window.

He stood up and pulled up the spare chair and sat himself just to the side of her line of sight outside. 'Hi, Mum, are you okay?'

Still she stared out the window. Not even a flicker of recognition. He took her by the hand and held it. He squeezed it gently, but couldn't feel any sort of reciprocation. It struck Colin that he could say more or less anything and there would still be no response. He decided to tell her about his week, which is what he did every time he saw her, but his summary was a complete fabrication. He told her how things were going well at work and how Robin was making good progress at school. He then made some tea, ensuring hers was lukewarm in case she spilled it, but she didn't drink any.

After a while he just sat staring out the window like his mother. He needed to remember to pay the invoice for this place, but there was also the worry of his mother's savings fast running out. What would happen then? He sighed, before drawing more of the heavily scented warm room air deep into his lungs.

There were now two goldfinches outside, dipping their heads periodically into the feeder, and a wood pigeon below, moving in a stately manner and combing for fallen seeds. He recalled how his mother had bought him his first pair of binoculars for his eighth birthday and they'd sat together at the kitchen table looking at the birds outside, his mother helping him identify them so he could write down the day and date and what birds he'd seen in his notebook. It was just one of so many happy childhood memories she'd helped create. He pictured now pulling on his wellies to go blackberry picking with her on Sundays in autumn, the thrill of finding clusters of ripened berries and filling up plastic bags, before returning home to measure out the flour and sugar for the crumble and licking the bowl. She'd been such a lively and enthusiastic woman, full of ideas and passions and interests, but to see her now…

His eyes were swimming in tears. He looked again at her. Does anyone ever love you as much as your mum? He'd once read a memoir of a soldier from the First World War, who'd said that on the Somme battlefield, as men were cut down by enemy machine-gun fire and lay in their hordes dying in bloody agony in the mud, those close to death mostly said the same thing: they called out for their mothers, always their mothers.

As tears ran down his cheeks he brought his hand to his face and used the fleshy part of his palm to wipe them away. Just briefly he sensed his mother's eyes on him and he turned to her, but she was already looking out the window again. Had there been a flicker of recognition?

He shifted his chair to bring himself closer to her and took both her hands into his. He looked square into her eyes. 'I don't know if this is the last time you'll ever be able to recognise me, Mum, or understand what I'm saying. I don't know whether you're still there, but I feel you are. I just wanted to say thank you. Thank you for everything you've done for me. I love you.'

～

'*PLEASE* CAN YOU DO YOUR TEETH?' ASKED COLIN, STANDING outside the bathroom holding his son's toothbrush.

'In a minute,' said Robin, walking away.

'NOW!' shouted Colin.

Robin stopped and turned, fear clenching his face.

'I've asked three times, just bloody do as you're told, for *once.*'

Robin hesitated.

'NOW!' screamed Colin so loudly it reverberated through the house, while bearing down on his son, who cowered against the wall, but took the toothbrush and rushed to the bathroom.

Colin instantly regretted it and stood panting outside the bathroom, his pulse pumping. On some subconscious level he knew he no longer had control of his temper.

His son emerged a few moments later sobbing, his face contorted in anguish. 'You *hate* me! You don't want me as your son!' He ran along the corridor to his bedroom.

'I'm sorry,' Colin said, following him, but as he reached his room its door slammed shut. He turned the handle and gently pushed but it wouldn't open as Robin was sitting just the other side. He could hear him sobbing. 'Just go away!' he shouted.

He paused for a moment, before retreating to his darkened bedroom and sitting down on the unmade bed with his head in his hands.

A short while later he heard his wife enter. 'What's going on?' she asked. He didn't look up, for it seemed to him that whatever he said would only make matters worse. 'Well?' she prompted.

He shook his bowed head. 'He never *listens* to me.' It frightened him how weak his voice was and how pathetic he sounded.

He felt the bed depress as his wife sat down next to him. There was a short silence. 'Colin, I've known you for almost twenty years and in all that time you've only lost your temper a handful of times. The trouble is, they've all been recently, and they're getting worse.'

He breathed out deeply through his nose. 'I don't know what came over me… he never seems to do what I ask.'

'He barely knows you these days because you're never here.'

'You *know* what it's like at work, I'm under lots of pressure.'

'I do know, yes, but it gets to the point where you've got to wonder whether it's all worth it.'

He sat up straight and stared at his wife. 'What do you mean, *you wonder whether it's all worth it?* What am I supposed to do? You say I work too hard, but then we forever need more things. We just booked a holiday, how are we going to pay for that?'

His wife returned his stare evenly.

'Well?' he asked.

'You're raising your voice again. Look, we can cancel the holiday if it helps. But what we can't have is you behaving like this. I'm already looking after one troubled child, I don't need to be looking after another. Let's discuss this later, I've got to help Robin get ready for school.' She stood up and left.

Colin's head dropped again into his hands. He wondered whether it was fair that he was allocated half the tasks at home despite working full-time. He worked under constant pressure all day and when he collapsed through the front door at 8pm each night he was expected to read bedtime stories and do the washing up. Who helped *him* with the stresses of work? No one, that's who.

He thought back through the insane amount of work he'd put in over the last year. All that worry, day after day: fretting over multiple large, complex and multi-faceted legal claims; the constant vigilance and sign-offs required to ensure compliance with risk procedures and external regulators; the continuous close surveillance regarding his sales, his margins, his personal profitability. And it wasn't just the last year, he'd had two decades of it: fitful sleep each night, waking immediately stressed every day, logged on and working by 7.30am, stealing a ten-minute sandwich break at his desk for lunch. Even then it wasn't over: after dinner he'd be checking his emails until late at night. His pulse never slowed. His brain never rested.

He stood up from the unmade bed, pulled a striped tie from his wardrobe and began tying the knot, only to get it muddled and yank it free from his neck in frustration.

'Have you done Robin's packed lunch?' came his wife's voice from the doorway.

'What?'

'I said have you done Robin's packed lunch?'

He shook his head and stared at her uncomprehendingly. 'I can't believe you're throwing this at me *now*.'

'But we agreed: I get him dressed and get his breakfast, and you do his—'

'Okay, okay,' he said, walking to the door. 'For fuck's sake,' he said as he passed his wife. Always one more thing. Always another obligation. He walked towards the stairs.

'Stop!' said his wife, coming up behind him. 'Just go and get changed and go to work, I don't want you upsetting Robin again. *I'll* do his lunch.'

Colin's head felt foggy and he wandered back to the bedroom and sat down on the bed again. He knew he needed to get on top of things, which in turn might help calm him down and free up some time to spend with his family. But he'd lost confidence in his ability to turn it around. There was too much to do. Even if he ticked say five things off the to-do list today, another seven or eight would invariably replace them, leaving him in deficit. It was a losing battle.

Once dressed, he walked downstairs and left for work without saying goodbye to his wife or son.

A SHORT WHILE LATER HE WAS STANDING ON THE TRAIN TO work, as usual squashed against the carriage door such was the weight of passengers. His thoughts turned to Robin. He bitterly regretted shouting at him. As if the boy didn't have enough problems. He'd always been a troubled child, and had turned out nothing like Colin had imagined. Everything with him had been a battle. Mealtimes, getting dressed, bedtimes, doing teeth, and the resigned and anxious looks on the faces of staff from nursery, and again at pre-school, and now at primary school, forced to deliver the news that Robin was struggling, Robin had upset another child, Robin's behaviour wasn't *as expected*. The visits to the pediatrician, and to the child psychologist, and to the Special Educational Needs officer, agonizing over what it might be: Attention Deficit Disorder? Dyspraxia?

He was now overheating badly; a bead of sweat gathered on his hairline before trickling irritatingly down the side of his ear. Why hadn't he taken his coat off before boarding? He was now too squashed to remove it. He pressed the back of his hand against the metal of the train door; that at least was cool to the touch.

His thoughts turned to his mother. Could she still recognize him? His visit to her on Saturday now seemed epochal; what was there left for her if she couldn't recognize her own son? But how could he be sure? Perhaps it was like Motor Neurone Disease when they're lucid within but completely unable to communicate? Or like Locked-in Syndrome, only able to communicate via blinking. Good god. And what if it was hereditary? He worried less about himself than about Robin having to look after him or coming to a care home to see him. Would Robin even be capable of making such a journey? What if Robin inherited it? Please god, no.

Sweat now coated his forehead, collar and back, causing a broiling nausea to choke up his head as the train ground to a halt just outside the station. The man squeezed next to him sneezed powerfully into his hand inches from Colin's face, before rescuing a soiled handkerchief from his pocket and blowing his nose vigorously wet and loud. Colin's oesophagus contracted. The train driver announced that they were held at a red light awaiting a platform to become available. 'For fuck's sake,' he muttered through clenched teeth. He was going to be late to his meeting now, which he hadn't properly prepared for in any case. Damn it. He'd just have to improvise. He had higher priorities than bloody margin improvement in any case.

'Nice of you to join us, Colin,' said Seb, sitting at the head of the table.

'Sorry I'm late, trouble with the trains,' said Colin, finding a seat.

Seb very faintly, almost imperceptibly, shook his head as

he closely watched Colin sitting down. 'Well,' he said, still eyeing Colin, 'a little birdie tells me that this isn't the first time you've been late recently.'

Colin stared back at Seb, expressionless. A silence fell across the room and as it lingered so the air in the room seemed to thicken.

'Right, shall we begin?' Seb asked, but didn't wait for a reply. 'As you all know, the board has designated margin improvement as one of the firm's key strategic priorities and you all agreed last time to come to this meeting ready to share three ideas whereby each of your departments could achieve efficiencies. Right, can I start with you Adrian?' Adrian headed up Procurement and launched into a detailed account of how his department was reviewing all its contracts and in the process of meeting suppliers to get them to reduce their prices. It was like a child summarising last night's homework, with Seb acting as teacher and busily scribbling down a mark. Next up was Human Resources, who were working up an idea to cut wage costs by getting staff to pay for their own benefits, such as additional holiday and workplace car parking, through an *options* scheme. Didn't the people in HR realise this would also reduce *their own* wages? Then came Phil from I.T., describing various new software pilots designed to increase effectiveness or productivity. It struck Neil that the meeting was less a genuine assessment of what was best, and more about showing an unthinking commitment to the firm by talking lots and talking earnestly, like endlessly repeating a liturgy to a priest. Come to think of it, every meeting was like this, people mindlessly saying anything as long as it was what they thought Seb or *the board* wanted to hear. Even if they'd been tasked with thinking up ways to kill their own families they'd still all be here, enthusiastically showing off their black-market revolvers and demonstrating how to remove the batteries from carbon monoxide alarms. What was wrong with these people? And to think he'd spent twenty years in this… this *cult*.

'Colin, your turn.'

'Sorry, what was that?' asked Colin.

'I said it's your turn. Can we have your ideas for margin improvement?'

There was a short silence. 'Well…' he said, searching his mind for something relevant to say, but finding nothing.

'I emailed you about this on Friday,' prompted Seb.

'Did you?'

'Yes, I did.'

'What time did you email?'

Seb's lips screwed into a tight hole.

'To be honest,' said Colin, 'as far as I can tell there's two ways to increase our margins: one is to charge our clients more and the other one is to pay everyone less. I don't think the latter is going to be too popular, so I guess we should charge clients more.'

'And how do you propose we do that?' asked Seb with a slowed-down delivery.

Colin shrugged his shoulders. 'I need more time to think about it.'

Seb tutted. 'You were supposed to come to this meeting with these ideas fully formed.'

Colin trained his eyes directly on the bridge of Seb's nose, like lining up the cross hairs in a rifle's sights. He stayed completely silent; all expression and movement fell from his face. He did not blink.

'Well?' asked Seb.

'Well *what*?'

'How do you intend to justify increased fees?'

Another silence settled across the room. Most of the other attendees now stared downwards or fidgeted with their pens, a few exchanging veiled glances. All his life Colin had been a shy and reserved man, such that a stand-off like this would have been excruciating for him. Not now. It was as if all his senses and emotions were suspended. The tension of the confrontation was simply being absorbed into the infinite mass of issues, obligations and unresolved problems now weighing him down to breaking point. In fact he welcomed it; perversely he wanted Seb to push him, so that the final justice when meted out in return would be so... so *definitive. Go on, Seb* he thought to himself, *ask for more money. Please ask for more. Please. Ask.*

'Look, how about we take this offline?' said Seb eventually, a look of concern visible on his face.

Colin still said nothing and simply stared, like a machine with a broken component unable to respond or function.

'Right, I'll think we'll end there,' said Seb, drawing the meeting to a close and standing. Everyone else also hurriedly stood, leaving Colin sitting perfectly still, staring straight ahead.

SITTING AT THE BREAKFAST TABLE GRIPPING A COLD METAL spoon, Colin stared vacantly out the window trying to remember what he had to get done that day. He couldn't focus and glanced down instead at the Weetabix in his bowl; after pouring the milk, he'd become distracted, so that the biscuits had now fully absorbed all the milk to become a grey, unappetising mush.

He tried again to concentrate. He knew three things had to be done today without fail. Firstly... oh yes, booking an appointment with the paediatrician to discuss Robin's behavioural issues again; this had to be done urgently as there was no telling how long the waiting list would be. Secondly... the car's MOT, yes that was it. It must have been more than a year since the last one, but when he'd checked the glove compartment yesterday for the papers for the due date they hadn't been there. What was the third thing? He rubbed his forehead. There was definitely three things... fuck it, he just couldn't retrieve it. How could he add it to the to-do list if he couldn't bloody remember it?

'Can you help me with this?' his wife said, holding up the jam jar which she'd been trying to open.

Colin stared out of the window, oblivious to his wife's question.

'Colin! I said can you help me with this?'

He stood, walked stiffly over to his wife and she handed him the jar. He tried to turn the lid but it was locked fast. He sighed.

'Here, I'll try again,' said his wife.

'No. I've got it.' The entirety of Colin's focus zeroed in on the jar. For some reason it seemed to articulate all that was against him in his life and he vowed to win this battle. Indeed, it was more than that. If he couldn't beat a jam jar then what could he do? He *had* to win. He'd rather break his hand than lose out to this fucking lid! He resumed his grip on it, this time so hard that a mesh of thick veins stood proud on the back of his hand. He tensed every muscle in his body, his whole frame vibrating with a humming electrostatic energy; it was almost as if he wasn't human anymore, but more like an industrial machine switched to its maximum setting, its pistons and rods about to be brutally released. He turned the lid with all his might; suddenly there was a sickening splintering sound as the jam jar broke in half. 'ARGH!' shouted Colin, dropping the jar and bending double, holding his hand.

'Shit! Are you alright?' said his wife, leaning towards him.

'I'm fine,' he said, but blood was dripping from the palm of his hand.

'Oh my god, you're bleeding.'

'It's okay, I'll sort it,' said Colin, before walking upstairs to find a plaster. He ran his hand under the tap, causing a red blush in the basin. He dabbed some tissue paper onto the cut, but it merely absorbed the blood until it became wet and heavy and he threw it into the toilet. Instead, he held his hand in the air, blood trickling down his wrist, and stared at himself in the cabinet mirror. He saw no colour: just the grey bristles on his sallow cheeks, his hair now entirely a gun-boat metal grey.

He walked downstairs and left for work without saying goodbye to his wife or son.

Sitting hunched over his desk at work, he stared at some crumbs nestling in between the letters on his keyboard left over from an earlier lunch. Lifting his eyes, his sight landed on the photograph he kept on his desk of his wife and Robin but, registering nothing, his attention focused back to the crumbs, examining their intricate shapes and their positioning relative to one another.

His phone bleeped; without turning his head, his eyes flicked to it on his desk where a message from his wife lit up on the screen:

Hi – the school want to speak to us again about Robin's behaviour.

Also, there's a letter from the care home saying we owe them a lot of money. A x

His eyes flicked back to the crumbs. His mouth hung open a little.

Sometime later his eyes flicked to the screen of his PC where he saw an email from a law firm they were in dispute with. He clicked on it:

Dear Colin,

Your recent claim to the County Court on behalf of your client is out of time. Under the provisions of the Limitations Act 1980, your client had until 31 March this year to bring their claim – whereas their claim was in fact only brought to the County Court on 8 April.

In the circumstances your client is time-barred and my client assumes that your client will now drop its claim in its entirety. Please confirm that you accept the above analysis. If not, my client reserves the right to seek its costs in dealing with this matter from your client in full.

Kind regards,

John Hammond

Partner

Colin sat staring at the screen. Oddly, he felt calm. His breathing didn't quicken. His temperature didn't rise. But in some deep, dark recess of his mind his subconscious was working through the full importance and implications of the email. As the processing began, so his body stiffened as more and more tension was absorbed.

An email appeared in his inbox from Seb. He clicked on it:

What the hell is this?! Please tell me you haven't made a huge mistake? Come to my office now.

He looked again at the email from the lawyers; Seb had been copied in. He scrolled through the prior emails in the file to find where they'd originally discussed the deadline. He was calm, controlled, even cold as he did so. He found the email and clicked on it. His eyes zeroed in with laser-like focus to the CC line: Seb had been copied in. He scanned the rest of the email, fully digesting its contents, before rising and walking to Seb's office.

'Sit down,' ordered Seb as Colin entered. He was pacing back and forth behind his desk restlessly, his face pale as paper, like he hadn't enjoyed any sunlight or fresh air in months.

Colin sat down.

'That's £4 million pounds gone,' said Seb, pulling a hand across his forehead. 'I can't fucking believe this!'

Ordinarily, Colin may have been thinking about the implications of the email on his career and reputation. Or else considering how he would deal with the long unravelling process to come: the confession to the client and the resulting explosion of anger, the endless explanations and excuses, the allocation of blame, the carefully drafted emails about restitution and compensation. Instead, he sat perfectly still, just his eyeballs swinging side to side as he tracked Seb's movements.

'What's gone wrong with you, Colin?' said Seb. 'Your behaviour at yesterday's margin improvement meeting was disgraceful and now this. What's got into you?'

Still Colin sat motionless.

'Have you told the client yet?' asked Seb.

'No.'

'Good. We need to think about how to positon this.' He stopped pacing and turned to face Colin square on. 'Why the fuck didn't you remember?'

Colin said nothing, his face completely expressionless.

'You do realise your career's well and truly fucked now? You do know that, don't you?'

Colin paused before replying. 'No.'

'*What*?!'

Colin now spoke in a flat monotone, like the voice on an answering machine asking you to leave a message. 'I will not take the blame. *You* should have remembered the deadline.'

Seb's eyes flared. 'How dare you try to offload the blame on me; it was *your* responsibility to get the application in on time.'

'No.'

'*What*?! I can't be expected to check every single client deadline. I wasn't even made aware of the deadline.'

'Yes, you were.' Colin's voice now sounded even more nasal and pre-programmed, like a Dalek.

Seb paused. 'You seem very sure of that.'

'I just checked the file. You were copied in on the email in which the deadline was discussed.'

'You fucking bastard. Not content with fucking everything up, you're now trying to blame me. How *dare* you. You *will* take responsibility for this.'

The muscles in Colin's shoulders tightened.

'Well?' asked Seb.

Colin said nothing. Rather, he stared at Seb like looking through a pair of binoculars, everything peripheral dissolving to darkness and focussing sharply on his facial features through a tunnel of amplified sight: his piggy, beady eyes and his twitching, shining with saliva mouth, both animated and agitated at this threat to their insatiable, sickening gluttony.

'I asked you a question, Colin. Do you take responsibility?'

Colin's body began mechanising: his stomach muscles clenched, his arms tensed, his hands gripped into fists, and his whole frame vibrated with a humming electrostatic energy

'Have you lost your voice or something?' asked Seb. 'Or perhaps your mind?'

Colin rose woodenly and walked rigidly around the desk towards Seb, who backed away while looking Colin up and down, but all Colin saw in front of him was a slippery, wriggling, filthy hog, snorting and groaning and grunting and wallowing, fighting for his turn to hungrily suck up more of the rancid swill from the trough…

'What is your malfunction, Colin?' asked Seb.

Colin snapped.

He grabbed Seb's throat, his fingers compressing into the soft flesh like a clamp; Seb's attempts to push his hands and arms away just bounced off, like hitting metal. Colin wasn't human anymore, he'd become an industrial machine, with pistons and rods which once set in motion could not be stopped. His only purpose was to eliminate Seb, ridding the world of evil and greed and avarice, to restore the natural order.

Seb repeatedly struck Colin around the head with his fists. Colin didn't feel a thing. Machines don't feel. He didn't register the cut on his brow which moments later caused a red blush of blood in his right eye. Rather he simply exerted full pressure through his arms to his hands, like a long, hydraulic lever lowering inexorably to its maximum setting: the tendons and muscles in Seb's neck began making sickening gristly noises as his cheeks turned purple and his body began to spasm and jerk, like a fish caught on the line.

From a far-off, distant place, a memory came to Colin of the birth of his son: the little but then growing bump inside his wife who for so long had been just a concept and a promise, before the rush to the hospital, and the waves of brutal pain washing through his wife, the contortions wrenching her face, the midwife's implorings and the final primordial cry as the bloody little thing slid out, even then still somehow a theory until his tiny body was lifted and he opened his eyes for the first time, wide and searching and staring *at him* such that he found himself staring into the eyes of God…

… he released Seb, who fell to the floor.

The door to Seb's office swung open and his secretary shrieked and shouted for help. Moments later a flurry of colleagues rushed in, two to Seb lying crumpled on the floor gasping for breath and one to Colin.

'Are you alright?' said the man to Colin, putting a hand on his back.

Colin turned to him, his face bloodied and bruised, but for the first time in as long as he could remember, his thought process was clear. 'I need help,' he said.

Thanks for reading. If you've enjoyed these stories, please spread the word and consider posting a review on Amazon, Goodreads, Waterstones, Kobo or any other suitable forum. These are immensely helpful to authors.

You can keep up to date with Dom's writing, and join his newsletter, at www.domhaslambooks.com

twitter.com/DomHaslam

instagram.com/domhaslambooks

Printed in Great Britain
by Amazon

57721167R00154